One
Hundred
Years
After
Tomorrow

One Hundred Years After Tomorrow

Brazilian Women's Fiction in the 20th Century

Translated, Edited, and with an Introduction by
Darlene J. Sadlier

Indiana University Press / Bloomington & Indianapolis

The paper used in this publication meets the minimum requirements of American National Standard for Information Sciences—Permanence of Paper for Printed Library Materials, ANSI Z39.48-1984.

Manufactured in the United States of America

Library of Congress Cataloging-in-Publication Data
One hundred years after tomorrow: Brazilian women's fiction in the twentieth century / translated, edited, and with an introduction by Darlene J. Sadlier.
p. cm.
Includes bibliographical references.
ISBN 0-253-35045-X (cloth). — ISBN 0-253-20699-5 (paper)
1. Brazilian fiction—Women authors—Translations into English. 2. Brazilian fiction—20th century—Translations into English. 3. Short stories, Brazilian—Translations into English. I. Sadlier, Darlene J. (Darlene Joy).
PQ9677.E5O56 1992 91-22132
869.3—dc20

1 2 3 4 5 95 95 94 93 92

For Doris J. Turner

mentor,

colleague,

and friend

Contents

Acknowledgments

A number of people from different parts of the world gave me help and support for this project. In Brazil, I wish to thank Monica Rector, Sylvia Paixão, Susana Bornéo Funck, Zahidé L. Muzart, Nelly Novaes Coelho, Bella Jozef, Rita Terezinha Schmidt, Cassiano Nunes, Nilo Scalzo, and Thex Corrêa da Silva. In England, I am especially indebted to Maggie Humm, who invited me to write an essay on Brazilian women writers for *Fiction International.* In the United States, I received important assistance from Earl Fitz, Maria Angélica Lopes, Lúcia Helena, and Fred Clark.

Heitor Martins, my colleague at Indiana University, was more than generous with his time and knowledge, and I thank him for his comments on the translations. I am also grateful to the Brazilian artist Yara Tupynambá, who graciously allowed me to use her work on the cover of this book. There are no adequate words to thank James Naremore, my husband and friend, who provided love, support, and invaluable editorial assistance. Finally, I wish to acknowledge the authors and the families of those writers no longer living for allowing me to publish my translations. I especially appreciate their enthusiasm, kindness, and prompt attention to my correspondence, all of which greatly facilitated my work.

I have made an effort to contact all holders of copyrights, and apologize for any that I have been unable to locate. I am grateful for permission to publish the following:

"A Fuga" ("The Flight") by Clarice Lispector. Copyright © 1979 by Clarice Lispector and Heirs of Clarice Lispector.

Éramos Seis (Selections from *We Were Six*) by Sra. Leandro Dupré. Copyright © 1943 by Sra. Leandro Dupré.

"No Silêncio da Casa Grande" ("In the Silence of the Big House") by Emi Bulhões Carvalho da Fonseca. Copyright © 1944 by Emi Bulhões Carvalho da Fonseca.

"Meu Tio Ricardo" ("My Uncle Ricardo") by Lúcia Benedetti. Copyright © 1950 by Lúcia Benedetti.

"Jovita" by Dinah Silviera de Queiroz. Copyright © 1957 by Dinah Silveira de Queiroz.

"Mundo Perfeito" ("A Perfect World") by Lia Correia Dutra. Copyright © 1957 by Lia Correia Dutra.

"Apenas um Saxofone" ("Just a Saxophone") by Lygia Fagundes Telles. Copyright © 1969 by Lygia Fagundes Telles.

"Coincidência Premeditada" ("Premeditated Coincidence") by Adalgisa Nery. Copyright © 1972 by Adalgisa Nery.

"Agda" by Hilda Hilst. Copyright © 1973 by Hilda Hilst.

"Oriente Próximo" ("Near East") by Nélida Piñon. Copyright © 1973 by Nélida Piñon.

"Dorceli" by Tania Jamardo Faillace. Copyright © 1975 by Tania Jamardo Faillace.

"O Frágil Equilíbrio" ("The Fragile Balance") by Elisa Lispector. Copyright © 1977 by Elisa Lispector.

"A Bela Adormecida (Roteiro de uma Vida Inútil)" ("The Sleeping Beauty [Script of a Useless Life])" by Edla van Steen. Copyright © 1978 by Edla van Steen.

"Menino de Vermelho, a Caminho da Lua" ("Little Girl in Red, on Her Way to the Moon") by Marina Colasanti. Copyright © 1980 by Marina Colasanti.

"O Vampiro da Alameda Casabranca" ("The Vampire of Whitehouse Lane") by Márcia Denser. Copyright © 1980 by Márcia Denser.

A Asa Esquerda do Anjo (Selections from *The Left Wing of the Angel*) by Lya Luft. Copyright © 1981 by Lya Luft.

"Toda Lana Turner Tem Seu Johnny Stompanato" ("Every Lana Turner Has Her Johnny Stompanato") by Sônia Coutinho. Copyright © 1985 by Sônia Coutinho.

One Hundred Years After Tomorrow

"*. . . it's good to eat at tomorrow's party, commemorating one hundred years of after tomorrow . . .*"

HILDA HILST, "Agda"

Introduction

This volume is a celebration of women's writing in Brazil over the past one hundred years. Like any other survey of the past, however, it calls attention to something in the present—in this case, to Brazil's emerging feminist consciousness. I have tried to recover a number of authors who have been "lost" by conventional literary histories and to revise the map of twentieth-century letters in Brazil; but in looking back over the past century, I hope to influence the future, creating a receptive audience for the writing we might enjoy one hundred years after tomorrow.

For much of the twentieth century, women authors in Brazil were denied cultural legitimacy; in fact, at the height of Getúlio Vargas's *Estado Novo* (New State) in the late 1930s, Brazilian historian and literary critic Olívio Montenegro remarked that women were biologically and psychologically unfit to be writers. They were better off channeling their energies into making babies:

> Let's be realistic. Fiction authored by the women among us has always been very weak. Sentimental and puerile. And when it contains some emotional quivers—at bottom it's just hysteria. Its exaltation doesn't come from the imagination: it's from desire. These authors are more faithful to sex than to literature. But literature isn't the best channel for sex—nor the most healthy. It's maternity that [these writers] understand well and from which they can benefit. (176, my translation)

According to Montenegro, the novelist Rachel de Queiroz was the only woman author of the period who did not "betray the sentimentalism of her sex." What made her fiction worthy of serious study was "the trace of a virile personality" (176).

Montenegro's overt sexism wasn't typical of the literary establishment, but it might as well have been. Until quite recently, it was difficult for most women to obtain any sort of recognition from the academic critics in Brazil. Prior to the 1980s, only three or four women authors were regularly discussed in standard reference works; the most frequently cited figures were Cecília Meireles, who wrote more than twenty volumes of poetry between 1919 and her death in 1964, and Rachel de Queiroz, whose 1930 novel, *O Quinze* (The Year Fifteen), vividly portrays the extreme economic hardships of people living in the *sertão*, or backlands region of the Brazilian Northeast. Interestingly, the inclusion of Meireles and Queiroz in the literary canon seems to have been partly determined by their ability to fit into aesthetic "movements" already sanctioned by criticism. For example, scholars generally referred to Meireles as a "post-symbolist" poet, and they usually placed the "virile" Queiroz in the tradition of nineteenth-century Brazilian regionalism. Even Queiroz's *As Três Marias* (1939) *(The Three Marias)*, whose plot centers on three convent-educated girls growing up in the provincial Northeast, did not escape this kind of classification. Upon its release, the writer and critic Mário de Andrade praised the author for writing a book whose style was similar to that of Machado de Assis (118). Only in the 1980s were Meireles and Queiroz talked about in terms of their "difference." As recent critics have noted, the introspective poetry of Meireles frequently turns on the question of female identity, whereas the fiction of Queiroz has as one of its recurring themes the problems educated women in general face in a traditional, Catholic society.

At various points in the century, we can find critics attempting to secure a reputation for women writers, but these attempts have been few and relatively far between. Historian and critic João Ribeiro, who wrote regularly for the *Jornal do Brasil* in the late 1920s and 1930s, dedicated several of his essays to women writers, including Cecília Meireles, the poet Eneida (de Moraes), and the novelist and critic Amélia Bevilaqua; and in a 1930 piece, he criticized the majority of his fellow members of the Brazilian Academy of Letters for voting against a proposal to admit women into its membership (39–41). His protest against the Academy was prompted by Amélia Bevilaqua's unsuccessful candidacy for a chair—a controversial event that was discussed extensively in newspapers at the time and documented in Bevilaqua's book, *Amélia Bevilaqua e a Academia Brasileira de Letras.* In the mid-1940s, the historian Olmio Barros Vidal devoted two chapters of his study, *Precursoras Brasileiras* (circa 1945), to the discussion of early women writers, including Teresa Margarida da Silva e Orta, whose *Aventuras de Diófanes* (1752) is considered by many to be the first Brazilian novel. In the early 1950s, the critic Lúcia Miguel-Pereira also cited the works of women authors in her studies of Brazilian literature, most notably in her *Prosa de Ficção (de 1870 a 1920);* and not long afterward, in 1959, R. (Raimundo) Magalhães Júnior published *O Conto Feminino (The Female Short Story)*—one of the first anthologies of women's fiction. Among the more than thirty writers included in Magalhães Júnior's volume are older figures such as Júlia Lopes de Almeida and Carmen Dolores, who were widely recognized in the early part of the century, and young authors such as Clarice Lispector, billed in a biographical note as "the sister of [novelist] Elisa Lispector" (58). Viewed from over thirty years later, *O Conto Feminino* is a reminder that there was a significant number of women writing during the first half of the twentieth century; and yet, unfortunately, most of the women mentioned in the anthology—among them Elisa Lispector, who today is described in passing as "the sister of Clarice Lispector"—have gone out of print.

My own anthology is an attempt to bring some of these writers back to critical attention. At the same time, I have tried to restore the balance of literary history by offering the widest possible sampling of twentieth-century literature by Brazilian women. There are, of course, necessary limits to any project of this type, and I am able to include only a fraction of the material that merits attention and translation. I can only hope that I suggest the considerable range and diversity of Brazil's rich literary culture and the important contributions women have made during the modern period.

At the very least, I expect readers in the United States will find the anthology informative. The writings collected here have never before been published in English. Of the twenty authors represented, all but two or three are virtually unknown in North America, and a few have been forgotten even in Brazil. Most deserve far greater attention than they have received. I should note, however, that I am not attempting to establish a canon of great but neglected artists. My chief purpose is to provide a historical overview of writing by women since the beginning of the century, in the process recovering some "lost" figures. I concentrate on women because, in Brazil as in most other nations, they have been somewhat marginalized. As outsiders and as relative newcomers to the literary scene, they have a critical perspective, and even when they do not write from an explicitly feminist point of view, they tell us interesting things about the dominant society.

The significance of these writings can best be appreciated if we understand something about the recent political climate of Brazil, particularly as it concerns women authors. The situation for women in general has improved considerably during the past two decades, especially since the declaration of the United Nations International Women's Year (IWY) in 1975, which stimulated important discussions throughout the country. Groups formed and conferences were held to study women's representation in all facets of Brazilian life, including literature and the arts. Two feminist newspapers appeared at that time—*Nós Mulheres* (We Women) in São Paulo and *Brasil Mulher* (Brazil Woman) in Londrina, in the southern state of Paraná—to keep women informed of activities throughout the nation. Little by little, a women's studies research began to emerge, and a few centers, such as the Carlos Chagas Foundation in São Paulo, became support units for the scholarship.

While the IWY opened the way for the study of gender issues in Brazil, the right-wing government's proclamation of a gradual return to democracy after more than ten years of intense political repression allowed women (as well as other opposition groups) to mobilize around "controversial" issues without fear of government reprisals. With *abertura,* the political "opening" declared in the 1970s, feminist and working-class women's groups were given a space in which to organize, to voice their concerns regarding the oppressive policies of the military regime, and to wage demands for better social services, including child and health care facilities.[1]

In the literary arena, the death of Clarice Lispector in 1977 brought increased attention not only to her work but also to women's writing generally. French critic Hélène Cixous's "discovery" of Lispector intensified the study of the Brazilian author; Cixous's now famous article "L'approche de Clarice Lispector (1979)," as well as her other tributes, most notably in *Vivre l'Orange* (1979) and *Illa* (1980), inspired within Brazil (whose intellectual life has long been influenced by France) a new form of literary inquiry based on *écriture féminine.*[2] In the early 1960s, critical studies of Clarice Lispector began appearing with some frequency in intellectual and academic journals. Most of those studies treat Lispector as something of a novelty, although she was far from being a new writer. (Her first novel, *Perto do Coração Selvagem [Near the Wild Heart]*, was published close to twenty years earlier, in 1944.) What attracted intellectuals is the "experimental" nature of her fiction, which was described in ways that facilitated her inclusion into the established canon. For example, the critic Massaud Moisés commented that her work reminded him of the introspective urban fiction of the 1930s (510), a genre overshadowed by the more popular social realist novel of the period. Others, including Álvaro Lins, talked about her affinity with such modernists as Joyce and Woolf (188). Giovanni Pontiero, the English translator of her *Laços de Família* (1960) *(Family Ties)*, saw in the angst and nausea of Lispector's middle-class characters the mark of existentialist writers Camus and Sartre (but not of Simone de Beauvoir) (Introduction, *Family Ties*).

Lispector was the best-known woman writing in Brazil during the early 1970s, but other women had been working longer and found scholarly recognition more elusive—although in a few cases they received major national and international literary awards. These included the short story writer and novelist Lygia Fagundes Telles and Dinah Silveira de Queiroz, a prolific author of realist novels, stories, *crônicas*, and science fiction. Fagundes Telles had begun writing in the late 1930s. She rarely received analysis in the learned journals (the essays by Fábio Lucas are among the exceptions), even though several of her works won major national prizes, and her "Antes do Baile Verde" ("Before the Green Ball") was awarded first place in a competition in Cannes for best foreign short story. Silveira de Queiroz, too, was seldom discussed critically until her death in 1982, in the midst of a women's literary boom that brought massive attention to her works.

The years following Lispector's death witnessed a budding of feminist literary scholarship in Brazil and a significant rise in the number of novels and stories written by women. By the mid-1980s, women writers were achieving a recognition that history had long denied them, and they became the topic of national and international conferences. At first, however, contemporary authors such as Hilda Hilst and Nélida Piñon did not fare much better than their predecessors. Hilst's writings, characterized by disjunctive language and controversial sexual themes, were generally ignored; and not until the appearance of Piñon's historical novel, *A República dos Sonhos* (1984) *(The Republic of Dreams)*, did critics begin to give her serious attention.

Other women writers could also be mentioned here, but I simply want to indicate that over the years Brazilian literary culture has been generally conservative. With the exception of a few authors, such as Meireles, Queiroz, and Lispector, the vast majority of women have remained outside the canon, although the social activities of the mid-to-late 1970s brought about a change in the way women writers were viewed. (Not coincidentially, in 1977 the Brazilian Academy of Letters elected the first woman to its membership.) Ultimately, it was the women writers and critics themselves who made the difference—building a cultural formation within the context of the more liberal political atmosphere, creating a literary "movement" of their own, and writing works that now draw widespread popular as well as critical attention.

As a result of *abertura* and the rising feminist consciousness, the Brazilian publishing houses began producing anthologies that promoted the new "women's literature." One of the pioneers of this anthologizing trend was the novelist and short story writer Edla van Steen, who in 1978 published *O Conto da Mulher Brasileira* (The Brazilian Woman's Short Story), an anthology of nineteen contemporary women, including such veteran figures as Lygia Fagundes Telles, Dinah Silveira de Queiroz, and Nélida Piñon, as well as recent writers such as Sônia Coutinho and Márcia Denser. In her preface to the collection, van Steen poses the question: why an anthology of women writers? In her words, "the idea, at first glance, doesn't seem justified, principally because I believe that artists, in their work, don't have a sex; they're artists" (5). In fact, however, women writers in Brazil have always been judged in relation to their gender; if van Steen seems cautious about acknowledging women's difference, that is partly because she wanted to avoid polemics, but also because she was reluctant to adopt a feminist label. (The word "feminist" is problematic for many women in developing countries, chiefly because of its "First World" connotations.) Despite her reservations, van Steen was obviously acknowledging the absence of women in Brazilian literary history and wanted to "call attention to and underscore not only the quality but also the quantity of women's production" (5).

Although there is no single theme joining together the nineteen stories in van Steen's anthology, most of the writings have female protagonists and deal with the problems of communicating with men. (Van Steen's own contribution, "Os Mortos Não Têm Desejos" [The Dead Don't Have Desires], which appears in the present anthology under its later title, "A Bela Adormecida" [The Sleeping Beauty], is one of the more formally interesting treatments of this theme.) Another, similar anthology that appeared in 1978 is *Mulheres e Mulheres* (Women and Women), containing stories by five men and five women and edited by a new writer, Rachel Jardim. The format of this book is significant. By alternating the women's and men's stories, Jardim provides an interesting juxtaposition of male and female images of women. The title of the volume alludes to its dual view. In her commentary on the book jacket, Jardim notes that the volume contains a variety of stories about women by men, ranging in style from the "scatological" to the "abstract" and preoccupied with "spinsterly types" and "prostitutes." While she does not go into detail, her description of the women's stories as closer to "flesh and blood" suggests her greater appreciation for what she regarded as the women's liberated, "true-to-life" characterizations.

A year later, in 1979, Edla van Steen published *O Papel do Amor* (The Role of Love), which, like Jardim's *Mulheres e Mulheres,* contains stories by both men and women. In the preface to the anthology, van Steen remarks on the new, more open political climate that allowed the publication of books on all subjects—including sex, a topic that had previously been discouraged by government censors. In an introduction to the collection, critic Fábio Lucas emphasizes the respectability of the entries, distinguishing them from the "erotismo comercializável," or "bankable eroticism," that was beginning to appear in bookstores. While he reassures the audience that there is nothing disorientingly experimental or gratuitously titillating about the collection, he calls attention to the stories about sexual love written by women—a phenomenon new to Brazilian literature, which became increasingly apparent during the 1980s.

Among those who took a more militant approach to describing women's sexuality is Márcia Denser, editor of *Muito Prazer: Contos Eróticos Femininos* (1982) (Very Pleased to Meet You: Erotic Short Stories by Women). In Denser's words, *Muito Prazer* is intended to prove that women have something to say about sex—especially sex between women. The stories of lesbian love in the volume are among the first on this topic published by women in Brazil, and the success of *Muito Prazer,* which features stories by Renata Pallotini, Sônia Coutinho, Marina Colasanti, Rachel Jardim, Lya Luft, and others, encouraged Denser to publish a second collection of erotic literature in 1984. *O Prazer é Todo Meu* (The Pleasure Is All Mine) features established figures such as Fagundes Telles, Piñon, Hilst, and Judith Grossman, who has been writing since the late 1950s, as well as Olga Savary, who that same year published *Carne Viva (Live Flesh),* the first anthology of women's erotic poetry.

In addition to works of contemporary fiction by women, new editions of books long out of print began to appear, and neglected authors such as Júlia Lopes de Almeida, Délia (Maria Benedita Bormann), Maria Firmina dos Reis, Albertina Berta, and Carmen Dolores found a new readership. As a result, the presence of women writers began to be reflected in literary histories and criticism. For example, in a recently published volume on Brazilian modernism, Massaud Moisés writes not only about such canonical figures as Meireles, Queiroz, and Lispector but also about novelists Lygia Fagundes Telles, Dinah Silveira de Queiroz, and Maria Alice Barroso; poets Olga Savary, Adélia Prado, and Ana Cristina César; and newer writers such as Sônia Coutinho, Edla van Steen, and Márcia Denser. This is a significant advance, especially if we consider that, some twenty years earlier, the critic Agrippino Grieco, in his *Poetas e Prosadores do Brasil* (a survey of writers from the colonial period through the 1960s), did not include a single woman author.

The extent to which Brazilian women writers are achieving serious recognition in their country is largely due to their counterparts in the scholarly community, who are becoming a major force in Brazilian literary criticism. In addition to Nelly Novaes Coelho, Maria Luíza Ramos, Bella Jozef, Eliane Zagury and Lúcia Helena, among others, a younger generation of women academics is beginning to write extensively about women's literature and to challenge conservative assumptions. These writers remind us that Brazil—like the United States, England, and France—has a long history of women's literature, much of which has been ignored over the years. The process of rediscovering and reevaluating women's contributions has only recently started, and the advances made in just the last few years suggest that a new Brazilian literary history is not far away.

As the foregoing brief survey of publications by women and responses by critics may suggest, the material collected here is symptomatic of Brazil's fitful struggle toward democracy and openness in the twentieth century. I allude to that struggle in some of the brief introductions to each of the authors I selected, but in general I let the stories speak for themselves. By way of conclusion, let me simply offer a few notes on the form and content of the fiction as a whole.

Not surprisingly, a great many of the writers I have translated have been concerned with domestic or "private" issues, especially with the relation between men and women. If we read the selections in chronological order, we can see that women writers in the early decades of the century often dealt with the manners and mores of the bourgeois family. Carmen Dolores was particularly adroit at describing the rituals of courtship and marriage in her narratives about middle-class urban and rural Brazil, while Júlia Lopes de Almeida, the oldest figure in the collection, wrote satirical monologues, alternately spoken by wives and husbands, which reveal the strains of conventional marriage. This theme persisted well into the modernist period. For example, "The Flight," an early story by fifteen-year-old Clarice Lispector, focuses on a woman's attempt to escape her constricting household after twelve debilitating years of marriage.

Some writers have addressed the mother-child relationship, as we can see in stories such as Tania Jamardo Faillace's "Dorceli" and, in some respects, in Hilda Hilst's "Agda." Notice, however, that a few of the stories in the collection are forthrightly devoted to what we normally regard as the "public" world. For instance, Rachel de Queiroz was one of the first writers in Brazil to document the devastation of the drought in the Northeast, and Dinah Silveira de Queiroz wrote novels and stories such as "Jovita," dealing with significant events in Brazilian history. Faillace's story, which concentrates on a mother and child, also convincingly portrays the struggles of young people living in urban poverty.

The collection inevitably mirrors the cultural diversity of Brazil, and it constitutes a sort of dialogue among many women's voices. But as already noted, the theme of erotic love seems to dominate much of the new writing. Hilda Hilst, Edla van Steen, Marina Colasanti, Márcia Denser, Lya Luft, and Sônia Coutinho have all written about sexual relations with men, and in a few cases, about sexual attraction between women. The implications of this phenomenon are complex. On the one hand, sex helps to sell books, and discussion of erotic themes involves a certain retreat into middle-class emotional experience, turning us away from open discussion of Brazil's severe social and economic problems. On the other hand, the new sexual explicitness is a healthy sign of women's growing independence and of the potential dissolution of the patriarchal order.

What is equally interesting about the more contemporary pieces is the range of formal experimentation that several of the authors employ. Narrative realism has given way almost entirely to surrealistic and self-reflexive writing, and in some cases to "magical" and "postmodern" techniques. In historical terms, one of the most obvious features of the collection is the movement from a relatively genteel realism to difficult, sometimes disorienting narratives. Júlia Lopes de Almeida's monologues, for all their sly wit, are considerably less free-associative and more decorous than the subjective fiction of such modern authors as Hilda Hilst, Elisa Lispector, Lygia Fagundes Telles, and Lya Luft. Notice, too, that while a great many of the stories focus on the inner lives of individual women, the ontological status of the thinking subject becomes more insecure as we approach the present. Internal monologue becomes completely decentered, or is framed by various forms of metanarrative; a concern with women's problems and women's subjectivity remains a dominant feature, but the contemporary stories are more radical in their attitude toward language.

Despite the many technical and stylistic differences among the writers, nearly all of the stories suggest an awareness of how the public sphere impinges on the quiet, "unspoken" experience of women. The fact that much of the fiction focuses on a traditionally private domain—and more recently, on such subjects as erotic love—does not mean that it is any less substantial. Women are opening a window into the deepest recesses of private life and making explicit the source of that "hysteria" noted by Olívio Montenegro in 1938. Meanwhile, they've always addressed a broad range of issues affecting men and women of different races and classes, giving us a sense of the entire Brazilian landscape. We in North America can learn a great deal from their stories—not only about Brazil's distinct culture and its history over the past hundred years, but also about its potential for change.

NOTES

1. For a detailed discussion of women's political activities during this period, see Marianne Schmink, "Women in Brazilian *Abertura* Politics, *Signs* 7, no. 1 (1981): 115–34.

2. Further information on the Lispector-Cixous relationship can be found in Carol Armbruster, "Hélène-Clarice: Nouvelle Voix," *Contemporary Literature* 24, no. 2 (1983): 145–57; Tilde Sankovitch, *French Women Writers and the Book* (Syracuse: Syracuse University Press, 1988); and Earl E. Fitz, "Hélène Cixous's Debt to Clarice Lispector: The Case of *Vivre l'Orange* and L'Ecriture féminine," *Revue de Littérature Comparée* 1, Janvier-Mars (1990): 235–49.

WORKS CITED

Andrade, Mário de. *O Empalhador de Passarinho*. 2nd ed. São Paulo: Livraria Martins Editora, 1955.

Barros Vidal, Olmio. *Precursoras Brasileiras*. Rio de Janeiro: A Noite Editora, circa 1945.

Cixous, Hélène. "L'approche de Clarice Lispector." *Entre l'écriture*. Paris: des femmes, 1986, 113–38.

———. *Illa*. Paris: des femmes, 1980.

———. *Vivre l'Orange.* Paris: des femmes, 1979.

O Conto da Mulher Brasileira. Ed. Edla van Steen. São Paulo: Editora Vertente, 1978.

O Conto Feminino. Ed. R. Magalhães Júnior. Rio de Janeiro: Editora Civilização Brasileira, 1959.

Grieco, Agrippino. *Poetas e Prosadores do Brasil (De Gregório de Matos a Guimarães Rosa).* Rio de Janeiro: Conquista, 1968.

Lins, Álvaro. *Os Mortos de Sobrecasaca: Ensaios e Estudos: 1940–1969.* Rio de Janeiro: Editora Civilização Brasileira, 1963.

Lispector, Clarice. *Family Ties.* Trans. Giovanni Pontiero. Austin: University of Texas Press, 1972. [*Laços de Família,* 1960]

Miguel-Pereira, Lúcia. *História da Literatura Brasileira: Prosa de Ficção (de 1870 a 1920).* Rio de Janeiro: José Olympio Editora, 1950.

Moisés, Massaud. *A Literatura Brasileira Através dos Textos.* 4th ed. São Paulo: Editora Cultrix, 1975.

———. *História da Literatura Brasileira: Modernismo.* São Paulo: Editora Cultrix, 1989.

Montenegro, Olívio. *O Romance Brasileiro: As Suas Origens e Tendências.* Rio de Janeiro: José Olympio Editora, 1938.

Muito Prazer: Contos Eróticos Femininos. Ed. Márcia Denser. Rio de Janeiro: Editora Record, 1982.

Mulheres e Mulheres. Ed. Rachel Jardim. Rio de Janeiro: Nova Fronteira, 1978.

Orta, Teresa Margarida da Silva e. 1752. *Aventuras de Diófanes.* 3rd. ed. Lisbon, 1790.

O Papel do Amor. Ed. Edla van Steen. São Paulo: Livraria Cultura Editora, 1979.

O Prazer é Todo Meu: Contos Eróticos Femininos. Ed. Márcia Denser. Rio de Janeiro: Editora Record, 1984.

Queiroz, Rachel de. 1930. *O Quinze.* 2nd ed. São Paulo: Companhia Editora Nacional, 1931.

———. *As Três Marias.* Rio de Janeiro: José Olympio Editora, 1939.

Ribeiro, João. "Amélia Bevilaqua e a Academia Brasileira de Letras." *Obras de João Ribeiro: Crítica.* Vol. 4. Rio de Janeiro: Publicações da Academia Brasileira de Letras, 1959.

Carmen Dolores

Carmen Dolores was the preferred pen name of Emília Moncorvo Bandeira de Melo (1852–1910), who also published under the pseudonyms Júlia de Castro and Leonel Sampaio. Historians are divided on her place of birth—São Paulo or Rio de Janeiro—but she lived in Rio and was a regular contributor to the newspapers *Correio da Manhã* and *O País.*

Writing at the turn of the century, Dolores was perhaps best known for her *crônicas,* or short commentaries on Brazilian life, which appeared in her weekly column in *O País.* In 1910, a collection of these writings was published (*Ao Esvoaçar da Idéia* [On the Fluttering of an Idea]), documenting her sustained interest in women's rights. In her *crônicas,* she advocated changing the law to allow divorce in Brazil, and she wrote passionately about equal rights—especially educational reform and the institution of fair wage legislation.

Dolores also wrote several volumes of short fiction and a novel, *A Luta* (The Struggle), which appeared shortly after her death in 1911. Her fiction tends to focus on middle-class women in urban Brazil, and her first book, a collection of short stories entitled *Gradações* (1897) (Gradations), explored women's largely dependent relationships with men. The title story of her second volume, *Um Drama na Roça* (1907) (A Drama in the Countryside), which I have selected for translation, is slightly unusual. Dolores shifts her focus from the urban bourgeoisie to the provincial middle class. She is especially adept at portraying the traditions and mores of rural Brazil, and, as in her stories about the city, she underscores the centrality of courtship and marriage in the lives of women.

A Drama in the Countryside

(1907)

On that Sunday, the village of——— awoke in celebration to the crackling of fireworks and the clanging of bells coming from the little white church at the top of the hill. No wonder! The month of Mary was coming to a close; there was going to be a mass sung, an auction of handicrafts and foods, a fireworks display, a dance in the main hall of the Municipal Council building, and everywhere people bustled about in great confusion. Already at ten o'clock that morning, Commander José Domingues, an important festival-goer, was climbing the steep, rocky hillside bathed in sun; worn out, apoplectic, he stopped from time to time to rest, saying to his wife in gasping, broken sentences: "Look at those girls, Leopoldina. . . . Call out to them to walk more slowly. . . ."

Gazing up toward the top of the hill, where two little shadows moved along protected by a single straw hat, Dona Leopoldina shouted with all the force she could muster: "Guilhermina! Laura! . . . wait right there. . . . Why all the hurry? . . ."

Reddened by fatigue and the heat, Dona Leopoldina's double chin unfolded onto a wide lace collar, where a gold brooch with the picture of the commander shone, and the body of her dark blue, grosgrain gown, which seemed about to explode, outlined in relief the enormous bust of a matron more accustomed to wide housedresses than to corseted party gowns.

Quickly waving in response to their mother's call, Guilhermina and Laura continued their ascent, and so engrossed were they in their conversation that they didn't even notice other groups who, passing by them in the same direction, greeted them with an affectionate "Good morning!"

Guilhermina, who was older, tall and spindly, with a pensive look on her gaunt face, seemed to listen as if in a trance as the shorter, blond, freckle-faced and petulant Laura spoke vehemently:

"I swear I'll do it, I swear. . . . If they continue like that, I'll let everybody know, even if it does cause a scandal. . . ."

"But what do you gain from that? . . . Then everything will be ruined."

"So be it! But if I'm to be disgraced as you were, I'll make sure to avenge myself first. . . . Oh, she'll see what I'm made of. . . ."

A group of young women interrupted their dialogue with embraces, kisses, exclamations, and news about the festivities: they were making their way up the hillside and joined the two sisters, who were now nearing the church square, where, since early morning, mobs of people had been waiting to enter the church. A giant, thatch-topped tent was open at the side in preparation for the auction; although the benches inside were empty, a large, rough-hewn table in the center was covered with roast turkeys, stuffed fish, boxes of rice powder, purses, velvet pin cushions, bottles of cognac, and hundreds of other objects of every size and shape—all of which was to be auctioned after the mass. Innumerable little stalls, housing games of chance, sweets and pastries, and a thousand local crafts, were scattered about the square, where the ground was carpeted with mangueira leaves. Here and there, priceless signs like "Nothing ventured, nothing gained" and "Big Jabiru's Place!" could be read on the front of the stalls; peals of laughter, accompanying the muted sound of the roulettes, were mixed in with the cursing of the players and the shouts of little black boys, creating a considerable racket, as skyrockets continued to climb into the air, becoming light smoky trails in the blue brilliance of the sky, and flags fluttered in the breeze, surrounded by palm trees and ornamental foliage.

As they approached the church, Guilhermina and Laura slowed the pace of their steps and rapidly exchanged glances—a pleading one from the first, a furious one from the second. Just then, one of the young women from the group said:

"Goodness, Laura! Isn't that your fiancé over there with your sister Hortense?! Look. . . ."

Her finger pointed toward a tall, dark-haired youth dressed in black, who was standing outside the church door next to a feminine figure, whose chic, elegant attire stood out from all the local women's frocks, which were pink and blue, pretentious and vulgar. The woman was tall, delicate, with provocative hips, and her fashionable dress, made of a white fabric with wide black velvet bands, fit like a glove around her round, protruding bust, giving total freedom of movement to her breasts. A little Medicis collar, high and overlaid with antique, scarlet-colored lace, enhanced her creamy complexion, and one look from her big, dark eyes was pure enchantment. All the other details of her dress—a long gold and pearl chain with a miniscule watch, little patent leather shoes and black silk stockings embroidered with tiny scarlet-colored stars, a discreet perfume that exuded from her entire being—everything denoted such a mastery of the science of pleasing that just seeing her there, in that quaint, provincial setting, was astounding.

What was such a creature doing there, in that corner of the world?—was the question on everyone's lips.

Laura approached the couple with a febrile step, and giving the fellow at her sister's side a hard, incisive look, she asked him crisply:

"What's the meaning of this, Novais? You said you'd wait for us at Chico Macedo's and instead you went looking for Hortense at Dona Fifina's to bring her here earlier? . . ." Embarrassed, the young man started babbling some lame excuse, but Hortense interrupted him, saying dryly that she was the one to blame. . . . She had seen him pass by Chico Macedo's store and had asked him to accompany her to the church.

What wrong was there in that? . . .

"But what about me? . . ." murmured Laura, her eyes still glistening with rage as Guilhermina, who was pulling at her sleeve, pointed to their mother and father, who were approaching the square, red-faced, panting, with their hearts about to leap out of their mouths.

Everyone grew quiet, and the villagers' grand entrance into the church was made under considerable visible constraint that was passed along to each new person who arrived.

Just as the orchestra broke out in dissonant chords and the strident voices of the public schoolteacher and her niece—combined with those of some singers from a neighboring city—intoned the first measures of the festive mass, Laura, unable to stifle her emotions, began to cry. The news spread quickly throughout the church:

The daughter of Commander José Domingues, fiancée of Dr. Novais, is crying because she's jealous of her sister! . . .

What a scandal in the village!

* * *

Hortense, the commander's second daughter and the prettiest of the three, had been married five years earlier to Dr. Miguel Marques, a prominent engineer, who had come to the village to inspect some railway lines and had fallen in love with her at a festival like the one going on now.

Recently, the couple had indulged themselves by spending over a year in Paris, enjoying all the refinements of a European civilization. Returning home, Marques was given an important commission in the northern state of Pará which didn't allow him to take his wife with him. Uneasy with Hortense's flightly manner, which seemed more and more pronounced, and fearful of leaving her alone in Rio de Janeiro, he had taken her to her parents' house to wait out the months of his absence.

Hortense's arrival was a major event in the life of the isolated, provincial village. Her boldness, her affected speech with its heavily pronounced *r*'s, the way she had of laughing at everything just to show off her white teeth, the lorgnon she impertinently raised to her eyes to look over things and people, and especially the Parisian chic of her various toilettes—everything about her scandalized the simple villagers, who began referring to her in undertones as the coquette.

Even Dona Leopoldina looked at her daughter sullenly; she didn't feel the least pleasure with her company, and instead preferred to sew with her other two daughters in the dining room, where she lazily buried herself in the wide, low chair that for more than thirty years had supported her bulk.

Hortense had returned home to find both her sisters engaged to be married.

Guilhermina, now in her twenty-sixth year, was about to marry the village schoolteacher, a tall, sallow-skinned fellow with eyeglasses and a pointed beard by the name of Jacinto Gomes, who took tea every evening in the house of his future in-laws. Following their betrothal, Laura would share her future with a young physician, Dr. Alonso Novais, who was currently in Rio with his elderly father, a rich landowner and friend of Commander José Domingues, who had been operated on for a cataract.

Both sisters were unhappy with the third sister, whose presence totally eclipsed their own; they saw in her a thousand new things that made her a stranger in the household and a threat to their most cherished dreams. Guilhermina, the sweeter and shyer of the two, managed to suppress her hostility, while Laura, who, at the rasher age of nineteen was more petulant, was constantly battling a growing antipathy that at times she was unable to conquer and subdue.

What had the intruder come there to do? And how could they now go to parties with their simple, hand-sewn muslin dresses when Hortense would always seem prettier with her Parisian toilettes adorned in lace and velvet?! . . . And that air of hers! . . . And the way she looked at men! . . . It was disgraceful.

A new situation arose that heightened the silent rage burning in the other two. While in Europe, Hortense had discovered she possessed a beautiful contralto voice and tried to cultivate it by studying with the best teachers—quickly learning, like a refined coquette, to make the most of certain notes produced from the chest, whose grave, sensuous, disturbing quality ran chills up and down the spine of all those who heard them. It would be difficult to describe the fear experienced by Hortense's family when she first began singing at home with that powerful and educated voice of hers, whose flourishes brought people to look through the Commander's windows.

Guilhermina's fiancé proved to be the most receptive to the electrifying tingle of the suggestive notes. Hortense had only to sit down at the piano and he would draw near, leaning on the old instrument, never turning away, his eyes fixed on her as quick, nervous twinges appeared on his livid, gaunt face.

Little by little, his backward shyness disappeared; now he spent hours talking with his future sister-in-law, who told him stories about Paris, slightly risqué anecdotes, things that happened to her and her husband, making him laugh as she twisted her sinuous body this way and that on the piano bench. Her fingers sparkling with rings, lying as if forgotten on the dingy keyboard or distractedly playing a scale, would often strike a chord in the heat of their conversation. The schoolteacher's glasses gleamed diabolically in the candlelight illuminating the sheet music on the stand. At times, he would translate the ardent lyrics in French and Italian with his head close to hers, breathing in the intoxicating perfume of her coarse, chestnut hair that brushed against his pointed beard.

Now Guilhermina spent the evenings alone, silent on the window seat where, prior to Hortense's arrival, she and her fiancé had spent such tender hours, planning projects, exchanging hopes, and looking out the window into the darkness at the small, whitewashed building in the distance—their future nesting place. How all that had changed! A gloomy sadness came over her as Dona Leopoldina nodded her head in sleep in the corner of the sofa, while Laura watched the entire scene unfold with hate-filled, penetrating eyes. One night, leaving a little later than usual for a lecture at the pharmacy next door, the Commander was shocked to find his eldest daughter abandoned, while her fiancé chatted with the other daughter, who already had a husband. Clearing his throat, he spoke angrily to the schoolteacher:

"What's going on here, *Mr.* Jacinto? There's your fiancée over there in the corner all alone and here you are jabbering with Hortense! . . . This is totally absurd. . . ."

And he left, slamming the door behind him.

About that time, some of the villagers had organized a picnic luncheon to be held on Colonel Juvenico's farm a half-league away. Since the road to his place passed near Commander José Domingues's house, everyone agreed to meet there. Some ladies would be traveling by buckboard, others on horseback with their parents or husbands—everyone was caught up in the whirlwind of the preparations.

Guilhermina awoke happier that day; her outlook was brighter because Hortense had declared she preferred the buckboard, and Guilhermina hoped to win her fiancé's admiration with her abilities on horseback. Her riding costume fit her perfectly, outlining her narrow, graceful waist.

She felt light, delicate, and far more animated. Her gaiety, however, quickly vanished at the parting hour: Jacinto Gomes calmly climbed up into the driver's seat in the buckboard where Hortense sat, and when those around him asked what he was doing there, he responded by saying that the horse promised him hadn't been delivered, and, moreover, he had awakened with a terrible headache and preferred the buckboard to the jolting trot of an unsatisfactory horse. There was nothing anyone could say to this, and with whips cracking, the party set off to the shouts of "Giddiyup Little Black One! . . . Giddiyup Dapple-Grey! . . .

Giddiyup Mulatta! . . ." The saddled horses whinnied as laughter, exclamations, and jokes passed from one group to another, their gaiety heightened by the beauty of the luminous March morning. The entrance into the backlands was delicious.

Soon the buckboards were passing silently over a bed of leaves that softened the jolts, and a penetrating coolness quickly replaced the intense heat of the nine o'clock sun. A balsamic aroma rose from the rugose trunks of giant trees, whose tops, melding together in the air, allowed but a tenuous light to shine through; rivulets of water moaned amidst the foliage, and a thousand mysterious sounds were heard: rustlings, the chirping of birds, the cracking of dried twigs, the furtive steps of pacas and armadillos—the voices of the forest violated in their secrets. Frightened by the invasion, the animals went invisibly scurrying. Little by little, the verve of the retinue subsided within the quasi-religious silence of the woods. The humidity, however, suddenly grew unbearable; here and there a few prosaic sneezes broke through, destroying altogether the romantic effect, and laughter filled the air once again until they reached the freshly cleared site where the outing was to take place.

The little black boys sent ahead were waiting there with baskets of food that were opened in the midst of the excitement, their abundant contents spread out on an enormous cloth extended on the ground; and the luncheon began, noisy and festive. They had placed champagne in a nearby stream to get cold. Colonel Juvenico, with a chicken thigh in his hand, told such funny stories that Commander José Domingues and two other old gents burst out laughing, their shiny bald pates turning red. Stuffing herself with turkey and *farofa* until she could barely breathe, the overweight Dona Leopoldina had to stand up and loosen her corset. As for Hortense, who was wearing a red blouse with little white dots, she had broken a branch from a tree and wound it like a garland round her head; having imbibed a little too much champagne, she now had two feverish red spots on her cheeks. Her crown of leaves gave her the appearance of a pretty bacchante.

The schoolteacher was sitting with Guilhermina, Laura, and some other young single women, but his eyes constantly searched for Hortense; his fiancée caught him several times being quiet and pensive, totally absorbed in the contemplation of her sister.

The picnic finally drew to a close. Groups of individuals stood up, their stomachs heavy from all the food, and they dispersed themselves among the trees, a few to exercise themselves, others to roam about in peace and freedom. The older women distributed food to the little black boys. Returning from washing her hands in a brook, Laura noticed that Guilhermina, Hortense, and Jacinto Gomes were gone. She looked around, a little confused, and walked through the woods, suddenly coming to a halt. . . . Guilhermina was up ahead, leaning against a tree, her body stretched forward, watching something in the distance that must have been terrible because she was trembling and her face was strained and livid. . . . Laura shouted:

"Guilhermina!"

Guilhermina turned, saw her sister and ran to her, crying out:

"Oh, Laura! . . . that good-for-nothing stole my fiancé! . . . She stole him. . . . I saw it all. . . . He kissed her on the mouth, there, under the mango tree, and then they walked on, their arms around each other. . . . I saw them, Oh God! . . ."

She threw herself down on the moist ground and, burying her face in the roots of a tree, began crying as Laura, shocked and pale, kneeled at her side, asking:

"But who did that? Who?"

"It was that hussy!" Guilhermina cried out again, as she lifted her contorted face. "It was Hortense! Who else?"

"That tramp, that evil, shameless woman! But keep your voice down. . . . If Papa were to come through here. . . ."

Frightened, Guilhermina got hold of herself and began straightening her outfit; suddenly she jumped up, and with a look of unbounded energy on her suffering face, she shook her fist at a point in the distance, and exclaimed:

"You can keep your Jacinto Gomes, traitor! . . . I wouldn't think of marrying him now. . . . We're through."

"But what about Papa and Mama? . . . Are you going to tell them what happened? . . ."

With two deep furrows running across her forehead and an absent look on her face, Guilhermina didn't answer right away; then she said, slowly:

"No! I won't say anything to them. I feel sorry for the two old dears.

What's more, it'd bring scandal to our good name! Dr. Novais might even decide not to marry you. . . . But marry Jacinto, that I'll never do!"

Later, she informed her father that an aversion toward her fiancé had gradually come over her, an aversion so great that she had resolved the marriage would not take place. No beseechings, arguments, or rebukes could break down the resolve into which she had retreated, very calm, cold, without giving any explanations, so that Commander Domingues was forced to bow to her iron will. Thus, Jacinto Gomes was dismissed; soon after, he requested a transfer to another school, and fifteen days later, his thin figure vanished from the village.

Oppressed by the hostile atmosphere in the house, Hortense now spent most of her time with Dona Fifina, wife of the tax collector, who had lived in Rio and regularly received fashion magazines and French novels from the city. They were good friends.

As for Laura, who had been looking forward to the arrival of her fiancé, who was coming in mid-May for the celebration, a curious apprehension now hovered over her spirit. When Dr. Novais finally arrived, all happy and effusive, housed in the home of his future in-laws so that he wouldn't be alone on his farm, she was moody and incommunicative, closely studying Hortense's every gesture and look.

Novais was a good-looking, well-traveled youth, who spoke with confidence. He had met Hortense when she was single and now found her changed, more chic, prettier, and he complimented her with the natural air of one who is completely innocent. But Laura was livid. Victim of a sick obsession that made her grow thin and caused her freckles to stand out on her face, she never once left him alone in the parlor. Perplexed, her fiancé was solicitous toward her, but her silent attitude began to annoy him; he found greater enjoyment in his pleasant chats with Hortense, in which they discussed Bourget, Maupassant, and Marcel Prévost. Little by little, their ideas and reminiscences of life in Europe drew them closer together. Laura sat in silence, witnessing their lively dialogues, in which she couldn't take part because she knew nothing of the subjects they discussed.

Toward the end of May, Hortense grew so close to her future brother-in-law that she even showed him her husband's letters, filled with intimate passages and amorous allusions. She laughed maliciously at the young man as he grew red and uneasy. At night, alone in his room, he thought: "*What a scandalous woman!* . . ." and he nervously chewed on his cigar, wanting to flee the house of his fiancée, who by now bored him completely. What an unfortunate choice he had made, opting for such a little bumpkin! Just the thought of Hortense filled his mind with a thousand details that evoked her entire being, which was provocative like a serpent, coiling itself around his body. One afternoon, while everyone was taking the customary nap, she knocked on his bedroom door, opened it a crack, and passed her arm through the opening—an arm that was bare, totally bare, white and fleshy, and whose hand offered him a tangerine. He took the fruit and grabbed hold of her arm, covering it with rapid, ardent kisses that made her warm flesh quiver. Oh, how sordid it all was, there, under the same roof with his fiancée! His reasoning told him to stop, but his nerves and feelings obeyed a slow, mysterious course of action that totally destroyed his energy and resistance.

It was then that the festivities celebrating the end of the month of Mary took place, and Alonso Novais, softened by the tears of Laura in the church and upset by his own behavior, swore to ignore Hortense's coquettish ways and to dedicate himself to his innocent fiancée. And, in fact, he stayed at her side throughout the auction and was all smiles as he purchased little things that he offered her in a loud, proprietary voice. But just as the fireworks began, their blue glow cutting through the darkness of the mountain, where people had huddled awaiting the display as little black boys ran back and forth, accompanying the spectacle of lights with whistles and applause, Novais began feeling tired, bored, and he sought out the profile of Hortense, who, gazing up at the starry sky with her white face framed by a lace bonnet, was transformed and idealized by the bursts of light. Without knowing how, he found himself next to her, taking advantage of the fleeting moments of darkness to squeeze her cold, trembling fingers under her cape. What did his fiancée matter to him now? . . . His confused feelings ignited an inextinguishable fire in his blood. He loved this woman. . . . He wanted her kisses, he wanted to touch her sinuous body, a body that was ardent, youthful and vibrant. . . .

Two hours later, with thoughts aflame as he stood in the vast salon of the Municipal Council building, where the dancing had already begun, he watched the Domingues family arrive, and he charged like a madman when Hortense appeared, dressed adorably in a pale pink silk dress, with her neck half-exposed and her hair piled up on top of her head and held in place by a jeweled comb. He didn't even look at his fiancée, who came in afterward, dressed all in white, and who, filled with anger, her face contracted, was speaking to Guilhermina in a low voice; he merely murmured an invitation to Hortense, put his arm around her waist, and together they launched into an American waltz, whose little, rapid steps no one else there knew.

What a shock that was!

It was scandalous! Embarrassed, Dona Leopoldina walked heavily across the room, found her husband, and whispered something in his ear that made his bald head turn bright red.

When the waltz was over, Novais withdrew to the buffet and began nervously drinking little glasses of cognac, one after the other. The trip back home—in the cold at two o'clock in the morning, under a chilling, dense fog and a deathly silence that fell over all the members of the family, who were inwardly upset—the trip back was lugubrious.

Once in their rooms, Laura, who no longer doubted her disgrace, sat down fully dressed in a corner of the room, where she remained stiff and immobile.

"Go lie down, sister!" murmured Guilhermina, who was filled with compassion, but who also feared provoking a teary, tumultuous scene at such a late hour.

A very dry *"No!"* was Laura's only response.

Guilhermina tried talking to her, even arguing, but her sister's decisiveness was impenetrable. Finally she gave up and went to bed, falling asleep instantly, having been won over by fatigue. Laura quietly took off her shoes, so as not to disturb her sister, and in her stocking feet and holding her breath, she silently went over and opened the door and looked down the darkened corridor. She had blown out the candle. A deep calm filled the house, now fast asleep; the rhythmic, monotonous tick-tock of the large dining room clock was the only sign of life. Although the minutes flew by, time seemed interminable to the impatient Laura; suddenly, her heart began beating faster and a cold sweat broke out on her face. A whitish form appeared at the end of the hallway, silently gliding along the wall; meanwhile, a door on the opposite side of the corridor opened a crack, the light from within revealing Alonso Novais, who had poked his head out of the door and had a smiling yet anxious look on his face.

The shadow moved toward him, slowly entering the area narrowly illuminated by the doorway; Laura, panting with rage, was able to see all too clearly the face of Hortense—that good-for-nothing, always triumphant in her perversity, who was incestuous, adulterous, forever starving for love, and was now about to steal the kisses of her fiancé and enjoy with him a night of fevered passion. . . .

Her blood boiled in her veins. . . . She was crazy with jealousy. . . . Hortense was passing by her, dressed all in white in a long negligee; Novais's arm was reaching out to her, eager to grab hold of her. . . . But Laura violently came between the two, and grabbing hold of Hortense, who was petrified with fear, she shoved her to the floor and began kicking and striking her, slapping her face, pulling out fistfuls of hair, and digging sharp nails into her chest, nails that tore her throbbing flesh like iron talons.

The uproar resounded terrifyingly throughout the sleepy house; doors opened, candles were lit, and Commander José Domingues came running in his underwear with a heavy cane in his hand, followed by Dona Leopoldina and some black servant women, who, wrapped in bedsheets and stricken with fear, were shouting for help.

Everyone was amazed and alarmed when they saw Hortense unconscious on the floor, her body all bloody and her clothing in tatters, and Laura struggling with Guilhermina, who had pulled her off Hortense and was holding her by the wrists. Overcome by rage, foaming at the mouth and with eyes glazed, Laura hoarsely shouted to them to let her kill the snake once and for all.

Novais had seen his fiancée leap at her sister, but he didn't have the courage to defend his accomplice. Frightened by the gravity of the situation and conscious of his own guilty actions, he had locked himself in his room, quickly dressed, jumped out the window facing the street, and sought refuge in a friend's house, where he arrived pale, panting, and cursing his bad luck.

* * *

Nowadays the estate of Commander José Domingues is closed, silent and deserted. . . .

The old gentleman has moved his family to Barbacena. After a long treatment, Hortense has gone back to Rio to await her husband's return; but she's disfigured, with deep scars on her face, and her lip, which had to have stitches, now stretches back toward her ear, giving her face a sardonic and highly disagreeable grin. She lives a sad and withdrawn life, attributing the ruination of her beauty to an incident she has invented: one day, having decided to pick some plums, she tripped and rolled down an embankment, suffering serious lacerations from the fall. . . .

Thus came to a close that year of festivities celebrating the end of the month of Mary in the village of______.

Júlia Lopes de Almeida

Born in Rio de Janeiro in 1862, Júlia Lopes de Almeida was the first woman to achieve a national reputation as a major writer in Brazil. The critic Lúcia Miguel-Pereira proclaimed her the most important novelist of her time, while historian José Veríssimo considered Almeida and her contemporary, Coelho Neto, to be the successors of Machado de Assis, Brazil's most distinguished nineteenth-century author.

Almeida's collected works, numbering over forty volumes, include novels, short stories, *crônicas*, plays, children's literature, and journalistic essays. Among her best known works are *A Família Medeiros* (1891) (The Medeiros Family), which takes place against the background of the abolitionist movement in the mid-nineteenth century; and *A Falência* (1901) (The Bankruptcy), which tells the story of the rise and fall of a contemporary bourgeois family. When the latter book was released, it was ranked by critics alongside two other works appearing in the same year: Euclides da Cunha's *Os Sertões (Rebellion in the Backlands)* and Graça Aranha's *Canaã (Canaan)*, both of which are now regarded as classics of Brazilian literature.

Unfortunately, despite the high praise Almeida received, only one of her works is in print today—an epistolary novel, *Correio da Roça* (1913; reprinted 1987) (Letters from the Countryside), which involves a correspondence between two middle-class women: Maria, a widow with four daughters, who is forced to move to the provinces, and Fernanda, her friend, who lives in the city. The novel is didactic, positing the benefits of life in the provinces, where women can supposedly live contemplative lives.

Perhaps the most interesting collection of Almeida's short fiction is *Eles e Elas* (1910) (He and She), a series of brief, tongue-in-cheek monologues about the tensions and conflicts between husbands and wives, alternately spoken by men and women. The two selections that follow are from this charming and unusual book.

From *He and She*

Did You Notice?

Did you notice? Well, friend, she's always like that, my wife is always like that. First she does, then she doesn't want what's proposed to her, or even many times what she herself invents. In fact, I'm convinced energetic resolution isn't possible among women, who lose themselves in a maze when they have to engage in the smallest acts. But my wife wins the prize when it comes to perplexities. She's indecisive enough to make a stone saint lose its patience. If I were made of granite, of the hardest granite, I'd become hard chips flying through the air; but I'm made of flesh. Unlike the obdurate materials of an insensitive artifact, human flesh adapts to suffering and to destiny's whims.

Frankly, there are days when my soul does so many flip-flops in my chest that I don't know why it doesn't come leaping right out of my mouth.

You know very well I've always been a practical man, calmly decisive, and an enemy of doubt. It irritates me that my wife makes me waste half my life with her harrowing perplexities; you can't imagine it, it's just too much! If she thinks about taking two steps forward, she immediately decides it's more prudent to take them back; consequently, we never move off the same spot. She concocts absurd, idealistic undertakings with extreme facility, believing that people needn't do much more than invent schemes. But when it comes to putting the most trivial action into effect, she'll spend an infinite time in discussions (like the one you just witnessed) that melt my brains, like fire melts wax.

The uncertainties of the meek are contagious, and that's one of the reasons for my despair. The funniest part, which you still don't know about, is that she was the one who proposed that we take advantage of today, Sunday, for a drive to Tijuca; and as soon as she saw me accept the invitation, the first objection popped out of her mouth—"But what if it rains?"

Observe them, and you will note that women are more concerned about rain than we are about war. I called her to my study and went to the trouble of examining the barometer and reassuring her. She still seemed unconvinced, looking one moment at the barometer, the next at me, when you arrived. Since it was agreed we'd go only after lunch, you didn't upset our plans; in fact, you could even have gone with us. As for the outcome, you saw it. Lacking faith in the barometer, she turns and half-consults the clouds and then runs through her rosary of fears—"Don't you think it unwise to leave the house for so long with just the servants around?" "And what if the automobile breaks down in the middle of the woods? . . . If I have to climb down the mountain on foot, I simply won't go down." "And what if Dona Estefânia were to come here this very day, she's been promising us a visit for how long?"

"And the price of renting an automobile, won't that represent a sacrifice for our modest budget?"

While I was trying to facilitate matters, she was creating new impediments: she feared a migraine . . . she didn't believe we'd be back by dinnertime. That's another of her manias: eating meals exactly at the same hour every day, as if we were a *pensão!* Her eyes burn with desire to go immediately ahead with the festivities she herself improvises; at the same time, her tongue sets up obstacles that impede them.

In this now-I'll-go, now-I-won't-go, which might seem to you an inconsequential game, enough hours are used up to execute a work of art worthy of eternal glory, or to realize a business deal yielding a pretty penny. It's virtually a waste of youth.

If today's incident were unique, I wouldn't say anything. But with very few exceptions, she's always like this. She greatly enjoys the theater. There isn't a woman in the world who doesn't. So if I invite her to go to some performance, she responds with a lively "Yes," then interjects "No . . . ," then signals me to wait a moment, and finally concludes with the dreaded word "Perhaps"! Her doubtfulness aggravates my temperament and at the same time softens my will.

I still can't make my wife understand that energetic actions enable life to unfold, while hesitation rolls it up and binds it tight. An indecisive person walks in tiny little steps, first one foot, then the other, instead of walking straight ahead with regular and firm strides.

—It seems to me that you're married to a woman of considerable reflection.

—Well now! It was hardly worth your being silent for so long, if you come up with such nonsense. Of course my wife has a lot of common sense. I couldn't live with her if I didn't think that. Only, she goes to extremes with her deliberations. . . .

—Do you think that's a defect?

—I believe that if before executing any act, even the most insignificant and commonly permitted one, we weigh it as scrupulously as the vendor weighs his butter, then we risk melting it into nothing.

That's just what happened to the drive to Tijuca. It melted just like butter. Do you want to know how many times I went to the phone to rent the automobile? Four.

Do you know how many times I went to the phone to cancel the same automobile that was coming to pick us up? Another four.

When my wife realized that her last refusal had been definite, she became sad. I perceived her regret; I saw her look at the sky in a final consultation and heard her sigh. The sky was never so blue. If I had wanted, I could have easily convinced her to go, but I was too tired. The devil is, I'd made plans that had to be abandoned because of a trip that never came off. I'd decided to look up Ramos. . . .

—Why didn't you just come out and tell your wife that?

—Because she would have complained from last night through this morning to late afternoon about not being able to go on her pretty and hygenic drive—all because of a visit between men. Anyway, I like her to enjoy herself.

—But then why didn't you convince her to go?

—Because by the time I had managed that, it would already have been too late.

Women persuade themselves that time is like rubber, which can be stretched according to one's whims. Few women have the skill to estimate the duration of a minute. One could say they expect time to serve them. It's their lack of methodic occupation that causes this mental quirk. Do you know of any more worthless object than a woman's watch? My wife's works only when I wind it. I know there are exceptions, but this is a rule; I believe I'm correct in saying that innumerable husbands, like me, set their wives' watches, but there probably isn't a single wife who does the same for her husband. I once met a poor soul who, before leaving for work every morning, would set seven watches besides his own: his wife's and those of his six daughters. This constituted a kind of hobby for him! Only in old age do women observe with exactitude the fleeing of the hours. But by then, time no longer waits for them. . . .

—It seems to me I hear your wife calling you.

—It must be to tell me that had we gone to Tijuca, we would be up there now enjoying this magnificent sunset, and that Dona Estefânia didn't come after all. As if the fault were all mine.

—Perhaps it's not for that reason. In any event, I'd better be saying goodbye. But before I go, give me just one word with regard to politics. Do you or don't you accept the commission from the House?

—Friend, if you want me to speak frankly . . . I don't know. . . . On the one hand, the thing suits me; on the other hand, it doesn't so much. You must believe I barely slept last night just thinking about it. What would you do in my place?

—I would accept without hesitation.

—Really? . . . well, I don't know . . . I'm horribly perplexed.

I Can't Have a Single Private Thought . . .

I can't have a single private thought, a moment's distraction that my husband doesn't try to penetrate, even to the recesses of my soul, with the authority of one who has absolute power and is an enemy of mysteries.

When I'm near him, I begin to worry about concealing even the inertias of my consciousness. He believes that, whether I'm speaking or silent, I should be concerned only about his person, and never allow myself the luxury of a single idea in which his image is not reflected. It's as if, in addition to the right to my body, he acquired the right to each thought budding forth or passing fleetingly through my brain; upset by daydreaming, he's like a farmer who becomes indignant when he sees tiny wildflowers cropping up among the wheat planted by hand on his land—something he hadn't counted on, blown by a mysterious wind, casting its seeds indiscriminately.

When from the fleeting moments of distraction I awake to his voice asking me:

—What are you thinking about?!—and I see his green eyes covered over with an uneasy curiosity, fixing themselves with sovereignty on mine, I shudder, as if I had been caught flagrantly committing an ugly deed, a crime I've yet to know!

Every generation has its particular dreams. . . . Who ordered him to marry a pretty women who's far younger than he?! If I were ugly . . . or if I were fifteen years older, which would make me his age, would he still ransack my soul with such desperation? . . . Who can say? Joanninha and Custódio are the same age . . . they're both thirty five . . . and do they go at it! Ah, but that's different; they quarrel about real problems and not phantoms. . . . Really, I don't know how to convince my rich little husband that at certain moments it's nearly impossible for me to say with any accuracy in which part of the unreal world my thoughts are hovering! If my head is lost in daydreams, it certainly isn't my fault.

. . . I believe the mind of men, or at least of married men, is far more exacting than ours, and that it never strays toward the unknown without considerable previous study, mapping the degrees, minutes, and seconds of the latitudes about to be traversed.

In or outside our radiant planet, there is certainly nothing so exacting as a husband . . . when under the conjugal roof. His life outside the home resembles certain landscapes viewed from the top of the mountain: some parts are clear while others are covered over by delicate, mysterious mists that our eyes vainly seek to penetrate. Try as we will, our fingers could never probe that moving, impalpable veil, woven by their ingenuity and our distrust, that wanders like clouds in the sky. . . .

When I ask my husband:

—Why did you arrive late today?

Or:

—Where are you going?

He smiles, attributing to my very natural curiosity a spot of jealousy; and I feel he's not always sincere in his response. At times I think he tinges his replies with a light malignance and a trace of reticence, making innocent motives seem treacherous, for the sole purpose of studying me; other times, these half-confessions, murmured with a playful air, are absolutely truthful.

He has carried out or will carry out everything that he confesses, even as he feigns amusement. . . . In such cases, the quality of my smile should be ambiguous, because when I realize the truth, I cannot help but allow a modicum of doubt to show. . . . Be that as it may, it's always easier to tell where a creature's coming from or going—its specific acts—than to describe what it's thinking about.

But husbands don't think like that: in the outside world, they're as malleable as wax, but within the home, their minds follow an ironlike logic. They insist on the "why" of everything done or about to be carried out, never overlooking the slightest detail as they dissect facts and demand minute and forthright information. Everything is subservient to their powerful will and their wise determination. . . .

Within the walls of my house or the keepchest of my brain, not a single incident occurs that my lord and husband doesn't demand scrupulous accounts of. . . . I wouldn't deny them to him so often if they weren't so difficult to explain. . . . But how can I answer him with truthfulness and clarity if I myself don't comprehend the tenuous course of the labyrinthine curves traveled by my poor ideas!

When my husband's pretty eyes—I can't help but confess that he has a marvelous pair of eyes—become covered over with that green light—so that they look like liquid emeralds—and stare at my pupils in search of the dream, desire, or fantasy passing through my imagination, my subtle intuition tells me that he's really seeking himself out, for he could never tolerate the idea that another image, no matter how fleeting, would inhabit my spirit! I quickly tuck under the uneasy wing of thought that is either agitating or refreshing me, and become so confused and muted by my own amazement at his egotistical curiosity that I'm unable to produce a sure, decisive, or rapid response. If by chance I should smile while silently sewing, having recalled some amusing yet insignificant detail, the glittering emeralds would swerve off the pages of the book they were reading and pursue in airy flight the shadow of my smile. Which way did it go? They don't know, and it's that destination they seek, flaming and silent, as they move from the solitude of the sitting room to the liberating light of the open window. . . . I become serious, and soon other concerns surface. The emeralds turn dark, as if a giant shadow had come between them and the luminous felicity. Perhaps they suspect my seriousness to be a sign of some moral effort to suppress guilt. . . . I've tried rehearsing a blank physiognomy in the mirror; but because of another misfortune that I seem unable to correct, every time I look in the mirror I can't help but smile or think of anything other than myself!

I really need to subject my spirit to rigorous discipline so that I can deny my face the most subtle or least discreet expression.

The woman who does not know how to dissemble seems insincere, because she betrays herself by flights of fancy. One could say that when the husband takes off his mask, the wife should put it on, so that there's always a little cloud of mystery and curiosity floating between them. Men are interested only in what they don't know. In the first years of marriage, women hurl their whole selves into their husbands' souls. It's a plunge that goes to the very bottom; we tell them everything: our secrets and those of others, original stories and extremely commonplace ones, what we said, what we heard, what we surmise—all in an unlimited declaration! They listen and smile from the heights of their prestige at us simple souls, who are spread at their feet like carpets. . . .

I was like that . . . my mother was like that . . . almost every woman is. . . . But . . . the hour finally comes when we women figure out that our husbands aren't telling us everything. . . . While we were making ourselves crystal clear, they remained flesh and bone. . . .

We trembled; the moment comes we weren't counting on, opening the door to certain wandering thoughts . . . in which the husband assumes various forms, ranging from a hero to a scoundrel; or he doesn't take any form . . . and. . . .

It's then that a woman who wants to keep peace in the home must learn dissimulation, in the event she's unable to make up something on the spur of the moment. That's my defect, not being able to improvise at the drop of a hat. If I could, then when he asked me yesterday, with a streak of anxious curiosity passing over his emerald eyes:

—What are you thinking about?

Instead of becoming embarrassed, wouldn't it have been so easy for me to answer him right away with some pacifying nonsense like, for example:

—I was thinking that a large bunch of dark purple violets would look magnificent in my blond hair?!

Rachel de Queiroz

In 1930, when she was twenty years old, Rachel de Queiroz published *O Quinze* (The Year Fifteen), a classic novel about the legendary drought of 1915 that ravaged her homeland in the Brazilian Northeast. Within a few years, Queiroz, and her fellow northeasterners Jorge Amado, José Lins do Rego, and Graciliano Ramos, were among the most important writers in the country, their novels documenting the economic hardships and class struggles in the least known and poorest region in Brazil.

A member of the Communist Party in the early 1930s, Queiroz was arrested and jailed for her political beliefs in 1937 by the Vargas government. Nevertheless, during this period she published a radical novel, *Caminho de Pedras* (Road of Stones), about political agitation and female independence. Like that book, many of Queiroz's other novels have strong women protagonists who, in different ways and in varying degrees, defy social conventions. Her 1939 novel, *As Três Marias (The Three Marias),* perhaps best exemplifies her preoccupation with the tradition-bound Northeast, where middle-class women struggle to find a life outside the home.

In the 1940s, Queiroz moved from the Northeast and settled in Rio de Janeiro, where she lives today. For many years, she wrote *crônicas* for magazines and newspapers in Rio, and she is considered one of the foremost practitioners of the genre. She also wrote two plays set in the Northeast: *Lampião* (1953), about a famous outlaw, and *A Beata Maria do Egito* (1958) (Devout Mary of Egypt), about religious fanaticism. Although Queiroz started her career as a communist, in later years she was outspoken in her support of the conservatives, and she was sympathetic with the military dictatorship that ruled Brazil between 1964 and 1985. During this period she published the novel *Dora, Doralina*

(1975), which deals with the experiences of a sexually independent woman from the Northeast.

Queiroz is one of the few women writers in Brazil to be regularly included in the canon. The recipient of several important literary awards, she became in 1977 the first woman elected to the Brazilian Academy of Letters.

From *The Year Fifteen*

(1930)

Now the only recourse left to Chico Bento was to leave.

He wasn't about to stay there dying of hunger, without grain, without work, without resources of any kind whatsoever. . . .

After all, the world was large and there was always the rubber trade in Amazonas. . . .

In the middle of the night, he and his wife planned their departure in their small, dark bedroom, where a dying lamp flickered.

As she listened, she cried, wiping her eyes blinded by tears on the hammock's scarlet-colored trim.

Confident in his dream, Chico Bento tried to cheer her up, telling her about the thousands of cases where *retirantes* had struck it rich in the North.

His slow, tired voice vibrated, projecting itself in dominating resonances, embarking upon ambitious projects. His incandescent imagination leveled torturous roads, forgot yearnings, hunger, and agonies, penetrating the green shade of the Amazon, conquering the brute forces of nature, dominating wild beasts and phantoms, and triumphantly snatching up the liberating and coveted gold. . . .

Cordulina listened and opened her heart to that hope. But as she ran her eyes over the walls of their hut and looked in the corner, where her son was fast asleep in his tiny, patched hammock, she felt, once again, a tug at her heart. She sobbed:

"Chico, I'm going to miss my little hut so! Where are we going to live in that far-off place of our Lord?"

The cowhand's sorrowful voice rose up again with consolations and promises:

"There's a branch on every tree for us to hang our hammock on. . . . And with nights as clear as these, it even makes one want to sleep outdoors. . . . Even if it did rain here, during the day or night, wouldn't we still have to leave to get some part-time work?"

Cordulina lowered her sad head. Chico Bento continued to speak:

"The animal I got in trade from Vicente will be here in the early morning. I'll ride it to Quixadá and see if I can get us some of those free train tickets the government's handing out. . . ."

Once he got the money from Zacharias da Feira, sold the mule, and killed the rest of the small animals for food to eat on the way, then he'd have everything he needed. Passage, food, money. . . .

Cordulina got up to rock the baby boy, who woke up crying.

It was dawn.

Little, dissonant birds, perched on a thorny bush in the front yard, sang intermittently.

The early morning light turned the sky red. The tiny birds continued to sing, more energetically now.

His wife put on her skirt and jacket and went to make the coffee.

Chico Bento was alone. Sitting up in the hammock, with his hands dangling as his wrists rested on his knees, his thoughts drifted into a confused daydream of adventure and good fortune.

However, as daylight entered the cracks in the walls of the tiny bedroom, the optimistic vision little by little grew dimmer and his magnificent wave of enthusiasm slowly disappeared; now the only thing left of his ambitious project was the painful sadness of their upcoming exile.

Sleepy-headed, the children got up, rubbing their eyes, and as they stretched themselves, yawning widely, their ribs stood out in relief.

Soon, the oldest boy left for the corral. Passing by the door of the tiny bedroom, he shouted:

"Papa! I'm going to take the man the cattle."

Chico Bento put his feet on the ground, dazed, as if he had just been awakened:

"Oh, yes! It's time. . . ."

The morning was cold, almost hazy.

The boy opened the gate and prodded the cattle that slowly left the corral.

Raising his hat in his hand, he asked for his father's blessing.

His father mumbled: "God be with you," and he remained there, watching the boy, who was softly whistling as he went down the rocky path.

The mule he got in trade for the cattle wasn't quite the old nag Chico Bento said it was on the afternoon of the negotiations.

It was young, a kicker, and still plumb.

Riding bareback, almost on the animal's rump, the boy made his way back, bouncing along to the mule's low, jostling gait.

Chico Bento took the animal, examined the spot on its coat to see if it was a birthmark or a badly healed bruise. He slapped its back and the animal flinched. Then he adjusted the knot in the reins wrapped around the post and walked away; just as he was about to enter the house, he turned to the boy and said:

"Come get breakfast and then saddle up the mule 'cause I need to go to Quixadá."

In vain, Chico Bento talked to the ticket agent about getting his family to Fortaleza. It was just him, his wife, his sister-in-law, and five little kids! . . .

The man wasn't helpful.

"It's impossible. You have to wait a month. All the tickets I've been issued to give out have been assigned. Why don't you go on foot?"

"But, sir, going on foot with that many little kids, why, we'd die for sure!"

The man shrugged his shoulders:

"What do you mean, die! Nowadays you *retirantes* have it so easy. Back in '77, there wasn't a train for any. . . . You'll just have to find another way, there's no more tickets. . . . "

Chico Bento was on his way out.

As Chico reached the door, the agent said, consolingly:

"If you want to wait, maybe I can arrange something for you later on. You know? I had to give fifty tickets to Mathias Paroara; he's hiring single men to work up in Acre!"

In Zacharias's store, the cowhand let off steam as he drank thirstily:

"The scoundrel! In the end, they go round everywhere saying the government'll help the poor. . . . The government'll help you all right, it'll help you die!"

Zacharias confided to him:

"But the government is helping. It's the agent who's the thief. . . . He's selling tickets to the highest bidder. . . ."

The cowhand's eyes gleamed:

"So that's why he told me he had given fifty tickets to Mathias Paroara! . . . "

"What d'ya mean, given! He gave them all right, but it was you give me this and I'll give you that. . . . Paroara told me he had to pay nearly as much as the regular ticket price. . . . It almost wasn't worthwhile. . . ."

His anger fueled by the drink, Chico Bento spat out:

"Bunch of thieves!"

Cordulina was mending some clothes when the cowhand arrived home. Just by looking at him, she knew immediately that things had not gone well.

Furious, spitting insults, he got upset with the mule as he took off the bridle:

"Damned she-devil, you're like riding a dog! Even worse than that old bag of bones back at the ranch!"

Cordulina got up, pushing away the little boy who was pulling at the lapels of her jacket and crying "Mama." She called to her sister in the kitchen:

"Mocinha! See if you can give this child some fish gruel, he's about ready to devour my breasts!"

Then she went over to her husband:

"How was it, Chico? Did you get the money and the tickets?"

"What tickets! We all have to go on foot, like animals! Nobody can get anything in this miserable place! God provides only for the rich!"

Cordulina knew from her husband's breath and from his furious outbursts, which were contrary to his naturally quiet disposition, that he had drunk too much:

She asked him:

"Chico, why do you drink when you go to Quixadá? You're like this every time you come back from there!"

"Nonsense, wife! . . . I didn't hardly drink anything! I just quenched my thirst! What I really wanted to do was get stinking drunk to forget how miserable everything is! . . ."

On the first night of the journey, they took shelter in an abandoned shack that suddenly appeared at the side of the road, as if some good fortune had put it there for the *retirantes*.

The cowhand went over to the saddlebags and came back with a slab of dried goat meat and a sack full of manioc meal with small pieces of hard brown sugar inside.

The women had already improvised a trivet and were lighting a fire. Cooking over the flames, the meat sizzled and the salt popped. When he put the first bite in his mouth, Chico Bento spit it out:

"Ugh! Pure salt! Tastes like a saltlick!"

Mocinha explained:

"We didn't have any water to wash. . . ."

Not caring about the salt, the children put their hands into the meal, tore off strips of meat and swallowed them, licking their fingers.

Then Cordulina said:

"Chico, see if you can't get a little water for coffee. . . ."

Despite his fatigue from the long day's march, Chico Bento got up and went out; his dry, burning throat felt as if it were on fire, and he too wanted water.

Having quieted their hunger, the children cried out for something to drink; they moaned, cleared their throats, swallowed more manioc meal, then licked a bit of the brown sugar, momentarily appeasing their dry throats with the sweets.

Patiently, their mother consoled them:

"Wait a little bit, your father'll be back any minute. . . ."

A half-hour later, he returned with a gourd filled with brackish water that he had gotten nearly a half-kilometer away.

Josias, who was the one who complained and coughed the most, ran to his father, took the vessel from his hands, and attached his impatient lips to its edge, sucking up the long-awaited water in long, delicious gulps. But the others came and took the gourd away from him.

Distressed, Cordulina intervened:

"You crazy kids! Do you want to go without coffee?"

Beneath a large jujube tree sat a whole band of *retirantes:* an old woman, two men, a young woman, and some children.

According to the position of the sun, it was eleven o'clock. When Chico Bento and his family appeared on the road, the men were skinning a steer and the women were boiling water in a kerosene can, waving the flame with a very dirty, patched straw hat.

For as far as the eye could see, there wasn't another tree in sight. Just that old jujube, devastated and spiny, its welcoming crown green against the ash- and tawny-colored desolation of the countryside.

Cordulina panted from exhaustion. The dog, named Cowcatcher, barked, then paused to lick his scorched paws.

The children whined, asking for something to eat.

Chico Bento thought: Why is it that the restlessness, heat, and fatigue in children always make them more hungry?

"Mother, I want something to eat . . . give me a little piece of brown sugar!"

"Ouch! Damned rock! I hurt my foot on the damned thing! Papa, aren't we going to eat with those people over there, under that tree?"

There was only one jujube. The cowhand felt he, too, had a right to his share of the tree's coolness and shade.

After setting down his bundles and unpacking the mule, he looked at their neighbors. The steer was almost skinned. Its swollen head didn't have any horns. Just two putrid, stinking holes from which a purulent water seeped.

Leaning against the trunk of the tree, Chico Bento addressed himself to the skinners:

"If you don't mind my asking, what did the calf die of?"

One of the men stood up, his knife dripping blood, his hands all red, a foul, bloody stench all about him:

"Horn disease. When we found it, it was already sick. We're going to eat it, before the buzzards do."

Nauseated, Chico Bento spit off to the side:

"You folks are brave enough to eat this? It makes me sick just looking at it. . . ."

The other man calmly explained:

"It's been two days since we've had anything to put in the skillet to eat. . . ."

Chico opened his arms in a large gesture of fraternity:

"But not that! Over there, in my things, I have the rest of some salted meat that'll be enough for us all. Leave that mess for the buzzards. It's already theirs anyway! I won't let a fellow Christian eat rotten meat as long as I've got a little something in my sack."

The animal gave off a rank smell because of the disease.

The large, skinned bloody mass was a delight for the vultures that eyed it, from up there, thinking about their sadly empty craw in the petty indifference of the clouds. To commemorate their find, they executed huge, festive circles in the air, their black wings growing blacker in their spiraling descent.

The dried goat meat was all gone. . . .

Cordulina was frightened:

"Chico, what'll we eat tomorrow?"

Ancestral backland generosity flourished in the cowhand's altruism:

"Who knows! God will provide! I wasn't about to let those poor wretches gnaw rotten bones. . . ."

Lying on a bed of rags, Josias, one of Chico Bento's little sons, panted painfully.

His stomach was swollen like a balloon. His face was bloated and a tired, anguished breath passed between his half-opened, purplish lips.

His mother came and went, putting a cloth under his head, stirring the fire in the corner, complaining, swearing, feeling as if she were about to lose her mind.

They had found shelter in an abandoned grain house that was cluttered with dismantled machinery.

Josias had been sick since yesterday evening.

Earlier yesterday, as they walked along filled with hunger, they had passed by an old plantation field, with a bit of cassava still buried here and there in the ground.

Josias, who was straggling along behind, dropped back further.

He saw his father wasn't paying attention to him since his thoughts were on finding shelter. His mother, with the little boy on her hip, marched along way in front.

Falling behind even further, he entered the field and began digging with a little shovel in a hole next to a manioc bush; with great difficulty, even hurting himself, he managed to dig up a root which the shovel had cut in half.

Beating it against a rock, he more or less stripped it of its bark and sank his teeth into the yellow, fibrous pulp, one end of which was already turning to wood.

He greedily gnawed the dry, yellow root, grinding his teeth into its hard fiber.

Then he threw the end of the root on the ground, wiped his mouth on the edge of his sleeve, and sprightly slipped through the opening in the fence.

When he joined the others, who had already gathered together, his mother, worried by his absence, asked:

"What happened, Josias? Are you playing dumb or are you up to no good? What were you doing?"

The small boy looked away:

"Nothing . . . I was over there. . . ."

Chico Bento, who had gone in search of something, also came upon the field; struggling, he managed to pull up some pieces of manioc root and he returned to the hut, carrying them in his bag.

As Cordulina scraped the miserable cache for a tapioca, Josias, silent at her side and stretched out on the ground, made a face from time to time. Finally, he told his mother he had a stomachache.

"What from?"

Then he told her the story of the poisonous manioc. Startled, Cordulina stood up:

"My son! For the love of God! You ate raw manioc?"

Frightened and feeling the pain even more now, the boy began to cry. Stunned, tripping over some wood, Cordulina went over to a clearing and searched the stark ground for some leaves with which to make a tea. Then, giving up, she went over to the bags and pulled out a handful of dried senna from the bottom.

As she made the tea, she cried out to her husband, who was in the distance, exchanging words with a passerby:

"Chico! Chico! Mother of God, help me! Josias has poisoned himself!"

The remedies were used up, all resources were exhausted, and she was alone and her husband was far away—he had left at dawn to try to find someone who might know of a cure. Squatting next to her dying child, her head almost between her knees, and with a child holding onto her skirts, Cordulina cried uncontrollably.

Seated on a heavy wooden beam, one of the other children looked at his brother as he sucked his finger. Pedro, the oldest, was seated on the other side, and, from time to time, he shooed away flies that tried to land on the sick boy's face.

The child was just skin and bones: the outline of his swollen stomach was like a deformity on his thin, dry, leathery body, which was blackened and fetid like a corpse.

By the time his father arrived with an old black woman healer, Josias, moribund and unconscious, was breathing noisily and the death rattle could already be heard.

The old woman looked at the sick child, shaking her white, kinky head.

"There's nothing more to be done. . . . This one's already in the hands of Our Lord. . . ."

Cordulina raised her head for a few moments, looked at the old woman, then lowered her head once again between her knees, and cried twice as hard.

To avoid the possibility of error, the old black woman began to circle the child, blessing him with a dried twig taken from a chain around her neck which jingled with medals. And she muttered the prayer:

" 'Where do you come from, Peters and Paul? I come from Rome. What's new in Rome, Peters and Paul? . . .' "

Chico Bento leaned against a pole from a manioc press, his hatless head bowed, wretchedly watching his son's agony.

As the death rattle grew louder and louder, the child slowly slipped away, his body taut like an overfilled balloon about to explode. . . .

Finally they arrived at the *retirante* camp in Quixadá.

The child who had once been so chubby in Cordulina's arms now clung to her neck. So thin, neither a ghost nor death, perhaps only a skeleton could be that thin. . . .

"You, here, *compadre?* When did you arrive?" Chico Bento heard the voice and raised his eyes with a surprised look:

"Oh, *comadre* Conceição! You, here? I got here yesterday."

The young schoolteacher addressed herself to Cordulina:

"And you, *comadre,* how are you? Frail, no?"

The woman responded, sadly:

"Oh, *comadre,* who knows how I am! . . . It seems I'm still alive. . . ."

"And this one, here, is he my godchild?"

Intending to pick him up, Conceição nevertheless stepped back from the squalor of the child, contenting herself with taking his hand—a dry little paw that was rough and shriveled. . . .

"Don't you want your godmother's blessing, Manuel? His name is Manuel, isn't it?"

"Yes, but the children call him Duca. . . ."

"Did you come by train, *compadre?*"

"Just from Acarape to here. From Aroeiras to Acarape we came on foot. . . ."

Conceição was horrified, looking at one of the children, who was naked and so thin that it was a wonder he could support his huge stomach on his spindly legs:

"Virgin Mary! How did this little thing survive! It's a miracle!"

Cordulina made a tired gesture with her hands. The cowhand murmured:

"Only God Our Father knows. . . ."

Seated in the tiny parlor on St. Bernardo Street, with his hat between his legs and a coarse shock of hair over his eyes, Chico Bento talked to Conceição and her grandmother, Dona Inácia, about his uncertain future. The perverse drought had added to the misfortunes on the road. He also spoke of the miserable promiscuity of the poverty-ridden camp.

Sadly, he told of the hunger suffered on the trip and the miseries that resulted from it.

The death of Josias, godson of his *compadre* Luís Bezerra, the government representative in Acarape, who had helped them in one of the most miserable periods in their lives!—the death of Josias, who, lying next to a girder in that old grain shed, with his stomach swollen just like those of the northeasterners from Pará about to die. . . .

And the incident with the goat—"God forgive me!"—it was the first time Chico Bento had begged another man. . . . And it had turned out badly, the man had taken him for a good-for-nothing, trying to steal his goat; he was so tired, so dead on his feet, that all he could do was cringe and take the man's insults. . . .

The young woman's eyes brimmed with tears; filled with emotion, Dona Inácia raised her glasses and wiped her eyes with her handkerchief.

Huddled over, the cowhand kept on talking, merely stretching out his withered arm from time to time to whip the air at some sharp image of misery or acute despair. . . .

Then his son, Pedro, had run away, and then there was the night on the road when his wife, stretched out on the ground with little Duca at her side, panted and made meaningless noises, like someone who's about to die. . . .

Squatting by her side, with the two other little ones holding onto his legs, he didn't have the strength even to look for help or try to find shelter. . . .

* * *

One afternoon in the camp, Chico Bento called Conceição aside with a worried look on his face:

"*Comadre,* if I might have a word with you. . . ."

She approached him and sat down:

"What is it, *compadre?*"

The cowhand cleared his throat and spat on the ground as he searched for the words with which to begin:

"*Comadre,* when I left my home I was all set to go north. When Josias died and the other one ran off, my wife lost heart and fell to crying all day long, fearing she'd lose the rest of them. . . . First, I'd like you to talk to her, and then to help me get some tickets for the boat trip north. . . . This thing of children dying is crazy. . . . "

Conceição pensively bit her lip:

"Not that trip, *compadre!* I think *comadre* is right. . . . These children won't make a trip like that, all caged up on a ship going from the Amazon north. . . . And even if they could withstand the journey, what would you do when they got sick?"

Then Chico Bento said:

"I also thought about Maranhão. . . ."

Startled, Cordulina turned around:

"Chico, what do you mean, Maranhão? Heaven help us! Haven't you heard them say that whole families die there from malaria, as if it were the plague?"

Conceição agreed, pensively tracing the folds in her skirt with her fingernail:

"Yes, I've heard the worst things about Maranhão. . . . I agree, it's no good for you. . . ."

Dispirited, Chico Bento let his thin arms fall to his side:

"Then what are we going to do? *Comadre,* you can see we can't stay here, in this misery. . . . There's almost no work left in Tauhape. . . . What can I do to feed the children, outside of begging?"

At that bitter and just question, Conceição kept quiet, then she slowly murmured:

"You're right. But Amazonas isn't worth your while either. . . . Even rubber isn't making money. . . . And going to Maranhão is like going to your death. . . ."

The three remained silent in their indecision: Conceição, observing once again the folds in her skirt, Cordulina with her hands crossed in her lap and her eyes lowered, and Chico Bento, sadly fingering his bony face, his gaze fixed on some indeterminate point.

Suddenly, Conceição had an idea:

"Why don't you go to São Paulo? They say things are good there. . . . Plenty of work, a healthy climate. . . . You might even get rich. . . ."

The cowhand raised his eyes and hesitantly agreed:

"Yes. . . . Could be. . . . I put everything in your hands, *comadre.* All I want to do is get away. To the North or South. . . ."

Cordulina asked, timidly:

"Is it very far, São Paulo? Farther than Amazonas?"

"Almost the same distance. And, there, there's no malaria, malicious dolphins, or alligators. . . . It's a rich, clean, healthy land. . . ."

Chico Bento added:

"I've heard a lot of good things about São Paulo. Land of money, coffee, lots of sailors. . . ."

Conceição got up, shaking her skirt:

"Well, then, it's decided: São Paulo! I'll try to get the tickets. I'll bet anything that in a few years you'll come back rich. . . ."

The tickets were secured, but at a price. . . .

She finally had the small blue-colored stubs in her hand:

BRAZILIAN LLOYD NATIONAL COMPANY 3RD CLASS ONE PASSAGE

Why was she so moved by the sad confusion with which Chico Bento greeted her when she arrived with the tickets?

He extended his bony hand, and a strange spark flashed in his sick eyes:

"Amen!"

* * *

It was late afternoon. When Conceição left, he remained there, immobile and stretched out on the ground, staring at the misery of the camp, which was bustling at that hour.

The last rays of sunlight cast a red glow on their filthy rags and emaciated bodies, as if they were open, bloody sores. . . .

Now Chico Bento looked at that all too familiar scene with the disinterested detachment of an outsider.

In one or two days, he'd never again see those people, who lived and bustled about him, with their bony bodies rattling and their voices rasping out sorrowful exclamations. . . .

An old woman, camped nearby, came up to him with a tin cup, full of coffee. She was a good and helpful woman. Cared for by one of the ladies, she always had presents—coffee, sugar, bread—that she shared with her neighbors.

She offered the coffee to the cowhand:

"A little taste, Mr. Chico?" He took the cup, and stopping his hand in midair, he stared for a moment at the old woman standing before him.

Just a few hours more and maybe he'd never see this good and caring woman again! And if he did return one day, many years from now . . . she was already so old. . . . Where would she be?—Under a small mound of earth with a cross without a name.

Wiping her eyes, Cordulina approached them:

"*Sinhá* Anninha, did you hear that we're going to São Paulo?"

Suprised and anxious, *Sinhá* Anninha clasped her hands:

"My God! When?"

"When, Chico?"

He had trouble answering her. Something was painfully lodged in his throat.

Was it possible that he was feeling sad to leave that misery and horror?

In his mind the cowhand visualized his closed, deserted home in Aroeiras.

"When, Chico?"

"After tomorrow. . . ."

* * *

It was the day they were to leave. Dona Inácia opened the shutter in her house. Filling the street and the sky, the sun blinded her:

"This is too much, Conceição! Must you go to the beach with such a sun outside! Can't those people get off without your being there?"

The young woman was stubborn; she was going. Her grandmother went on:

"And you're going alone! You'll come back with a head cold and get even more sunburned!"

Conceição laughed:

"Now, now, Mother Nácia. Why all the fuss? Say it's all right. You always do in the end!"

Looking into the mirror, she put her hat on.

The clock struck the hour.

Conceição hurried along.

"Holy Mary! It's late. See you soon, Mother Nácia! Don't be angry! . . ."

The old woman made a gesture to hold her back. But when her granddaughter kissed her and marched toward the door, she shouted her consent at the last minute:

"Well at least show some good sense!"

There, from up above, the young woman watched them go, clutching one another as they looked out to the sea, with the same anguished and startled look in their eyes.

They were heading toward the Unknown, toward a *retirante* camp and the slavery of sharecroppers. . . .

They were headed toward their Destiny, which had called to them from so very far away, from the tawny, drought-ridden lands of Quixadá, and had brought them through hunger and death and infinite anguish, to here, only to take them up once again, onto the green shoulders of the sea and on to far-off lands where there was always manioc meal and cool, rainy weather. . . .

The boat in which they sat was now a small dot, a black wart pulling alongside the ship.

Conceição slowly turned away, drying her teary eyes on the handkerchief she had waved toward the sea.

Clarice Lispector

Clarice Lispector was two months old when her family left the Ukraine in 1925 and emigrated to Brazil. Recife, in the northeastern part of the country, was her home until her family moved to Rio de Janeiro in 1937. There she attended law school and worked as a translator alongside the writers Lúcio Cardoso and Antônio Callado. After securing a position at the newspaper *A Noite,* she began writing her first novel, *Perto do Coração Selvagem* (1944) *(Near the Wild Heart),* which Cardoso helped her to publish. The book was a critical success, and its title, which is taken from James Joyce's *A Portrait of the Artist as a Young Man,* caused several reviewers to comment on her affinity with the modernists.

In 1943, Lispector married Mauri Gurgel Valente, and the couple traveled extensively for the next fifteen years. In 1946, she published her second novel, *O Lustre* (The Luster), and three years later, *A Cidade Sitiada* (The Besieged City). During this period abroad, which ended with an eight-year residence in the United States, she also gave birth to two sons.

Shortly after returning to Brazil in 1959, Lispector published a collection of stories entitled *Laços de Família* (1960) *(Family Ties),* which became one of her most widely admired books. The stories in this volume deal with the inner lives of relatively commonplace characters, but they also have a heightened, surrealistic quality that became a typical feature of Lispector's mature work. In the 1960s, in addition to *Laços de Família,* Lispector wrote two other volumes of short fiction, four novels, and two children's books. Perhaps the most important of these publications was *A Paixão Segundo G. H.* (1964) *(The Passion According to G. H.)*—a powerful novel that describes a middle-class woman's surreal encounter with a cockroach.

As I've pointed out in the introduction to this anthology, Lispector's reputation among critics grew enormously during the 1960s. By the time of her death in 1977, she was already translated into several languages and was the most celebrated woman author in Brazil. Her best known fiction is structured around small, epiphanic moments; the story translated here, from her earliest period, helps to illustrate her preoccupation with characters who are imprisoned both by the society and by their own anxieties.

The Flight

(1940)

It began turning dark and she was afraid. The rain fell without respite, and the moistened sidewalks gleamed in the light of street lamps. People in a great hurry passed by with umbrellas and raincoats, their faces tired. Automobiles skidded on the wet asphalt, and one or two horns sounded softly.

She wanted to sit on a bench in the park, because, in truth, she didn't feel the rain and she didn't care about the cold. She felt only a tinge of fear, because she still hadn't decided what path to take. The bench would be a resting point. But the passersby looked at her strangely, and she kept walking.

She was tired. She thought over and over: "What's going to happen now?" If she were to keep on walking. That wasn't a solution. Return home? No. She feared some force might push her back to where she had started. Dazed as she was, she closed her eyes and imagined a great whirlwind coming out of "Elvira's Place," violently sucking her up, sitting her down next to her window at home with a book in her hand, and recomposing her daily scene. She was frightened. She waited for a moment until no one was passing by, and then she said firmly, "You won't go back." She grew calm.

Now that she had decided to go away, she seemed reborn. If she weren't so confused, she would have infinitely enjoyed what she had come to realize after the past two hours: "Well then, things still exist." Yes, the discovery was simply extraordinary. She had been married for twelve years, and three hours of freedom restored her almost whole unto herself—the first thing to do was to see if things still existed. If she were acting out this moment as tragedy on the stage, she would touch herself, pinch herself, just to make sure she was awake. But acting was the last thing she wanted to do.

Besides, it wasn't only happiness and relief she experienced. Also a tinge of fear and the memory of twelve years.

She crossed the promenade and leaned against a wall to look at the sea. The rain continued. She had boarded the bus at Tijuca and had gotten off in Gloria. She had already walked beyond Widow's Hill.

The sea churned forcefully, and when the waves broke against the rocks, salty foam sprayed over her. For a moment she wondered if that part of the sea was deep, because it was impossible to guess: the dark, gloomy waters could be hiding the infinite, or they could be centimeters above the sand. Now that she was free, she could try the game again. She had only to look lingeringly at the water and imagine a world without end. It was as if she were drowning and would never touch the bottom of the sea with her feet. A heavy anguish. Why search the bottom?

The idea of not finding the bottom of the sea was an old one, dating back to childhood. In grade school, while reading a chapter on the force of gravity, she had invented a man with a funny disease. The force of gravity had no effect on him. . . . Thus, she saw him falling off the earth and continuing to fall, because she didn't know what fate to give him. Where was he falling to? Then she resolved: he would keep on falling, falling and growing used to it; he would eat while falling, sleep while falling, live and even die while falling. And would he then keep on falling? At this moment in her life the memory of the falling man didn't pain her—on the contrary, it gave her a sense of freedom that she hadn't felt for twelve years. Because her husband had exerted a singular power over her: his mere presence was enough to paralyze the slightest movement of her imagination. At first, this had brought her a certain peace, for she used to grow weary of thinking about amusing but useless things.

Now the rain had stopped. The coolness felt refreshing. I won't go home. Ah yes, this thought is infinitely consoling. Will he be surprised? Yes, twelve years are a heavy weight, like kilos of lead. The days melt together, fuse, and form a single block, a large anchor. And persons are lost. Their eyes are like deep wells. Dark and silent water. Their gestures become empty and they have but one fear in life: that something will come and transform the stillness. They live behind a window, looking through the glass at the rainy season that covers over the sun, then summer returns and afterward the rains begin again. Desires are phantoms that dissolve when the lamp of good sense is barely lit. Why is it that husbands have so much good sense? Her husband's attitude is particularly solid, sound, and he never makes a mistake. The kind of reasonableness that people have who use only one brand of pencil and know by heart what's written on the bottom of their shoes. He can tell you exactly about train schedules, about which newspaper has the largest circulation, and even name the part of the world where monkeys reproduce most quickly.

She laughs. Now she can laugh. . . . I was eating while falling, I was sleeping while falling, I lived while falling. I'm going to find a place to plant my feet. . . .

She found this thought so amusing that she leaned over the wall and began to laugh. A fat man stopped some distance away and looked at her. What should I do? Perhaps go up to him and say: "My dear, it's raining." No. "My dear, I was a married woman and now I'm a woman." She started walking and forgot the fat man.

She opens her mouth and feels the fresh air flood inside. Why did she wait so long for this renovation? Only today, after twelve centuries. She had stepped out of a cold shower, put on a lightweight dress, and picked up a book. But today was different from all the afternoons of the days of all those years. It was warm and she was suffocating. She opened all the windows and doors. But no relief: the air was immobile, serious, heavy. No breeze, and the sky was low with dark, thick clouds.

How did it happen? In the beginning, just a sense of uneasiness and heat. Then something within her began to grow. Suddenly, in slow, minuscule movements, she pulled off her dress and tore it into long thin strips. The air closed in about her, squeezing her. Then a loud rumble shook the house. Almost at the same time, large, warm raindrops began to fall here and there.

She remained still in the middle of the room, panting. The rain increased. She heard it drumming on the metal roof in the back and the maid's cries as she gathered up the clothes. A fresh breeze circled through the house, soothing her warm face. She was calmer then. She got dressed, gathered together all the money in the house, and left.

Now she was hungry. She hadn't felt hungry for twelve years. She'd go into a restaurant. The bread is fresh, the soup is hot. She'd ask for coffee, a strong and aromatic cupful. Oh, how everything is pretty and delightful. The hotel room has a foreign air, the pillow is soft, with the perfume of clean linen. And when the darkness overcomes the room, an enormous moon will appear after the rain, a fresh, serene moon. And she'll sleep covered with moonlight. . . .

She'd get up early. She'd have the morning free to buy the essentials for the trip, because the ship leaves at two in the afternoon. The sea is quiet, almost without waves. The blue of the sky, violent, screaming. The ship moves away rapidly. . . . And soon the silence. The waters sing in the hull, softly, rhythmically. . . . Seagulls soar all about, white specks of foam fleeing the sea. Yes, all that!

But she doesn't have enough money to travel. The tickets are so expensive. And the rain that soaked her has left her with a sharp coldness inside. She can go to a hotel. That's true. But the hotels in Rio aren't appropriate for an unaccompanied lady, except for the first-class ones. And in a first-class hotel she might run into one of her husband's acquaintances, which would certainly hurt his business.

Oh, all this is a lie. What's the truth? Twelve years are a heavy weight, like kilos of lead, and the days close around one's body, squeezing harder. I'll go back home. I can't be mad at myself because I'm tired. Everything is merely happening to me, I'm not provoking anything. It's twelve years.

She enters the house. It's late and her husband is reading in bed. She tells him that Rosinha was ill. Didn't he get her note saying she'd be late getting home? No, he says.

She drinks a glass of milk because she isn't hungry. She puts on her blue flannel pajamas with the small white dots, they're really quite soft. She asks her husband to turn out the light. He kisses her on her face and tells her to wake him up at seven sharp. She promises, he turns off the light.

From behind the trees appears a large, pure light.

She keeps her eyes open for a while. Then, wiping her tears on the sheet, she closes her eyes and arranges herself in bed. She feels the moonlight slowly covering her.

In the silence of the night, the ship moves farther and farther away.

Sra. Leandro Dupré

Sra. Leandro (Maria José) Dupré was among Brazil's most popular and prolific writers of the 1940s and 1950s. Born in 1905, in a small town in the state of São Paulo, she published her first story, "Uma Família Antiga de Jaboticabal" (An Old Family from Jaboticabal), in a 1938 edition of the newspaper *O Estado de São Paulo.* Shortly after the publication of her first novel, *O Romance de Teresa Bernard* (1941) (The Romance of Teresa Bernard), she wrote *Éramos Seis* (1943) (We Were Six), about a struggling middle-class family in São Paulo. (The title is poignant, because midway through the book the father dies, and from that point the family slowly disintegrates.) Hailed by writer and critic Monteiro Lobato, who is credited with "discovering" Dupré, *Éramos Seis* became a best-selling novel and was awarded the Brazilian Academy of Letters' Raul Pompéia Prize as the best work of 1943.

The majority of Dupré's novels, which include *Luz e Sombra* (1944) (Light and Dark), *Gina* (1945), and *Os Rodriguez* (1946) (The Rodriguezes), are concerned with everyday life in lower-middle-class families, and their central protagonists tend to be women. Among her most successful creations is Dona Lola, the narrator in *Éramos Seis,* whose strength, good humor, love, and ingenuity make for a compelling image of the "ordinary" wife and mother. This character was so popular with the Brazilian public that, in 1949, Dupré published a sequel to *Éramos Seis,* entitled simply *Dona Lola.*

Dupré's books saw numerous reprintings, and several of her novels were still available in the 1970s. Despite having been one of the most widely read authors in the country, Dupré is rarely mentioned in standard reference works on Brazilian literature.

From *We Were Six* (1943)

In the beginning of December, my sisters arrived from Itapetininga. I went to the station with little Júlio and we all returned home by trolley car because a coach was too expensive and we needed to economize. We put their two small suitcases in the front of the trolley car; I soon regreted having brought Júlio along; my sisters had brought several packages filled with eggs and sweets that Momma had sent me, and Júlio only caused more confusion by wanting to help carry the packages that he dropped with every step.

Clotilde and Olga were anxious to see our new house; the year before, when they had come to spend the holidays, we still lived in Bom Retiro, in a tiny house that barely accommodated our family of six. My sisters had had to sleep in the small bedroom with the older boys, where the four of them barely fit, even with Carlos and Alfredo sleeping on a mattress on the floor.

When I wrote telling them that we had moved to Avenida Angélica, into a fine house that we were intending to buy, they wrote me from Itapetininga, saying: "So, it's only mansions for you now?"

On the way home in the trolley car, they kept asking me questions:

"Are you happy in your new home?"

"How many rooms does it have?"

"Do you own it yet?"

"Does it have a garden out front?"

I answered their questions, paying more attention to my son, who was trying to conceal his desire to open the box which he knew contained a cake. I asked for news of Momma.

They said she was doing fine, but was complaining of rheumatism in her legs caused by so much work; she always had a lot to do. From time to time she would also complain about a sharp pain in the pit of her stomach. We were silent for a few moments, thinking about Momma's pain and wondering what it could be.

When we arrived home, my husband, Júlio, and the other children were waiting at the front gate. There was much talk and many embraces:

"Look how Isabel has grown!"

"And Júlio gets fatter every time we see him!"

"What a pretty house!"

They went inside and glanced into all the corners, while Júlio carried the bags to their room and Durvalina took the baskets and packages to the kitchen. They hugged Durvalina:

"Even Durva is fatter. Just one look and you can see things are going well here."

They went through the entire house, finding everything perfect. In their room, which was my sewing room, I had covered the sewing machine with a small embroidered cloth so that it could be used as a table. There were two beds, a chair, and a small mirror hung on the wall. They took off their hats, went into the bathroom and returned, combing their hair, all the while keeping up a steady stream of conversation:

"What a wonderful bathroom! If only we had one like that at home!"

Later:

"Do you know who got married? I bet you can't guess! Maria da Glória!"

I opened my eyes wide in amazement:

"You don't say! Maria da Glória? But to whom?"

"A salesman employed by some important firm, they say he makes good money."

I sat down on the bed, stunned, and stared at Clotilde, who had broken the news:

"Why she must be forty years old, Clotilde! More than forty even; I remember I was just a child in short dresses and she was already going to dances! She's more than forty, I'll bet she's forty-five!"

Olga intervened, saying maliciously:

"That's right. Imagine, old and ugly and yet she got herself a husband. I told Clotilde we shouldn't lose hope."

Clotilde scoffed:

"Ha! Don't talk nonsense!"

Isabel appeared at the bedroom door eating a piece of candy; I was furious:

"My God! Look at that child eating candy and it's almost supper time. Who gave that to you?"

She didn't answer, and before I could take it out of her hand, she put the whole piece in her mouth, looking at me with eyes that started to tear from her efforts to chew. The aunts laughed, enchanted:

"Isabel's a delight; she looks like Júlio."

"But she has Lola's eyes."

"Her eyes and her mouth; her mouth is just like Lola's."

"Then she looks like Lola."

"No. She has Júlio's forehead and nose. Look close."

Isabel became impatient and ran out of the room; then Júlio appeared in the doorway, smiling:

"Aren't you done telling your news? Is there much more?" And turning to me, he asked:

"How's dinner coming along, Lola? Isn't it ready yet?"

I scurried out of the room and told Durvalina to put dinner on the table.

After dinner we continued to talk in the living room about acquaintances and relatives from Itapetininga. I asked:

"And Aunt Candoca, how's she doing? You wrote me she had taken a fall. Is she better?"

"She broke her leg, but now she's almost good as new. You knew that Juquinha fell off a horse?"

"No. You didn't write about that. Did he get hurt very badly? Why didn't you write and tell me?"

"He didn't break a single bone, but his forehead and nose were pretty scratched up; his face was swollen for a few days, but then got better. We didn't write about it because we were about to come here."

Suddenly, Olga recalled another incident and began talking with renewed enthusiasm:

"Do you know that Doca made peace with Gumercindo? They're going to get married next month."

"No! When they were fighting she said she'd rather die than marry him!"

"That's just talk. She says things without thinking. Now they're really excited about the wedding."

"Who would have thought?"

The children, sleepy-eyed, sat round us listening to our stories and refusing to go to bed; later, I carried them quickly to their rooms, tucked them in, and returnèd to the living room to hear more news. With his pipe in the corner of his mouth and the newspaper on his lap, Júlio exchanged a few sentences with my sisters, asking them about his uncle and other acquaintances. I looked at the sweets Momma had sent: six little cans of guava paste in syrup, six little packages of sugared figs; six jars of peach preserves and a marble cake; I mentally calculated how many days those desserts would last. There was a pause in the conversation, a resting period, then Júlio started it up again:

"And how's Soares doing? Still playing the part of the Romeo?"

Clotilde and Olga looked at one another and blushed. It was as if they were asking: should we tell them or not? Clotilde decided to break the news:

"Nowadays he's chasing after Maroquinhas."

Júlio took the pipe out of his mouth; a look of amazement came over his face and his eyes opened wide. I had a can of sweets in my hand and was so taken back by the news that I didn't know what to do with it. Olga added:

"That's right. That's what he's up to these days, the shameless man. He's a good-for-nothing."

Júlio finally managed to speak:

"He's that for a fact. Imagine, Maroquinhas, Chico's wife. Isn't it a shame?"

We all sat still without saying a word, feeling the tragic news spread through the air like smoke; we started up the conversation again, but the most shocking story of the evening returned as the overriding theme. I spoke in a low voice as if I were afraid to hear my own words:

"This world is lost. I can hardly believe it, it seems incredible. And Maroquinhas?"

"Maroquinhas is responding. So they say."

Disgusted, Olga said:

"Women are idiots, they believe in men; I always had a funny feeling about Maroquinhas, she was always so fired up around men."

For the next half-hour we commented on the situation, anxiously wondering how Chico would react.

Finally Júlio got up and stretched his arms over his head:

"Well now. Shall we turn in? It's almost ten o'clock!"

We all went our different directions; but before going to bed, I sought out Olga and asked her privately:

"How's Zeca doing?"

Olga made a face and turning away, responded:

"I don't know. We had a fight."

"You fought? But why? I don't believe it!"

Clotilde overheard us and came into the conversation:

"A lovers' spat, Lola. Any day now they'll make up."

"But what was the reason for the fight? You two were so close!"

Olga explained, her voice sounding somewhat upset:

"He didn't want me to come here to São Paulo. He wanted me to spend the holidays right there. Imagine! I insisted on coming and he got mad. He didn't show up for two days, but I came here anyway. Why didn't he ask me nicely? If we were engaged, I wouldn't have come."

Smiling, I said:

"These little tiffs are nothing, any day now you'll be engaged."

And saying good night, I withdrew to the bedroom where Júlio was already fast asleep. I laid down and in the darkness replayed all the stories I had heard and visualized all my friends and acquaintances from Itapetininga. I saw Maroquinhas flirting with that good-for-nothing Soares; Doca marrying Gumercindo; Momma mixing a large pan of guava paste, or peeking in the giant clay oven in the backyard to see if the powdered biscuits were browned. Flushed, sweating, a towel wrapped around her head, and with the lid of the oven in her one hand and a little stick in the other, she was turning the biscuits over one at a time, wrinkling her forehead and keeping her eyes half-shut because of the heat. Aunt Candoca with her broken leg stretched out on a chair, moaning from time to time: Oh, my God! They all went through my mind and stubbornly returned over and over until, finally exhausted, I closed my heavy eyelids and went to sleep.

* * *

The week following my sisters' arrival, we began working on their hats and dresses so they would look presentable when they went out. They were last year's hats and were ugly and faded; we changed them, using wire and canvas, covering everything with satin, which was in style at the time. Clotilde's hat was gray satin with a cherry-colored ribbon; Olga's was blue satin with tiny blue flowers around the brim. Then, after their dresses were ready, we went to visit Aunt Emília, our "rich aunt," as Júlio used to say. She was my father's oldest sister and had married a very wealthy and important gentleman, although she had been a widow for some time now. She lived on Guaianazes Street; one of the questions my mother repeatedly asked in her letters was: "Have you visited your Aunt Emília?" Our visit to her was a necessary duty since Momma owed her many favors. One beautiful day, just after lunch, we went to Guaianazes Street. On the way, I warned Olga not to laugh or look at me if we were served *orchata,* a drink made of crushed melon seeds, or if Aunt Emília started talking about the origins of the different Paulista families. It was funny, that mania of hers: she knew by heart every important family in the city and had a prodigious memory for names and dates. She had even made a notebook in which she had written down the histories of São Paulo's founding fathers, and whenever she saw people interested in the subject, you couldn't get her to stop talking. Olga promised not to look or laugh.

The mansion on Guaianazes Street commanded respect and instilled fear; as we arrived and rang the doorbell, I mentally calculated how many times our house—it still wasn't ours and we didn't know when we would finish paying the remaining twenty *contos* we owed on it—would fit inside those gardens. Aunt Emília was very rich and to us her house—with its legion of servants, its stiff, smug housekeepers, its thick carpets that your feet would sink into, its curtains heavy as lead, and varnished tables with their legs filled with carved balls and people's faces—was like a dream from the thousand and one nights. And the horses? She had a carriage pulled by two brown horses and driven by a straight-back coachman whose large, shiny top hat was tipped at an angle on his head. She said she would use a carriage as long as she could, she detested automobiles. And whenever she visited me, which was once a year, her coach would stop in front of our house, and the neighbors' windows would fill with curious faces staring at the majestic horses as they stamped the ground with their powerful hooves.

The children would get excited and go in and out of the house, which made me quite nervous. Carlos and Alfredo would stand with their hands in their pockets and walk from one side of the carriage to the other with an imposing air, challenging all those who passed by with their haughty eyes, as if they were saying: "We aren't just anyone; look at the visitors our mother receives." And they would cast admiring glances at the coachman, who looked just like a king on a throne. Happily, her visits were brief; I was always embarrassed, because I was only able to offer her coffee, which she didn't always accept.

In the mansion, a servant took us to a private parlor where Aunt Emília received her intimate friends and relatives. We sat with great ceremony on the edge of the velvet chairs, and when our aunt entered with her majestic air, we got up to greet her respectfully. She was already in her seventies and was tall and had an imposing air that kept everyone at a distance; she always seemed to say implicitly: "You don't need to get close, talk right from there." She politely asked about our mother, my husband, and the children, then we asked her about her children. She told stories about her oldest ones and her grandchildren, and said that her two unmarried sons were traveling in Argentina; if it weren't for the war, they'd be in Europe. Then, she rang a bell and when the servant appeared, she ordered him to call the girls; a little later, her two daughters, who lived there with her, entered. The "girls" were over fifty years old, one a widow and the other a spinster; they were both quiet and pensive. Aunt Emília ordered one of them to ring the bell, and turning to us, asked gently:

"Do you like *orchata?* I'll order some for you."

I looked at the design in the carpet, and with my lips pressed together, made a tremendous effort not to laugh; I soon sensed that Olga's chair was shaking and then she began to cough; she coughed so hard that everyone began recommending cough syrups; one said that eucalyptus was better, another advised something else, and finally the coughing ceased. We drank the *orchata* and then Aunt Emília paid me the money for the slippers I had made for her. I protested:

"I didn't come here for this, Aunt Emília. I'm in no hurry for the money."

But she paid and placed another order for her prospective grandchildren, whose births were imminent. She then informed us that the wedding of her youngest granddaughter would take place at the end of the month at her house, where they would also have the reception. There was a pause, then suddenly she said:

"I know the history of the Lemos family since 1624; they're from São José de Atibaia and had a farm in Paraíba. There was a Dom Francisco de Lemos born in Castela and he married Isabel in the year 1640. Isabel died and Dom Francisco married Catarina de Mendonça and they had two children, Baltasar and Jerônimo. . . ."

One of the girls interrupted:

"Didn't one of them marry a daughter of Bartolomeu Bueno de Camargo?"

"That's right, Baltasar. They had seven children. . . ."

Olga gave me a pleading look as if asking: "Can it be she'll name all seven?" I shook my head "yes" and Olga gave a deep sigh.

Aunt Emília continued:

"One of the daughters of that couple was Leonor, who was married three times; the first time she married a widower, Machado da Borba Gato (she paused to appreciate the effect of that name); with Borba Gato she had four children."

One of the girls, who was counting on her fingers the number of children Leonor had had, raised her hand and showed seven fingers. Aunt Emília went on, undisturbed:

"One of the children from the second marriage was also called Baltasar, and he married Francisca de Souza in 1710, in the village of Santo Amaro. They had three children, I believe that the Lemos name of Lola's husband comes from that branch of the family. One of the children got married in Vila de Itú, which at that time was called Outú.

Clotilde couldn't help but exclaim:

"What a memory you have, Aunt Emília! How do you manage to keep everything straight? Names and dates?"

Aunt Emília laughed, pleased with herself:

"Ah! It's because I like those things. Just one of my many manias. There are people who like to collect stamps, or fans or coins; I collect the origins of the Paulistas. I love it and have everything written down in notebooks. Ever since I was a young girl, I've been interested in family trees; didn't your father tell you that?"

"Papa told us, but I never knew your memory was so marvelous. Is that Borba Gato the same one mentioned in Brazilian histories?"

Aunt Emília became more animated and turned toward Clotilde:

"Yes, the very same. Baltasar had a daughter, Isabel; another daughter was called Mariana; she was married to an Alcoforado, then she married a Baião. They had a son called Baltasar too, and he married Isabel Monteiro and. . . ."

At that moment some ladies entered the room and Aunt Emília stood up to receive them. She introduced us, saying we were members of the Barros family from Itú, and went on to explain to the visitors:

"I was telling my nieces about the origin of their mother's family, which also happens to be that of the husband of the second daughter, this one here (and she pointed to me). I was just talking about the Lemos family. I have everything written down in notebooks. The Barros family is also among my acquaintances; there's the Pais de Barros family, the Aguiar Barros family. . . ."

One of the ladies replied:

"Your memory is extraordinary. I'm amazed that you know everything in such detail, with dates, without forgetting a thing. You should write a book about the families of São Paulo, it would be extremely interesting."

Everyone agreed and Aunt Emília smiled, saying that she had already considered that. Another lady said:

"Our family is descended from the Barroses from Itú."

Aunt Emília became excited:

"Rightly so. Captain Fernão Pais de Barros married Ângela Leite Ribeiro in 1781, and they had several children; the seventh one was Captain Francisco Xavier Pais de Barros from Itú, his nickname was Captain Chico de Sorocaba. . . ."

One of the ladies interrupted, smiling:

"That was our grandfather. How did you know?"

Aunt Emília continued, becoming more excited by the minute:

"He was married three times; the first time to Rosa Cândida de

Aguiar Barros, the second time to his ex-sister-in-law, Maria de Aguiar Barros, and the third time to Andreza Lopes de Oliveira."

Clotilde exclaimed in admiration:

"That's wonderful, Aunt Emília!"

Another lady asked:

"Wasn't it one of those who had a gold mine and managed to extract an *arroba* of gold out of it?"

"Yes indeed; with that *arroba* of gold, he bought land in Itú and returned to São Paulo, where he married Maria Paula Machado, the daughter of. . . ."

One of her daughters interrupted:

"The first of those Barroses came to Brazil centuries earlier, didn't they, mama?"

"Yes. The first one was called Pedro Vaz de Barros. He arrived in 1601 and was a councilman in the House in São Paulo. Imagine, he was already a councilman then, see how old the family is?"

We were all impressed; Aunt Emília continued:

"He married here into the Leme family, who are descended from a Flamengo family, and the couple's fifth child was Fernão Pais de Barros. He brilliantly defended the town square in Santos from an attack launched by the Dutch, and received letters from Prince Pedro in his own hand. . . ."

"Your memory is as marvelous as your modesty," one of the ladies said vehemently.

Another one declared:

"It's a true treasure having in one's head the family trees of the Paulistas!"

They all smiled; the servant entered and announced more visitors had arrived. My sisters and I took our leave; we talked about the visit all afternoon: Aunt Emília's memory, her granddaughter's wedding celebration—everything that had happened.

Some ten days later, a servant delivered an invitation to the wedding; the house broke out in total confusion. After a while I said:

"I'm not going; I need so many things that I can't go. I don't have a good enough dress or hat; in fact, I only have one pair of new shoes. I don't even have any stockings."

There were strong protests:

"It would be absurd if you missed that magnificent party! Don't even think that way; we'll figure out something, but you and Júlio have to go."

When Júlio came home that afternoon, we talked about the party and showed him the invitation to the reception. Dismayed, Júlio scratched his head:

"Rich relatives are only good for making people spend money. Imagine how much this is going to cost us just to go there and stay half an hour: the clothes, shoes, car. . . .

Olga replied:

"*Noblesse oblige,* I think you two should go. Be patient, Júlio, just think how pretty the party will be and all the yummy things you'll have to eat and drink!"

I said:

"No, it's better if we back out. I don't want to think about how much the things I need would cost; with that money I could buy clothes and shoes for the children."

My sisters continued to argue:

"No, you have to go. What are you thinking about? Aunt Emília would be offended."

Júlio ended up agreeing with them:

"Let's throw caution to the wind and go, Lola."

Clotilde looked at me and said:

"I have some new stockings I'll loan you. I haven't even worn them yet."

Olga said she would loan me a small beaded bag she had gotten from a friend long ago, and Júlio gave me fifty *mil réis* to get a dress.

Three years earlier I had bought a dress with maroon lace for the wedding of one of Aunt Candoca's daughters; I took this dress to the seamstress to see what she could do with it. She took off the old trimming that was falling apart and decorated the dress with canary-yellow velvet ribbons; in those days they wore that color a lot. With the rest of the money, I bought some new flowers for my black silk hat, some gloves, and because Júlio was grumbling that his tie was too ugly for a wedding, I got him a new tie. He also bought a new pair of high laced shoes.

On the day of the wedding, early in the morning, I called the beautician to come fix my hair and by noon she was done; she spent an hour rolling and pinning the curls around my head. My hair was long, to my waist, and the woman had a terrible time pinning it all up and giving it a fashionable look.

After my hairdo was ready, I felt sad, my face looked enormous and my hair resembled a hornet's nest. But I didn't say a word because my sisters were busy praising my hairstyle, saying it had turned out beautifully. I was unhappy and had to endure it the entire day, because the wedding wasn't until six. Clotilde and Olga were nervous, trying to remember every detail, and they went around commenting with little cries and exclamations. They took care of the children so they wouldn't bother me; they rubbed cold cream on my face and neck, and made me take a lukewarm bath so that my features would look rested; and at four o'clock, they helped me get dressed. First came the corset; they cinched it so tight that the staves poked into my flesh—I'd gotten quite a bit heavier in the last few years. Putting my dress on was a struggle because we were afraid of ruining my hair. The children kept peeking in, asking if they could see "Momma ready," and by then I was really impatient. It was the end of December and the day was exceedingly hot; I wasn't even dressed and I was sweating so much that the cream Clotilde had put on my face had run, making me look hideous. Then Júlio arrived and began to get dressed; he said he had hired an automobile to pick us up at five-thirty, and the children ran to wait for it at the gate.

Olga wiped the cream off my face with a bit of cloth and then put on another layer; I sat down in a living room chair to rest and try to stop sweating; I felt like sending everything to the devil by then, taking off my clothes, taking down my hair, sitting on the floor dressed only in a slip and robe, and having a cup of coffee with bread and butter.

The moment finally came for me to put on my hat; with Olga on one side and Clotilde on the other, they placed the enormous black hat on my head and secured it with the pins Dona Genu had loaned me; one pin was made of ivory in the shape of a horse's head and was very pretty. They let me fasten the collar of my dress at the last minute; there were five staves in the collar that kept my neck long and stretched. Then I put on my gloves and picked up the beaded purse with a little lace hankie inside. When I looked in the mirror, I barely recognized myself; I was so different from my usual self, with all those trimmings and trinkets. Clotilde and Olga were tireless in their admiration and they called to Dona Genu to come over and see me. In came Dona Genu, her young daughters, and the children; everyone stood around me, talking and commenting; Dona Genu said it was a shame I didn't have any jewels, but Olga responded, saying that Cinderella didn't have any either and she was still the prettiest one at the ball, and that once in Aunt Emília's house, everyone would ask:

"Who's that woman in the maroon dress with the canary-yellow ribbons? The one with the black silk hat?"

Such was the impact I was going to have. Júlio appeared in the living room, limping a little and complaining that the wedding was going to be a bore because he didn't know anyone, and besides that, his new shoes were too tight; rich people were only good for making poor people spend their hard-earned money. He promised he wouldn't limp once we got there. Everybody praised his dark suit and new tie; I noticed that his shoes squeaked and was horrified. We weren't even close to being Prince Charming and Cinderella. At the last hour, a small problem arose; my sisters were of the opinion that the rented automobile should wait at the entrance to the mansion until the festivities were over. Júlio thought that was extravagant and would be extremely expensive. Olga reasoned:

"But when the party's over, you'll be tired and won't find an automobile to bring you back. It would be unattractive for you to walk home through the streets dressed like that. . . . *Noblesse oblige,* I think that's what you should do."

Júlio scratched his head with care so as not to move the hairs out of place:

"But how much will the fellow charge? It's going to cost a fortune, and I've had so many expenses."

Clotilde said:

"Wait here, I'll go talk to the chauffeur."

Soon after, she returned saying that she had haggled a bit with the fellow, an Italian, and that he had agreed on twelve *mil réis;* at first he wouldn't budge from fifteen, but he finally gave in.

Júlio took out all the money he had in his pockets and counted it, but it wasn't enough. I went to my drawer where there were always a few coins lying about, and putting it all together, we managed to come up with the exact amount. We climbed into the automobile waiting for us at the gate, while the whole neighborhood stood round watching us leave, smiling and waving goodbye and at the same time envying our good fortune at having been invited to a high-society celebration. I didn't move during the entire trip for fear that I'd muss up my hair or tip my hat.

A never-ending line of automobiles majestically drove up Guaianazes Street, whose occupants were left off at the door to the mansion. A bit nervous, we got out of the automobile and with small, solemn steps, we crossed the garden and entered the main hall, which was filling up with guests. In the distance we saw Aunt Emília and one of her girls, who smiled at us.

We looked around, and because we didn't know anyone there, we stood silently in a corner of the room awaiting the bride and groom. Suddenly soft music began playing and a glass door in the hall was opened. We saw the bride give her arm to her father and walk slowly toward the altar that had been erected at the back of the room.

There was a long silence, then the ceremony began. We couldn't hear anything clearly because we were so far away from the altar—just the murmuring of voices—and we saw the bridal couple's heads move. From time to time Júlio whispered in my ear:

"What a bore! And my corns are killing me in these shoes."

"Who told you to buy shoes too tight for your feet? You bought them, now suffer the consequences."

Soon afterward, everyone was embracing each other as they moved about and talked. Other doors in the hall were opened and we all followed the bride and groom to the dining room. Here there was an enormous table filled with beautiful pastries. With some difficulty, we managed to make our way through the crowd to the newlyweds, who were seated at the center of a long table; we shook their hands and wished them happiness. They didn't know us, but they smiled politely and thanked us. . . .

By nine o'clock that evening, the newlyweds had disappeared and many of the guests were beginning to leave. We said our goodbyes and left as well. Júlio was limping horribly and his shoes squeaked as he walked, but he didn't care. I pushed my hat back off my sweaty forehead to give it some air. We found our Italian driver, who looked a little nervous and was excitedly talking to his compatriots. Júlio asked him what was going on and he responded:

"Don't blame me, but the price, she's gone up. I had to drive the priest home and come back. You owe me another five *mil réis.*"

Júlio stared at him with his eyes opened wide:

"What? You drove the priest? What's that got to do with me? I'm paying what we agreed on and that's that."

"But who's gonna pay for the priest? I can't take no loss. I'm no budge 'til I get my money."

Júlio was getting more excited:

"What do you mean? You're crazy. I'll pay what we agreed on and not a penny more. Get in, Lola."

The driver raised five fingers in Júlio's face and said, angrily:

"They order me to take the priest home. I'm wanting my money."

He cleared his throat and hiked up his pants with both hands. I grabbed hold of Júlio's arm:

"Stop arguing and let's go. We're not getting anywhere."

Furious, Júlio turned to the driver and said:

"Look here, I'm not to blame if they told you to drive the priest. I didn't have anything to do with it. I'll pay you what we agreed on. Now let's go."

"I'm no budge without five *mil réis.* Who's gonna pay me?"

The other drivers, passersby, and guests from the party began gathering around us. I tried pulling Júlio away, whispering:

"Please, Júlio. Stop arguing and let's go. Don't make a scene."

But Júlio shouted even louder:

"Who'll pay you? I don't know who's gonna pay you. I'm paying what I owe. Crank up this rattletrap and take me home."

The driver looked at him angrily and spit on the ground:

"By God, I'm no leave without five *mil réis.* I drive the priest. They order me."

"And I'm responsible? I don't even know the priest. Come on, let's get going."

The people around us began discussing the situation in loud voices; some were against Júlio, others were in his favor. The driver wasn't budging and, from time to time, he yanked up his pants. Clearing his throat, he raised his arm and stuck five fingers almost in our faces.

I was getting more and more nervous. Grabbing Júlio's arm again, I begged him to leave. Angry, he asked me:

"Leave how? This wretch wants more money and I don't have a cent in my pocket!"

I was sweating. Guests coming out of the mansion looked at us curiously. The driver was becoming bolder as Júlio got more irritated. Júlio said:

"Let's stop gabbing and go."

"I want my money for drive the priest."

"I don't have your money."

"I don't hire out for to take a loss."

"But I didn't ask you to drive the priest. I had nothing to do with that."

The circle of people around us was getting larger and everyone was commenting on the case:

"By God, I do the job and I no take a loss."

"But I had nothing to do with that."

"By God, I want my money."

At that moment, one of my aunt's servants came out to see what was going on: I thanked God. The servant told the driver that he'd get his money right then if he wouldn't argue any further. The servant left and came back with the money. Then we got into the automobile and were finally on our way home. My sisters and the two older children were waiting up to hear our news. When we arrived, Júlio paid what he owed and seemed ready to start up the argument again, saying:

"Now look here. . . ."

But I grabbed his arm and shouted, "Júlio!"

He gave up. Greatly relieved, I got out of the automobile with my hat in my hand. He went up to the house in his stocking feet, carrying his shoes. Before entering, he turned and shook one of his shoes at the automobile, which was pulling away. Once in the house, we sat down. Júlio propped up his feet on the chair in front of him and we both gave a deep sigh.

Olga asked:

"Did everybody comment on your dress? Was it a big success?"

I didn't have the heart to tell her that no one noticed me or the dress:

"It wasn't exactly a success, but they noticed it and several ladies asked me where I got it."

Clotilde said:

"You looked beautiful. A real Cinderella."

"No, Clotilde. No way. There were some beautiful dresses there from Europe . . . silver, gold, a few had jewels. . . ."

My sisters' eyes opened wide. Júlio and the two children got up to go to bed, but I stayed and talked without stopping until very late that evening.

Emi Bulhões Carvalho da Fonseca

Like Sra. Leandro Dupré, Emi Bulhões Carvalho da Fonseca was a prolific and widely read author of the 1940s and 1950s. A Carioca by birth, she published her first book, a collection of stories entitled *No Silêncio da Casa Grande* (In the Silence of the Big House) in 1944. That year, the book was awarded the Afonso Arinos Prize for best fiction. Two years later, in 1946, she published the novel *Mona Lisa*, which was followed by *O Oitavo Pecado* (1947) (The Eighth Sin), *Jóia* (1948) (Jewel), *Pedras Altas* (1949) (High Rocks), *Anoiteceu na Charneca* (1951) (Nightfall on the Moors), and *Lua Cinzenta* (1953) (Gray Moon). Among her best known works is *Desquite Amigável* (1965) (Friendly Separation), about the difficulties couples endured in a country where divorce was prohibited.

Carvalho da Fonseca's career spanned nearly four decades, and her fiction provides insights into important aspects of the Brazilian experience. Unfortunately, like several of her contemporaries, she is now an almost forgotten author.

In the Silence of the Big House

(1944)

It is the moment near dawn. The sleeping world gives a kind of grimace, anxiously flutters its eyes, opens its mouth and gulps. Everything is in a state of suspension, palpitating, as it senses the agony of a land turning cold, fading, and growing pale. . . . But there, up ahead, trembling and indecisive, is a promise of resurrection and life, a rustling. Day is about to begin.

In bed, still unconscious, Natalina feels the grazing touch of the cold wings of the angel of death, who shoulders the night, and she pulls the red coverlet's thick baize up under her chin. She has slept soundly and is about to awaken. But she doesn't feel the pleasant sensation that comes with a good night's rest. A painful feeling weighs on her chest, at a point directly over her heart. She's still asleep. Only the first layer of her being is awakening as it rises out of some deep thing that suffocates and anguishes her. And unpleasant memories come forth, one by one, like bubbles rising to the surface. . . . Suddenly, the memory of her disgrace, of the horrible suffering she endured, chases away all sleep. She awakens in agony, trying not to accept the reality of the cruel scenes she recalls so vividly. Turning her face to the side, she feels relief as she lets the tears stream down her face and onto the pillow, whose thick fabric absorbs them completely. In the darkness, much calmer now, she remembers the horrible scene that seems to have happened yesterday, or perhaps it was a few days ago, she's not sure, having lost all sense of time. But what comes to her mind are older memories, much much older. She sees herself as a little girl. How old must she be? Three, four. . . . She's with the other slaves and at the side of her mother, who, always busy and burdened with work, rails at her continuously. Her mother's hands. Large, very dark on the back, the palms almost white—active, thick hands. As if hypnotized, she follows their movements as they plunge into the blue water of the washing tub, then pull out the undergarments, soaping and pounding their twisted form, then soaping them again and going back into the water. From time to time, the hands busy themselves over her; she feels their roughness as they rapidly dress her or take hold of her arm. Utilitarian gestures. Never an embrace. But then she doesn't know about that kind of thing, so she doesn't find the absence of any affection strange. She learns her first lesson in life—that the rough hands of the poor are instruments of work and nothing more.

She sees herself sitting on a stone step. She's wearing a little white shift, a weightless rag on her body. The garden is filled with sun. She feels intensely happy to be alive and is enchanted by the pebbles she's gathering from a crack near the door. Further ahead, she spies a gray one, a veritable treasure. She moves quickly in order to grab it before someone. . . . She takes off running on little crooked legs whose small black feet are smooth, flat, and dirty from the soil. But just as she bends over, her face filled with happiness, she stops, confused. A white hand, small and chubby, appearing out of nowhere, picks up the coveted pebble before she can get to it. She raises her eyes. A little blond girl, squatting on the ground, looks at her defiantly, now the owner of her treasure. Natalina doesn't hesitate. The stone is hers, she saw it first. Bracing herself on her sturdy little legs, she thrusts out her arm and pushes the little girl, who, awkward and taken by surprise, loses her balance and falls to the ground, screaming. Natalina takes advantage of the moment to grab the stone and clutches it in her tiny hand. Seeing the other girl crying, she begins to cry too, and sits down on the ground in front of her. At the sound of their cries, shapes come running, first two, then three. . . . Then Natalina learns her second lesson in life. Everyone shouts at her, and they shake her hard, while they hug the other one, the little white girl. Why? She was in the right, the stone was hers, the other child had just come along to provoke her. The two wanted the same thing, the two ended up crying. But it was to her that they said: "What nerve, a little black girl carrying on like that! That's all we need!" And they continue to soothe the other one, who is crying even more than she is.

From that day forward, she played silently, distrustingly. If the little white girl demanded her playthings, Natalina gave them to her, though her heart revolted against it. Curiously enough, after their violent encounter over the stone, she felt drawn to her adversary—who was none other than Yaya, the daughter of the house. They must have had certain affinities; it wasn't by chance that both of them coveted the same plaything. Thus, Natalina was constantly taken from the slave quarters and brought to play with Yaya on the veranda of the big house or in her bedroom, where there was a doll dressed in blue silk with marvelous eyes that opened and closed. Finding herself alone one day, Natalina gently touched its face, very gently, for fear of soiling it. The face was cold, delicate, and exceedingly smooth. She quickly withdrew her hand when someone opened the door; seeing her frightened expression, the person standing there said: "It's absurd having this little black girl inside the house. She's up to something bad." She still recalls how her heart, filled with fear, beat frantically at that moment.

In spite of everything, she grew up "inside the house" and became a young woman. She no longer came to play; rather she came to sew, to tidy Yaya's drawers, to shine her shoes and put buttons on her clothes. They said she was handy. From time to time, Yaya would give her a dress. And her life went by calmly, although she was expected to behave with considerable humility.

Now her memories focused on more recent events. She was always at Yaya's side. Yet Yaya never showed the slightest interest in poor Natalina, nor did she express any fondness for her constant companion. On the contrary, she treated her dryly, with condescension. To Natalina, Yaya seemed a bad person, a heartless, self-centered creature who always demanded everything for herself. But she had every reason for self-absorption. She was so pretty! If only she knew how Natalina admired her! Natalina loved to watch her at the piano; she'd spend enormous amounts of time looking at Yaya's perfect profile from afar. There was nothing quite so beautiful. It took her by surprise one day when she heard one of the ladies say to the other: "Yaya would be a real beauty if it weren't for her teeth. Why doesn't our brother take her to the city to see a dentist? Who knows, maybe they could be fixed." Natalina was intrigued. She had never noticed Yaya's teeth, and thought of her face as physical perfection itself. Why were teeth important anyway? She had never even noticed her own. Then she remembered looking at them for the first time in the mirror hung in the parlor. She went on tiptoe. She recalled the scene as if it were happening now. The smell of a long-abandoned room and the silence filled with tiny noises as she approached the oval-shaped mirror there in the back of the room and examined her two rows of closed, white teeth. She was anxious to compare them with Yaya's and didn't rest until she saw her again. Then she looked at Yaya with different, scrutinizing eyes. When Yaya laughed, throwing back her blond head of hair, Natalina felt her heart leap from the shock. It was true, they were ugly, twisted, and gray. Life had taught her a third lesson: from time to time God balances out his favors.

From that moment on, she felt a certain pride, a secret vanity. The pride of her teeth, the vanity of her smile. She loved to display them and was content because she knew she was showing something pretty.

One day she almost died from happiness when Zé Cândido—that handsome black fellow, who had once danced with her—watched her pass by and shouted to his friend, so that she could hear him: "Lookie there, that black gal has some pretty mouth!"

Now the scene, the recent, horrible scene. Her tears flow again and a wave of rebellion comes over her heart. For several days she had noticed something was different. The man, the owner who never looked at her and had never said a word to her, had ordered her to come to his office. He was a brutal, authoritative man. There wasn't anyone on the plantation who didn't fear him. He was always dressed in riding clothes with boots and a caved-in hat, and she had grown used to seeing his outline in the distance, standing with his legs spread apart, giving work orders, or on horseback riding through the fields. She rarely encountered him in the house, because whenever she heard his thick, gruff voice, she'd hide in fear. Rarely would they call for her to accompany Yaya when he was in the house. Consequently, she began to tremble when they told her he wanted to see her. She clasped her arms around her shaking body and vaguely repeated an Ave Maria, wondering what she could have done wrong. When she reached the door to the office, she stopped, frightened. A tall man was standing beside the owner. The two fell silent when she appeared and they studied her for a moment. Then the owner spoke up and his voice didn't seem so bad. First he said her name, which won her over a little: "Come here, Natalina, so this man can see you." When she got close, the man looked at her, took her chin in his hand and mumbled something like: "Good, good." The two men looked at each other, pleased, forgetting all about her being there. Then the owner asked: "Is it best to tell her now?" "No, what for?" replied the other man. "She'll find out soon enough. Let's make it the day after tomorrow." Natalina was confused and intrigued, but not sad because the owner had dismissed her with what looked like a smile.

What did they want of her? Strange. The day after tomorrow. What could it be? Ironically, she looked forward to the appointed day. If only she had known, if only she had foreseen! . . . She would have run away, preferring to face hunger, death, any imaginable disgrace. Anything would have been better.

The day finally arrived. They came for her in the morning. As she walked, she was more interested in solving the mystery than in feeling apprehensive. The owner smiled at her, he couldn't want to harm her.

They took her to a room at the back of the house, a large, almost empty room that nobody ever entered. They had opened up all the windows and had placed two armchairs alongside a small table covered with a white cloth, upon which were sitting a liter of alcohol and a package of cotton. When she entered, she saw the man who had looked at her mouth putting on a white apron and taking some strange instruments from a bag that he had placed on the table beside the cotton. They made her sit down in one of the chairs. Lacking the courage to ask what they wanted of her, she began feeling nervous. Those gadgets held her attention. She felt a tremor in her legs, a coldness in her body, and a desperate desire to cry. Then she recognized the owner's heavy footsteps in the hallway. She remembered that he had treated her almost kindly. She thought about asking him. . . . But she was taken aback when she saw his reddened face and his hardened eyes that passed over her without looking at her directly. He said to the other man: "Do you guarantee the results? And my daughter, she won't suffer a lot, will she?"

Yaya! What was wrong with Yaya? Natalina felt relieved when she saw her enter the room. Thank God, they wouldn't do anything bad to her in front of Yaya.

The young woman seemed to avoid her gaze. She was pale and agitated, but her face had a cold, decided look. She approached her father and the other man, who looked like a doctor, and when the three of them began talking in low voices, Natalina felt she was doomed. She realized some danger was imminent and threatening her and that she was alone, desperately alone. Overcome by a nameless horror, she finally sensed what it might be. She heard a word. Her teeth, they were going to pull out her teeth. They're talking about pain, how many they're going to extract. . . . Her eyes wide with fear, feeling nearly insane, she tries to get up from the chair. Suddenly, out of nowhere, a man appears and grabs hold of her arms, rendering her immobile. Someone passes a belt over her chest and straps her to the chair. Another man appears, then another. . . . My God! Suddenly there are a lot of people in the room and they're all against her! Natalina cries out: "Yaya, for the love of God!" Just then, the man with the white apron walks toward her and says in a rough voice: "It's better not to make a fuss, otherwise I'll give you a drug." A drug! What had she done? It's impossible! What are they going to do to her?

Yaya is already seated in another chair and is looking very pale. Her father comes up to her and takes her hand. Natalina barely sees all of this because a cloud has come over her eyes. One of the men holds her head. She tries to struggle free, but the pressure keeps her immobile. They force her to open her mouth. The doctor approaches her with an instrument in his hand. Reliving all this in memory, Natalina now recalls how, in her desperate struggling, she bit his finger. He groaned under his breath and stepped back, but soon after returned, determined and brutal. She felt the cold metal grip the gums of her teeth; a piercing pain shot through her brain and she lost consciousness.

When she came to, she was lying in bed. At her side was old Inácia, who had placed salt-water compresses on her mouth. She felt an incredible aching in her mouth, whose gums were swollen large. She moved her hand over her mouth. . . . And thought she'd die from the coldness in her heart. Her mouth, her beautiful mouth, her pride, was now a horrible, empty hole, tragically empty and covered over by her withered lips. Then she heard Inácia speak of her martyrdom. They had pulled out her front teeth, one by one, in order to put them, alive and pulsating, in Yaya's mouth, whose own ugly and useless teeth had been extracted, one by one.

Old Inácia consoled her. Needless to get upset, what was so important about teeth? They didn't do that to her to punish her. The owner had chosen her because the dentist had told him to look among the slaves for the one that had the most perfect teeth. And Yaya looked so beautiful now, she'd seen her. It was even a good thing for Natalina. Surely they'd give her something, some present as compensation. What importance did teeth have anyway? And the old woman laughed, displaying a ravaged mouth: "People end up losing them in the end anyhow."

Now, in the sad white light of dawn, the image of that gaping mouth is what most tortures Natalina's grieving heart. As it appears before her, she remembers a healthy face of a muscular man turning and saying to his companion: "That black gal has some pretty mouth." She can't stand it anymore and something grows and breaks inside her chest, and waves of crazed, convulsive, heaving sobs come, suffocating her and heightening her agitation, and in an attempt to stifle them by covering her face with her hands, she rolls her body from one side of the bed to the other in desperation and delirium, like a woman gone mad.

Lúcia Benedetti

Lúcia Benedetti's literary debut was somewhat unusual. In 1935, at the age of nineteen, she entered a competition organized by the newspaper *A Noite*, for the best love letter written to actor Ramón Novarro. She won second prize, but more importantly, she became a regular contributor to *A Noite* and two other Rio-based newspapers, *Carioca* and *Vamos Ler*, whose editor-in-chief, the playwright Raimundo Magalhães Júnior, she married in 1936.

In 1940, Benedetti and her husband traveled to the United States, where they remained for two years. During this period she continued to write for newspapers in Brazil, and she finished her first novel, *Entrada de Serviço* (1942) (Service Entrance). Despite Benedetti's considerable work in fiction, which also includes the novels *Três Soldados* (1956) (Three Soldiers), about World War II, and *Chão Estrangeiro* (1956) (Foreign Ground), about her life in the United States, she is perhaps best remembered as a playwright and is widely regarded as the creator of a children's theater in Brazil.

In 1950, along with Lygia Fagundes Telles, Benedetti was awarded the Brazilian Academy of Letters' Afonso Arinos prize for short fiction. In her prize-winning volume, *Vesperal com Chuva* (Vesperal with Rain), she draws from her experiences as a child growing up in a small town in the state of São Paulo. The story "Meu Tio Ricardo" (My Uncle Ricardo) is from this collection.

My Uncle Ricardo

(1950)

My Uncle Ricardo always arrived at night. No one would ever say anything to me about it, nor would I ask. But I would guess from the happy look on my grandmother's face. I could also tell by the nervous way she ordered the coffeepot left on the stove, the sewing things removed from the front bedroom, the windows cleaned, a thousand other chores done one right after another, that my uncle would wake up at home the following day. I never saw him arrive. Or leave.

One beautiful morning I would awake to find my uncle seated at the table, rolling his cornhusk cigarette and telling incredible tales about the *sertão*. I loved listening to my Uncle Ricardo's stories. He spoke slowly, pausing at length as he crushed the tobacco leaves in the hollow of his hand and searched for the matches in his pockets; then he'd light his cigarette and inhale deeply. We sat there, waiting, with our hearts racing. A little while later, as if noting our presence just then, he'd take up the thread of his story once again. I knew Uncle Ricardo wasn't telling those stories to me. He was telling them to the older people, who understood everything. But whenever I heard my Uncle Ricardo's grave, unhurried voice, I'd run to a corner of the room and humbly curl myself up on the floor so as not to miss a single word.

I remember one story about a jaguar. That was the best one of all. Uncle Ricardo told it like no one else could. One evening a jaguar stopped in the middle of the road to look at the moon. That very afternoon, Uncle Ricardo had gone out to pick the fruit of the jaboticaba trees that grew in the woods. He had had difficulty finding the place where they grew. When he finally came across them, it was already growing dark, but that didn't stop him. He had brought an empty kerosene can along with him in which to carry the *jabuticabas* back to the camp. He filled the can and was contentedly walking back. Uncle Ricardo said that the moon that night was the prettiest thing you could imagine. No one in the whole world had ever seen anything like it. The moonlight was so intense that it seemed as though day were breaking. Uncle Ricardo was merrily walking along when he spied a bright shape in the middle of the road. He didn't give it any importance. He kept walking toward it. When he was practically on top of it, he stopped dead in his tracks, because the shape turned out to be a jaguar. An enormous jaguar, spotted all over, that had made its way to the middle of the road to look at the moon. At this point in the story, Uncle Ricardo would roll his cigarette. Then he'd look for his matches. Everyone was tense, waiting, their hearts beating anxiously. Uncle Ricardo didn't have a single weapon on him. Not even a stick of wood. Just the can filled with *jabuticabas.* What did he do? He silently emptied out the can of *jabuticabas* on the ground. Then, he approached the jaguar, getting closer, closer. The jaguar was distracted by the moonlight. When my uncle got right up next to the animal, he gave the can a powerful sock—pow! Frightened, the jaguar ran away. Uncle Ricardo said he ran too. Each of them ran in the opposite direction.

That's what my Uncle Ricardo's stories were like.

He never stayed with us for very long. Three, four days, then he was off again. He'd leave at dawn, and I never saw him go. Once he brought me a rag doll. I almost died from happiness. I remember one time he came back rich. I was there when they read the letter he had written to my grandmother. He had sold some lumber for a fabulous price. My grandmother took off her glasses, wiped her eyes with her apron, and exclaimed:

"He's rich!"

I skipped merrily out to the backyard. From time to time I burst out laughing as I ran around the house. But that wasn't enough to release all my happiness. I went from door to door, telling the whole neighborhood. I'd clap my hands, someone would come to the door, and I'd tell them the news in a loud voice:

"Know what? My Uncle Ricardo wrote to say he's rich!"

I was certain the neighbors liked him. They visited him whenever he arrived, and he said goodbye to them whenever he went away. At night, as they gathered outside my grandmother's door to talk, they always asked about him. My grandmother, poor thing, would sigh as she reported her uncertain news of him. Uncle Ricardo wrote only when there was something very important to tell. And now he was coming home a rich man. . . .

I didn't see him arrive. My mother made me go to bed because it was cold that night, and I had been coughing a lot the whole day. But the next day I woke up very early and ran to the dining room. Uncle Ricardo was there, eating breakfast. He was the same Uncle Ricardo, his forehead criss-crossed with wrinkles, his moustache a bit darkened by tobacco, and he was wearing khaki linen pants. He had on the same yellow leather boots he had worn when he left. I expected him to return covered with jewels and wearing clothes made of silk, like the prince in fairy tales. But he came back looking the same as always. Meanwhile, my grandmother had said he was rich! My disappointment was ten times greater than my happiness. I went to the backyard and cried. But at night, the neighbors came by, laughing and noisy, and my Uncle Ricardo told new stories. This time he had acted in a play. He was in a town where a company of actors arrived. He made friends with the director. On opening night, one of the actors fell ill and the director sent for him. It was a small part. He had just two scenes and very few words to say. In one of the scenes, he had to ask for secrecy over something or other, it was very important for the development of the plot. The dialogue went something like this:

"I wonder if you can keep a secret?"

"My mouth is a graveyard. . . . ," the other fellow responded.

"Bravo, Jeremias. You're a good man and I trust you!" my uncle would say.

But on opening night, at the very moment when the other fellow said, "My mouth is a graveyard," my uncle looked out at the audience. A few of his friends were there. He got a bit confused. The other actor repeated his line, trying to get my uncle's attention:

"My mouth is a graveyard. . . . I give you my word that my mouth is a GRAVEYARD. . . . ," he shouted.

A bit annoyed, my uncle turned and shouted back:

"I know that, I can see the skulls!"

The neighbors almost died laughing at the story. My grandmother shook her head, sorrowfully. My uncle was famous for his lack of good sense. He was constantly worrying the family. My other uncle, Gustavo, had arranged an excellent job for him at the post office. It was steady employment with a future, and if he wanted, he could move up. My uncle refused. I heard bitter arguing that evening. My uncle defended the *sertão:*

"I know you all don't understand! But is there anything healthier than sleeping in tents, breathing in the fresh air, the scent of resin, the boundless oxygen? And the sunshine I get. It can only be good for me. Besides, I'm always moving about from place to place, making friends, meeting different people. You're the ones who are stuck here as if you had rocks tied around your necks! Let me tell you, I've only met good, honest folk in the *sertão!*"

"What about those thieves you talked about, Ricardo?" my grandmother interjected, timidly.

"So? What of it? Thieves help people become more active, more daring, they break up the monotony of the place. God help me if I have to live in a place where there aren't any thieves!"

My uncle was like that.

Once, he stayed away a long time before returning home. I saw my grandmother wipe her eyes on her apron, sigh, and look distractedly at the ground. Then, one afternoon, I noticed they were readying the back bedroom. They carried Uncle Ricardo's bed in there as well as his wardrobe and night table. Uncle Ricardo in the back of the house! And no one was happy. It was clear to me that he was about to arrive. But why didn't they bustle around like always? My mother had a sad, grave air about her. My grandmother gave orders in a strange, wasted voice, like someone who had spent the night crying.

I wasn't wrong. When I got up the next day, Uncle Ricardo was eating breakfast. I studied him from afar. He was the same. I crossed the room, went over to him, and looked closely. There wasn't any difference. Even his boots were the same as always. I sighed in relief. Uncle Ricardo coughed from time to time and looked at me, smiling. At night, the neighbors came by, as always. Uncle Ricardo greeted them from a distance:

"Don't get too close, because I'm a sick man now!"

One of my grandmother's friends began to cry. Uncle Ricardo sat down a few feet away and said:

"What nonsense, crying about a thing like that. I confess I was pretty annoyed when the doctor informed me. I went and got the medicines he prescribed, and I began watching my diet. You want to know something? I wouldn't change places with anybody. Why, only an English lord is as well off as I am!"

My grandmother looked at him and shook her head.

"I used to come here all the time, right?" he said. "And where did they put me? In the front bedroom. I can't begin to tell you how many sleepless nights I spent because of the buses in the street making noise, and because in the early morning, when it was still dark outside, first the milkman would come with his little milk cart, then the baker, and who knows who else? A horde of people without anything to do. Now that I've got this little bacillus, where did they put me? In the back bedroom where I always wanted to sleep! Before, I used to get up and you know what I'd eat? Coffee with bread. Now do you know what I have as soon as I open my eyes? Porridge, a glass of milk, and then, coffee. Before, when it got to be ten o'clock, my stomach would be growling away, but I'd have to wait until eleven o'clock for lunch. Now, every hour on the hour they've got some tidbit on the stove for me. Cooked banana, rice porridge, chicken soup. . . . If I'd known that, I would have gotten sick a long time ago."

The neighbors laughed. My grandmother accompanied their laughter with a faint smile.

One day my uncle stopped going out. He stayed in the house, stretched out in the easy chair, and said funny little things and told stories about the *sertão* he loved so much. The doctor liked him and always told him not to smoke. Smiling, my uncle said:

"When the bacillus entered, they found the smoke already there. Now they leave with the smoke. They ought to be used to one another by now. . . ."

One morning, my uncle didn't get up out of bed. He explained to everybody that it didn't matter where he stayed put. He chose to stay in bed, which, according to him, would be less work for everybody and was more comfortable.

One afternoon, I brought him a large, fresh, ripe guava that I had picked in the backyard. He refused the fruit, shaking his head. I noticed he was having a hard time breathing. He tried to say something to me. He still had the strength to smile at me. His breathing made a strange noise in his chest. I asked him to eat the guava. I insisted. My uncle raised his hand, but he didn't have the strength to take hold of the fruit. He shook his head. I ran out, calling, crying, nearly shouting for my mother.

That same afternoon, they sent me far away to my godmother's house, which was on a farm outside the city. I liked it there because there were other girls to play with. I returned home two days later. Uncle Ricardo's room was empty. As always, I didn't see him go.

Dinah Silveira de Queiroz

I

Dinah Silveira de Queiroz was born in São Paulo in 1911 and made her debut as a writer in 1937, when her short story "Pecado" (Sin), appeared in the newspaper *Correio Paulistano.* A few years later, the story appeared in English translation in *Mademoiselle,* having been selected for special recognition in a competition for the best short fiction from Latin America.

Silveira de Queiroz's first novel, *Floradas na Serra* (Blossoms on the Mountain), published in 1939, was a realistic narrative set in a tuberculosis sanatorium; a highly popular book that has recently been published in its twenty-sixth edition, it provided the basis for a movie and a radio and television series. From that point on, Silveira de Queiroz experimented with a variety of forms. In her second novel, *Margarida La Rocque: A Ilha dos Demônios* (1949) (Margarida La Roque: Demons' Isle), she anticipated "magical realism" by blending fantasy and verisimilitude to tell the story of a woman stranded on a deserted island. She wrote a historical novel, *A Muralha* (1954) *(The Women of Brazil),* about the discovery of São Paulo, and was credited with introducing "serious," or literary, science fiction to Brazil in a 1960 collection of stories, *Eles Herderão a Terra* (They Will Inherit the Earth). She was also drawn to religious themes, as in her two-part novel, *Eu Venho: Memorial do Cristo* (1974, 1977) *(Christ's Memorial),* the story of Christ, narrated in the first person.

The short story collection *As Noites do Morro do Encanto* (1957) (Enchanted Mountain Nights) contains some of her best fiction, including the piece translated here—"Jovita," which Silveira de Queiroz selected for inclusion in an anthology of her work published in 1974.

Silveira de Queiroz was the recipient of several major literary awards, including the Machado de Assis Prize, given to her collected works in 1954. In 1981, one year before her death, she became the second woman to be elected to the Brazilian Academy of Letters.

Jovita

(1957)

From his window up above, the Governor saw the town square and surroundings move up and down as he went back and forth in his rocking chair. Sufficiently accustomed to the malicious stares from behind neighboring shutters, he had taken precautions on that damp, warm afternoon: he had put a coat over his large nightshirt so that whoever looked at him from outside would see him dressed to the waist in perfect governmental dignity.

It was four o'clock in the afternoon and the town square was beginning to come alive. People were leaving their houses to take their afternoon refreshments. Slaves loaned out for hire strolled among the groups of people selling orangeade and lemonade. A beggar dressed up as a saint, who took advantage of the moments of collective good humor following dinner time, leaned against the Church door dressed as St. Roque, with his tunic, dog, and staff. Someone in the Church was rehearsing a vigorously sung litany dedicated to the Virgin Mary. The Governor looked at all this and thought: "Shameless land! No one would ever think we were at war."

The movement of his rocking blew air up his nightshirt, shaping it like a barrel; and yet, despite the fact that he was only half-dressed, His Excellency began thinking grave thoughts. He supposed it was the paltry number of recruits sent by his State to fight in the Paraguayan War that had motivated the most humiliating letter he had ever received in his whole life. It had been sent to him by a Senator:

It appears that Your Excellency has still not awakened: our State is the disgrace of the North. I went to the docks to wait for the volunteers. I saw a half-dozen yellowish blacks and a few weak-kneed whites come off the ship. Three had fever, but the doctor told me it wasn't because they were sick—they had put garlic in their armpits to make their temperatures rise. They're making fun of me at Court. I live miserably, like a rat afraid to come out of its hole. Excellency, isn't there some way of stirring up these

> *people's patriotism? Haven't even the most recent echoes of battle found their way there? I know very well that the Brazilian* sertão *is rich with proud men. Why hasn't the Governor followed the example of the other state leaders and dispatched people he can trust to round up volunteers?*

The Governor mulled over this extremely grave matter as his traveling eye went up and down, taking in different portions of the square. Over there, two young women were talking, showing off their lively embroidered shawls as they sipped their orangeade. They laughed, then whispered to one another and to the young men who were gathered in a corner, watching the people pass by.

"A disgrace!" the Governor murmured to himself. "So many louts around here, sighing, serenading, and reciting poems, when they're not flirting in the square . . . and we're at war—a sacred war against the tyrant López!"

At that point in his sad meditation, the Governor saw that something extraordinary was going on below, at the far end of the square. A strange band of ragged men came into the street alongside the Church. One of them cried out in despair, looking like a madman. People went running; the group stopped, and one man, who was on horseback accompanying the group, began gesturing and shouting to the people as the street grew more and more crowded with curious bystanders.

The Governor got up out of his chair and watched as the angry man on horseback whipped the crazy-looking fellow, who was crying out in desperation. Shortly thereafter, the leader prodded the human agglomerate forward and positioned it in front of the Palace. It was then that the Governor recognized the man on horseback as his friend, Captain Jonas, who had gone into the interior in search of volunteers.

Excited, he called to a slave and quickly began to dress. A few minutes later, he was going down the Palace steps. Captain Jonas greeted him effusively as he dismounted and began showing him the men he had brought:

"Governor, forgive me. *This* was all there was, all I was able to round up. Only God knows with what difficulty! Look here, these ten are slaves; these twenty, here, came because they wanted to come—and more than half of them regretted it on the way. You know that in order to travel seventy-two leagues, a man has to be a man! Seriously speaking, there's only one, this young fellow here, who's a real man. If it's not too much to ask of you, shake his hand as an example to the others!"

"But he's not a young fellow . . . he's a child!"

"By your leave, sir, I ain't no child. I already turned seventeen!"

As the small recruit answered on behalf of Captain Jonas, the Governor took in the whole of the fellow's fragile body and was amazed:

"Come up here on the sidewalk, my son. All these people need to see what a patriot looks like. You sir," the Governor said in a loud voice, "are invited to stay at the Palace. I want everyone to admire your courage."

At that moment, one of the recruits fell to the ground. It was the same one who had shouted as he came into the square.

"I can't take any more, have pity! . . ."

Captain Jonas snorted:

"There's nothing wrong with this good-for-nothing. He's pretending just so he won't have to ship out."

To which the young fellow responded, with a sympathetic smile that showed his teeth filed to a point:

"Governor, this man's so scared of war he cut off his little toe. Take a look there. Tell him to take off the bandage."

The sign of cowardice was laid bare. The recruit had used a knife to cut off his little toe, and once the sandal was removed and the rags were unwrapped, the mutilation was exposed.

"Have pity on a poor wretch," he said to the Governor, "have pity on a wretch who tripped over a rock and pulled out his toe! For the love of God, have pity on me!"

The Governor had no doubts about what he should do in the face of this depressing scene. He launched into a energetic speech to the people of his city about the bravery of the recruits from all over Brazil. Then, he added:

"Thank God that some of them salvaged the honor of our land. I present these few for veneration by this city, which is redeemed by these brave men and ennobled by the act of this young fellow here, who fearlessly traveled seventy-two leagues to come here and embark on a ship to go to war!"

Addressing himself to the lad, whom the young women and men looked upon with admiration, he asked like a proud schoolmaster:

"Son, tell these people why you want to fight!"

With a singing, childlike voice, the young fellow responded:

"I'm going to defend the honor of the Brazilian women!"

The Governor kindly spoke up:

"You mean . . . the honor of all Brazilians, don't you?"

"No, sir. I mean the *Brazilian women.* I curse those Paraguayans who're goin' around insultin' the young women of Brazil. In the *sertão* there's a whole lot of stories bein' told and by people who don't lie. What I'm really gonna do is defend the honor of Brazilian women!"

"Wonderful!" exclaimed the Governor, who was moved. "That's a fine reason that all men"—and he shot a heated look at the group of young men—"should hear. The honor of the Brazilian woman has been trampled by our enemy, who sacks cities and violates defenseless young women from way over in Mato Grosso, whose brothers are fighting for the cause of freedom against tyranny."

An emotional moment followed. The young fellow had said something far more important than the Governor's haranguing. Everyone thought about the young man's words; saddened, forgetting the pleasant peacefulness of the square, they were shaken to their very souls and brought closer to the war, which, just a little while ago, had been insignificant.

Suddenly the woman schoolteacher, who also carried out the duties of midwife and had attended the noblest ladies in the place, strode up the sidewalk and, grabbing the youth by the shoulders, proclaimed:

"Governor, look for someone else to serve as your hero. I doubt if this recruit will because . . . this one has a pierced ear! It's a girl . . . not a man." (Then, she pinched the chest of the recruit.) "Governor, let the truth be told. This is no man, no sir!"

The youth raised a hand to his face. The schoolteacher went on in her metallic voice:

"I swear it's the truth; you can order an examination. It's a young lady. . . ."

A wave of astonishment spread over the square. Even the beggar dressed up as a saint, pretending he was crazy, prodded his dog; and with lucid, piercing eyes, he approached the sidewalk where a great confusion had broken out. In the midst of the hubbub, a redheaded woman yelled out:

"This is really shameful! The hussy wants to be right in with the men. . . ."

But the girl, who was trying to find a way to escape the public's curiosity and was already slipping away, was struck still by the insult and turned to confront the situation:

"Captain Jonas," she said in a loud voice. "Gimme your rifle." Defying the curious onlookers and the woman who had offended her, she insisted as Captain Jonas looked on half-perplexed. "Gimme your rifle, Captain!"

Captain Jonas didn't wait for permission from the Governor. Confounded by the situation, he pulled his weapon out of his saddle and handed it to the young woman. Throughout the trip he had deeply admired this youth, who had been so reserved, so stalwart and firm. Trembling with rage, her eyes shining wet and dark, the girl took the gun and shouted, spitting in her rage:

"Get outta the way, people, I'm gonna shoot!"

A clearing suddenly appeared in the square. Looking at the shocked Governor, who was about to call in the police to take control of the situation, she said:

"Pick out some branch over there, on the other side of the square. Where you want me to aim?"

The trembling in the Governor's legs was replaced by a general feeling of ease. He now sympathized with the brave young woman and said:

"Look, I want a difficult target. Do you see that dried branch, there, on the right? Look closely. Is that all right?"

Just as the last women were racing away, screaming, the *cabocla* raised the rifle to her shoulder, took aim, and rapidly fired in the direction of the trees. She hit the target. Then she handed the gun to Captain Jonas, saying in a loud voice:

"I just wanted to show that freckle-faced redhead what I wanna do in the war!"

Then she made another attempt to flee from the crowd, but it was the Governor himself who stopped her:

"Come here, my child." The crowd blocked her way. She had to make peace with the Governor.

"Your Excellency ain't gonna arrest me, are you?"

"Because you wanted to pass for a man?"

"But if I'd dressed in a skirt, they wouldn't have let me go to war. A soldier even told me so."

Once again, the circle of people began to close in tighter around the girl. At this point, the police had to intervene. Some of the women shouted. Others said harsh words in defense of the girl. The men were quiet. The Governor finally managed to raise his voice above the noise:

"Go back to your homes," he said. And to the soldiers, "Look over there! Keep an eye on those recruits, they're getting away!" He took the girl's hand, paternally. "I stand behind what I said: you are my guest at the Palace!"

It was a hectic night. Jovita—which was the young woman's name—had difficulty sitting at the table and taking part in the dinner. She didn't know how to use a fork. Finally she declared:

"There's no way I'm eatin' with this stick, no sir."

The Governor made her feel at ease. He told her he had a daughter her age, who was with her mother in Rio de Janeiro. Jovita could sleep in her room, he said. With considerable skill, Jovita formed little mounds of food on her plate and quickly raised them to her mouth. She talked about how the idea for the trip came about:

"I got boilin' mad. I called my older brother—we're orphans—and said: 'It's about time you got your things together and paid the bill at the store.' My brother pretended he didn't know what for. That got me mad. But because my older brother is, to my way of thinkin', second to the Lord Our Father, I told him what he already knew: 'It's time to go to war; all the good men have left!' Then he began a long speech: 'And who'll take care of my goat house? And who'll keep an eye on my vegetables? And who'll take care of the newborn calves?' I said: 'Your sister. Me. The one you're lookin' at. . . .' But he wasn't satisfied with that and began tryin' to make excuses. I wasn't rude to him 'cause I owe him respect, but I said to him real calm: 'Captain Jonas'll be back here in ten days; either you go or . . .' 'Or what?' he asked, in a louder voice. '. . . or then I'll leave. You'll never set eyes on your sister again!' "

Jovita carefully formed a little ball of food with her fingers and swallowed it. Then she finished the story:

"That's it, Governor. My brother's probably hightailin' here after me."

"You didn't have anyone else, a fiancé? You're just about at the marrying age."

"Properly speaking, I don't have a fiancé; but there's a fella who lives near me by the name of Pedro, who I know likes me. All the girls are crazy about him. I don't mean to offend you, but he was always wantin' to put his arms around me. Then one afternoon he stopped me on the road and said some things to me in a low voice. But I'm a bit contrary and I threw water on his fire: 'Go put your arms around your grandmother. Next time you come lookin' for me, you best be wearin' a uniform. . . .' "

They had reached this point in the conversation when a group of women asked to enter the dining room. The Governor got up to go to another room, but the ladies rushed in, the most important one exclaiming as she spied Jovita:

"We came to make amends with our heroine!"

Jovita looked all around her, curious, in search of someone. What had the ladies come there to do? This strange talk couldn't have anything to do with her. The spokeswoman, followed by the other ladies, proclaimed to the Governor:

"We're here to ask in the name of all the women in this country, who are against the invader, that Your Excellency allow this courageous young woman to follow her destiny and defend us since the men from this place haven't shown themselves to be up to their role. We also wish to say that we are in solidarity with this brave young girl, that we are proud of our sex, and that we deplore the attitude of certain ladies in the square today."

The women began talking all at the same time. They spoke not only with words, but with fluttery gestures and the rustlings of their skirts and shawls. They smelled of jasmine and nervous perspiration.

Jovita only vaguely understood what was happening. She got up from the table:

"Governor, sir, you wanna tell me what these ladies are talkin' about?"

"They're honoring you; they came to ask me to allow you to go with the other recruits."

"Well, Governor . . . I'm just a poor Christian—as you can see—and these ladies here ain't no poor folk. But you ain't goin' let me go, are you?"

It suddenly occurred to the politician, who had suffered so much because of the troop situation, that this young woman could very well become a symbol of patriotic pride. He affably designated places for his visitors to sit down at the table, and then he said, vehemently:

"Jovita doesn't want to go any longer. She's going to return home tomorrow."

The little *cabocla* jumped up, passionately:

"Governor, sir, is it so, you wanna send me back?"

The Governor subtly provoked the girl:

"No woman is going to war. Since you don't have a mother or father, I should watch out for you and send you home tomorrow."

Her eyes welling with tears, the little *cabocla* said:

"You don't have to take care of me. There's somebody greater than you who'll take care of me."

The ladies thought she was referring to God, but the *cabocla* surprised them:

"The Emperor'll take care of me! If he goes to war . . . I'll go too. I'll dress up like a man, I'll wear a skirt . . . don't interfere, sir, I'm goin' no matter what!"

At that point, the Governor's voice grew louder:

"My child, I was just testing to see how far your courage to fight went." He chuckled affably in the direction of the ladies:

"Our State is going to teach a lesson to those who don't know how to be good Brazilians. This girl is going to leave tomorrow on the ship, and when she does, she'll be wearing a sergeant's uniform."

* * *

And that's just how she shipped out: wearing a sergeant's uniform. The troopship was supposed to leave at two in the afternoon, but it didn't depart until five. An emotional revolution shook the little city. The Governor made fiery speeches. Something unexpected happened: six young men from the area joined the recruits. Away they went, waving goodbye, still dressed in their civilian clothes, which varied from the doctor's coat to the stripped outfit of the baker's assistant. Women wept profusely; children threw flowers at Jovita, who was stunned. Later they saw her, half-lost in her uniform and with her tanned cheeks shaded by her cap, take a seat in the last boat heading out toward the ship that had cast anchor in the distance. And everyone cried when the band from the Theater struck up the Anthem. Finally, the ship turned around, slowly heading south on its way to war.

There had never been anyone whose absence created such a voice in a city as Jovita. When she was gone, they painted an embellished portrait of her, in which she was no longer the little *cabocla* but a fair girl with rosy cheeks, and they presented it to the Governor. A young poet wrote the lyrics of a song entitled "Jovita," which was quickly set to music by the band conductor and sung throughout the city.

Two weeks later, workers building the new annex to the Church could be heard whistling the tune.

And young girls at home would sing the rousing creation:

Who inspires us to bravery?
Jovita!
Who in uniform is the prettiest?
Jovita!
Who is blessed by the Country?
Jovita! Jovita!

The Governor was happy. This girl had been sent by his guardian angel. A wave of civic pride inundated the little city; the young men enlisted; there was even the beginning—and in just a few days!—of antipathy toward those who, able to leave, sent their slaves instead. The square had turned into a sadder place, but at night, meetings were held;

the women smiled and wept and the men were moved when anyone spoke of Jovita.

Two more ships had left with volunteers when the Governor received a troubling letter from his friend, the Senator:

> *Jovita is a guest in our home; she is unable to accompany the batallion; she's waiting for permission to embark. She called upon the Marquis of Caxias, but until today we haven't received a response. But Your Excellency need not mention this to the people of our land; she was at the dock to see our courageous volunteers off—they made a wonderful impression here. Jovita unexpectedly met up with her brother and her fiancé. It was an emotional scene. Your Excellency, think about the consequences if word reached there that Jovita didn't set off with the soldiers. . . .*

He read the letter two or three times, then he tore it up. That day he restationed himself at his observation post—his rocking chair. He thought about the brave girl and about his own role. The Emperor had left for the war. The Governor felt ill at ease, unprotected.

From the heights of his observatory, where he was dressed in his coat and nightshirt, he let the breeze and the comings and goings of the rocking chair cool his concern. "There must be a solution," he said. "As they say, there's a solution for everything."

At night, instead of sending a public employee to announce the war news, as he normally did on a daily basis, he himself ascended the small bandstand and gave enthusiastic reports. He ended by saying that Jovita had been cheered by crowds of people in Rio de Janeiro; he read an article from the *Jornal do Comércio,* which praised the young woman's civic virtues. The townspeople's hearts were set on fire, and at ten o'clock when they dispersed, they spontaneously began to sing "Jovita."

Months passed and new letters from the Senator arrived at the Governor's Palace. They no longer praised Jovita so much. Because of the difficulties she'd encountered, the girl had become ill-tempered. *I'm very unhappy: if I send Jovita back, I fear what might happen in our land. If I don't, I displease my wife, who, if you'll pardon me, Your Excellency, thinks that Jovita's a bit off in the head. . . .*

This letter was like a stab in the Governor's heart; he remained still in his chair for a long time, lacking the courage even to rock. At times he linked his longing for his daughter to a curious longing for the little *cabocla*. He almost confessed to himself: "I was a rascal! I knew she couldn't go." But he didn't have the courage to tell himself the truth. He sent Jovita one hundred *mil réis* that afternoon by way of Captain Jonas, who had finally departed with the last of the territory's recruits. His most pressing problem was finding a way to announce Jovita's return. The poor girl couldn't be kept waiting indefinitely in Rio. He even prayed to the Virgin Mary, his baptismal godmother. Jovita's case represented a political crisis about to explode and—who knows?—affect the prestige of his party, bring about the Ministry's collapse. This "national heroine" he had created could end up toppling him.

The Governor spent two sleepless nights; the newspaper accounts and the enthusiastic references to Jovita no longer had the same effect. She was having difficulty leaving; but the legend of Jovita was by now so powerful that it seemed the very moment she arrived on the battlefield, the war would be won. All the city's hopes rested on her youth and grace highlighted in the pictures they drew of her.

The Governor finally received a letter:

> *I'm taking the liberty of sending Jovita back on the 10th.* By the time the Governor read it, Jovita was already on her way back to his land. He was moved by the Senator's words: *She is resigned to waiting there for the response to the letter she sent by way of my intermediary to the Marquis of Caxias. She hopes he will be her protector and that he will understand what the others don't want to understand.*

The Governor took a dose of chloral in order to sleep and, on the following day, he announced to the people:

"I bring you glorious news: We've won the most extraordinary field battle . . . Brazil has won in Tuiuti!"

Applause and shouts burst forth. The Governor let the wave of cheers dry up and said:

"I bring you other news, equally good. It has to do with our beloved Jovita." And without giving them time to ask "Has she gotten off to war?" he rapidly continued: "The heroine of our land has set out . . . to raise the spirits of those who still lack the will to fight, who don't have our civic pride and aren't making any effort on behalf of our Country!"

Then, raising his voice in order to hide, with sheer volume, the deception he felt aching inside of him like the threat of a heart attack:

"Our Jovita, the modern-day Joan of Arc, is traveling from port to port, from city to city, raising spirits and sowing enthusiasm. In this way, she'll be helping in our Country's last effort toward a decisive victory over the infamous López!"

There was a moment of silence. The Governor held his breath with the anguishing expectation that, at the very least, someone would ask him questions difficult to answer, or, that one or another person might loudly voice their disappointment and contaminate the populace with a dangerous pessimism. He might even be insulted. And . . . if he were? But suddenly a woman's voice shouted out: "Viva Jovita!" Then a mute and unintelligible uproar gave way, which spread around the square. Soon it was pandemonium. Orators followed orators, and they began to prepare for Jovita's arrival. The joy of receiving her was combined with celebration of the victory won. With steady legs, the Governor made his way to the Palace.

It rained that night and he slept peacefully, something he hadn't done for a long time.

Jovita finally arrived. She was received like a conqueror, but she was no longer a slight young girl; she had matured and was somber. The Governor went to meet her on board ship. He was amazed how his scheme had come true. Wherever Jovita went, she was greeted with a fiery enthusiasm, a frenzied popularity.

It was difficult to convince her to accept the presents they offered her; in vain, the Governor asked her to smile at the people who happily welcomed her. She was downcast, suspicious—her eyes sunken in her drawn face. But she hadn't lost her hope of leaving. She felt the Marquis of Caxias had to oppose the order from General Headquarters, which was explained to her at length by the Senator . . . *As a woman, you can accompany the troops but not fight in battle; that is, your services need to be compatible with the nature of your sex.* A pretty and polished way of being denied . . . but what good were nice words when the attitude was condescending?

Accompanied by an enormous crowd, Jovita walked alongside the man who had made her believe in her own dreams. She couldn't bring herself to tell the multitude that she hadn't been commissioned to make speeches in order to seduce people and that she was simply waiting for the Marquis of Caxias to answer her letter.

The Governor was disturbed; he now felt a deep remorse. As much as he tried, he couldn't carry out this painful farce. The ladies accompanying the "heroine" had given her a gold necklace with a cross, which was to protect her in battle. The more Jovita's popularity grew, the more distressing the potential end of all this scheming seemed to the Governor.

At his request, they were left alone in the large hall of the Palace. He showed her the enormous portrait adorned with garlands of flowers.

"Who's that girl?" asked Jovita, whose eyes smarted from the light.

"It's you."

"But I'm not pretty like that."

"You are to the people, my child."

She continued to look without understanding, staring at the lofty figure that looked back at her, dressed in a beautiful ceremonial uniform. She couldn't find any explanation for so much pageantry and so many presents. She said to the Governor:

"I only ask that you lend me a horse. I wanna wait for the Marquis of Caxias's letter back home. I got faith in God that I, a young virgin maiden, might still avenge the honor of the Brazilian women."

"Of course," said the Governor. "I'll do as you ask. I'll even provide you with an escort. The new vicar from your parish; but first, let's eat dinner."

The two of them dined almost in silence. Jovita spent a long time arranging little mounds of dried beef, beans, and manioc on her plate, but she ate very little. The Governor didn't eat either because of the lump in his throat that prevented him from swallowing. The letter from the Marquis of Caxias had arrived on the same boat in which Jovita had traveled.

At the end of the dinner, the cheers of "Jovita! Jovita!" burst forth from under the window.

"Jesus!" she said. "This'll never end!"

"Be patient just this one time. Come say goodbye from the window."

And the city voraciously took hold of her in her guise as a youth dressed up in his father's uniform. She took off her cap, waved it in the air, and without wanting to, as if frightened, she let it drop. Many people ran at once to pick it up.

She murmured:

"These people're crazy. . . . I can't take it no more. Please. . . ."

They went back inside. A slave closed the window; the cheers were muted. Then, putting some courage into his weakened heart, the Governor took a deep breath and finally said:

"There arrived . . . a present for you from the Marquis of Caxias."

Jovita's lips turned white:

"A present . . . for me? I knew he was gonna help me . . . that he's not just brave, but he understands too. He's good to all the soldiers. . . ."

"Yes . . . yes . . . a present for you that you'll receive on behalf of your brother. A medal for bravery . . . that was conferred upon him in Tuiuti!"

"Holy Virgin!" Jovita said at last. Her eyes filled with tears. Pounding the table with her fists in an attempt to subdue a wave of emotion, she tore the painful words out of herself:

"You mean to say my brother, who didn't wanna go . . . was a real man. . . ."

"Your brother was a hero!"

She made an enormous effort to understand. She knew this wasn't good news. She knew . . . and she didn't have the courage to ask: If the Marquis of Caxias sent the medal, was it because my brother died?

The Governor rushed through what he had to say. And with a furrowed brow, he confronted and overcame his final hesitation:

"You are courageous like a good soldier and you ought to know. . . . Your brother died!"

But his sad mission still wasn't over. He saw the little *cabocla,* who looked like a stubborn child with her lost gaze welling up with tears, strike the table with her fist, rebelling against her own fear of the cries that begged to pour forth. Jovita clenched her teeth, believing that she was a good soldier.

He couldn't stop now. He'd have to be merciless to the end.

"On the list of those killed in combat in Tuiuti, there also appears another acquaintance of yours. . . ."

"Pedro?"

"Yes."

She went limp, no longer concerned with balling her fists or struggling against the weakness. She sat down and remained quiet. She recalled a day long ago, when the cheerful Pedro had caressed her, saying words of love. She moved her hand over her arm, feeling the thick fabric of the uniform, and inside her flesh trembled as she remembered that irreclaimable day when Pedro's fingers had touched her.

"Can I go, Governor?"

"We're waiting for the vicar, my child. I said he'd accompany you. Don't you remember? But before he arrives, I'm going to read the Marquis of Caxias's response."

> *Though I have nothing but complete admiration for such a noble, unselfish gesture as yours, nevertheless, the Brazilian Army's laws are rigorous. So that you will not be downcast by this denial, which we issue with the greatest feeling of sorrow, let us remind our fearless comrade that, thanks to God, Brazil has enough soldiers to defend it and lead it to a final victory. We pray to God that He give you long life; we are grateful and wish to reward you because of your lofty expression of patriotism, which elevates and dignifies the women of our land. . . .*

Jovita didn't want to understand. She stammered:

"Does this mean the Marquis . . . says no?"

The Governor let all his anxiety out in a long sigh. Unburdening himself, he announced:

"It means no. He sent an award; some money to reimburse your trip. . . ."

Emerging from the silence that had fallen over her like an absolute inertia, the young woman felt a vehement desire:

"Governor, will you loan me some clothes from one of your slaves? I don't deserve this uniform."

The Governor called for the black housemaid and ordered her to give Jovita one of his daughter's dresses. He wanted to thank this worn-out, wretched girl, who had barely heard the order given to the slave and dragged herself in the direction of his daughter's room with the feeble steps of an old woman. He wanted her to stay; he wanted to ask for her forgiveness; but he did nothing. When the priest arrived, a half-hour later, Jovita asked:

"I wanna go out through the slave quarters. Gimme permission, Governor; I don't want 'em to see me."

The weather turned cold at the moment of her departure. He let her pass through the large door that led to the kitchen and from there to the slave quarters; he didn't detain her any longer. He no longer thought about political complications. He no longer cared about what might happen tomorrow when everyone found out that the fabricated heroine had not been allowed to go to war, would never be allowed to go, and that everything was nothing more than a petty, stupid scheme. Jovita had been nothing more than a means to an end.

The new vicar, who had donned a cassock just the month before, rode silently behind Jovita. She was riding sidesaddle, and her wide flannel skirt undulated to the rhythm of the horse's gait. It was already dark, the day having ended suddenly in one of those rapid, equatorial nightfalls. The priest had been filled in quickly by the Governor. He felt so sorry for this poor young girl that he fabricated ingenious plans to console her. If she had a good voice, he'd arrange for her sing in the Church choir.

Just as the sudden and thick cover of night descended upon them, the riders came to a crossroads. Jovita hesitated, moved to the priest's side, and the two of them began discussing which road to take.

At that point they heard a far-off singing that was growing louder, bursting with enthusiasm. They noticed some white shapes in the distance; they were new recruits coming from the *sertão* on their way to war.

Now the shapes could be distinguished one from the other. A few sang and then others responded with the refrain:

Who is blessed by the Country?
Jovita! Jovita!

Passing by so close that their horses' breathing could be heard, one of the young men asked, coming up to Jovita and studying her in the light of the lamp:

"Praise be Our Lord Jesus Christ! Is this the road to the city?"

The road along which the men had come was the road to the *sertão,* there was no longer any doubt.

As the priest and Jovita headed in the direction of the *sertão,* he answered the fellow:

"The road to the city is over there."

When the riders withdrew, once again singing the song about Jovita, one man who had seen her up close and illuminated by the lamp fell back, distracted, and didn't enter the chorus. He said to his companion:

"That girl's the spittin' image of Jovita."

The other one laughed:

"Whoever heard of Jovita wearin' a skirt?"

Immersed as they were in the darkness—before the moonlight could illuminate the endless road of return—the priest nonetheless knew Jovita was crying. Her body was shaking and giving sudden little jerks; she desperately struggled against her own sobs, pressing her mouth closed, squeezing her eyes shut, lashing at herself. She would never again see her brother, who loved her as well as everything God had given them. He must be rotting away in that far-off, foreign land by now. Never again would she see Pedro.

"I'm dyin' of shame. Please, Father, gimme absolution, I sinned for being proud. I lost my brother . . . and I lost the one who loved me, but they went on to the very end. They avenged the Brazilian women, and here I am. In a little while, everyone'll be makin' fun of me. . . . The people on the streets called me a *heroine.* Such a pretty name, it's killin' me now."

With infinite caution, the priest searched for words. This would be his first job as a pastor, with his first lamb. An inexperienced young fellow, he didn't know how to talk to Jovita. He spoke half ingenuously to the night, to the clearing, there, at the end of the road where the full moon, rising, was revealed:

"Heroine or hero, female or male saint, you don't need to do great things. Saints were always defeated by the battles they waged in the world. What remains of them is so very much, yet they did almost nothing: a gesture, an example."

A little while later, the moon defied the sad, wartime night. Blood-red moon of the dead, bountiful moon of the glorious light of the living that travel toward victory.

The priest and the young girl went deeper and deeper down the road, disappearing on the moonlit ribbon that uncurled up to the horizon.

Farewell, Jovita. Jovita, farewell.

Lia Correia Dutra

Lia Correia Dutra began her career as a poet, and her first book, *Luz e Sombra* (Light and Shadow) was pronounced the best collection of poetry for 1931 by the Brazilian Academy of Letters. She was also a critic, and in 1938, during the heyday of the social realist novel in Brazil, she published a study of José Lins do Rego, a celebrated northeastern novelist.

Like many writers of her day, Correia Dutra abandoned poetry for fiction, and her first collection of stories, *Navio sem Porto* (1943) (Ship without a Port), was awarded the Humberto Campos prize. Many of her stories were published in *Leitura* (Reading), a left-wing journal she worked for over the years, and several have been anthologized, among them, "Mundo Perfeito" (A Perfect World). This story appears in Graciliano Ramos's *Contos e Novelas* (1956–1957) (Stories and Novellas), a three-volume collection of Brazilian fiction.

A Perfect World

(1957)

Shaken by his companion on the bench, he woke with a start. The man yelled, "Run, run! Here comes the police." Further away, a shrill voice confirmed the warning: "Look out for the cops! Look out for the cops!" Startled and still dazed, he took off, following his companion in and out of the park benches, until they came out in Lapa. There they stopped to catch their breath, and said goodbye to one another. The other fellow slapped him on the back and raised his hand to his greasy felt hat. They separated. Only then did he think about what had happened. He had run away as if he had had some crime to pay for, some offense to hide. But he was just there, sleeping on the hard bench, because he had been kicked out of the basement in which an old acquaintance had sheltered him, and he had been roaming the streets for two days now. He hadn't killed, robbed, or offended anyone. He had always been a timid, well-behaved creature. As a child, he rescued abandoned kittens from the gutter, he took flowers to his teacher, he never threw stones, he put burlap covers on his books and notebooks, he never wrote dirty words on the walls, he took a beating from the older children without telling on them, he respected his elders. After he grew up, he greeted everyone, thought well of the things they said to him: "That's it exactly, yes sir. . . . Perfectly. You're absolutely right." He waited for the traffic light before crossing the street, he always walked on the right-hand side, he got in lines without complaining, he justified class differences, he never mistreated animals, he never stepped on flower beds, he never spit on the ground or smoked in movie houses, he never nudged the women passengers on trolley cars or made love to married women. He was an individual with good intentions, fearful of God and the laws of his country, whose political opinions, because of his desire to please, were the same as those of the person speaking to him; at bottom, he was a supporter of the government, regardless of the government in charge. Possessed of the most commendable civic virtues, he remained standing whenever they played the national anthem (which he knew entirely by heart), he took off his hat to the flag or when passing a church, he loved to accompany parades and processions. He listened to speeches with pleasure; the longer the speeches, the more convincing they seemed to him. He worshipped Hierarchy and the Family; he believed in Justice and had a love of Order.

Thinking more clearly now, he saw that, despite all this, it was a good thing he had fled. If the police had caught him sleeping on the bench, they'd have asked the same old questions: "Name? Profession? Residence?" and, in the end, they would have taken him to the police station, where they would have written in the books: a bum. He found that designation especially hard to take; but, after all, that's just what he was. The park benches seemed made for people to sit on; there wasn't any law, not even a municipal ordinance prohibiting a man sitting on a bench from giving way to fatigue and falling asleep. Although in the beginning it seemed illogical to him, now he understood that the only people who had a right to sit on the benches at night and take a nap were the ones who had a permanent residence, a profession or an income that ensured them a roof over their heads and food—in other words, only those who didn't need benches because they had a bed waiting for them at home. Anyone who doesn't have any legal residence can't sleep anywhere.

Had he been dressed in good clothes and shoes, when his companion awakened him, had his face been shaven, and had his billfold in his pocket been filled with money, he wouldn't have needed to run (besides, the other fellow wouldn't have dared to arouse him); he'd wait for the policeman and say, as he stretched: "I was here enjoying the cool night air. . . . Don't ask me how, but I fell asleep." The policeman would find it quite natural: "Of course, my dear doctor. . . . The heat this evening is stifling and before you know it, you fall asleep." He would address me just like that: "my dear doctor," and would leave with his billy club to drive away the bums fast asleep on the other benches.

Without getting upset, the man drew his coat more closely over his shirtless chest, refastened the rusty diaper pin that had served him so very well, put his hands in his pockets, and started off down the sidewalk of the Passeio Público. He was falling asleep on his feet. He looked longingly at the lawns, shook off the temptation, and dragged his tired feet. The holes in his shoes hurt his toes; each step brought new pains, and the skin of his blistered heels stuck to the dried and cracked shoe leather. He walked by the same places he had passed earlier that night. As he walked, he noticed the clock on the skyscraper: it was two-thirty in the morning. Dawn was still a long way off. A night in the out-of-doors seemed to last forever when one didn't have the right to stop walking. Everything was much easier in the daytime. He would sit down. Watch people. The movement on the street distracted him. But the night unwound itself slowly, like a spool from which he silently pulled an endless thread. At night, the hours and minutes stretched out and multiplied; the duration of the hours and minutes changed. It seemed to him that he had passed by this same place long ago; but only a couple of hours back, at midnight, he had stationed himself, here, in front of the Municipal Theater, waiting for the opera to let out in order to make a bit of money by opening and closing car doors. It hadn't been a success. His dirtiness, his rags, his five-day-old beard hardly impressed the ladies, who were dressed in ball gowns and wrapped in furs. He had heard one of them say to her husband (for him, every man accompanying a lady in the street was her husband): "Disgusting! He looks like a tramp in the movies." And, in fact, his utterly miserable apparel did seem almost artificial, as if it had been arranged by a competent stage designer. Another woman, a chubby little lady with fair hair and roses in her décolletage, felt sympathy for him and said to the prosperous old gentleman giving her his arm: "Poor thing! He must be tubercular! João, give him something." But the old fellow said in a loud voice, as he entered the huge black automobile with a gray interior: "Child, you're so naive! You don't know anything about life. Those people have money stashed away. This one here might have even more than I do." The chauffeur had intentionally closed the door on his hand; the bloody pinch mark was still there, next to the fingernail on his index finger. The brutal gesture hadn't provoked any rage or feelings of revolt in him; the car was luxurious and it seemed natural that the chauffeur, who was responsible for its upkeep, should defend it. He merely blew on his finger and ran to pick up the forty cents the chubby woman had thrown to him behind the old man's back when the car started to move. This almost got him run over by a Ford that was coming up from behind. "Fool! Are you trying to get yourself killed?" yelled the driver, while he stood there, in the middle of the road, blanched from fear, gripping the money in his battered hand.

The man in charge of the cars had sent him away, and he had nearly been beaten up by a tall fellow with a numbered cap on his head, who told him that a particular spot in the street was taken: "I'm the one who calls for the automobiles around here, do you understand? Beat it, this spot is mine. I've got a permit from the police." Apparently you needed a special permit to close car doors. He was perplexed for a minute, but, because he was a well-behaved citizen, a lover of Order, respectful of Hierarchy, he acknowledged the perfect social organization of the street. He went on walking, submissive, clutching in his hand the eighty cents that his intrusions into the business of others had yielded him—for he had earned forty cents more from the owner of a roadster. Later on, a man with a white scarf around his neck, who had seen everything, gave him a coin, with the accompanying advice: "Don't spend it all on drink." He took the money uneasily because it was charity; he hadn't done anything to earn it. He had closed two doors, almost getting his finger mangled in that simple task, and that seemed to legitimize his previous earnings; but he hadn't given a pretense of assistance to the man with the scarf. The man had advised him not to spend the money on drink. And, in fact, he didn't spend it on drink—although, considering everything, it would probably have been better if he had. He spent it on food, a bowl of hot soup that dropped heavily into his empty stomach, and a piece of bread he gnawed later on, as he sat near the beach. The food had given him some relief, but not the dreamy anesthesia or the moment of euphoria that the same money, spent on booze, could give him. He didn't drink. But he saw drunks pass by, happy and laughing from time to time, muttering confused sentences, singing loudly, venting their innermost thoughts, addressing everyone, rich and poor, white and black, men and women, free of any inferiority complex or class prejudice, fraternizing with the whole of humanity—or, in the same carefree manner, slighting the humble and powerful, as if they were looking down from some Olympian height. He was deathly afraid of drink; nevertheless, he realized that, given the depths he had fallen to, the only way he could experience a return to dignity, a reintegration into the world, was through a few shots of whiskey. He'd love to forget, for even a few minutes, that new sensation brought on by poverty, of being rejected, feared, moved to the side like some useless object, avoided like a noxious thing. Respectful of others, he felt the painful need for them to respect him, to take him seriously. The need to belong to a group, to own his own place, to move within the well-defined borders. A gregarious being, he loved to say: *we*. He had said *we* many times before; he had spent his entire life saying: *we*. "We, those in our house; we, the students; we, the businessmen, we, we, we, of the petit bourgeoisie. He no longer had any family, or house, or profession; and he wasn't part of any social class. That made him feel extremely isolated. Solitude was distressing. He didn't have anything to fall back on.

He reconsidered certain things in his life—he was always so serious, so docile, so full of good will—he couldn't understand how he could have fallen so far. He had failed, he had closed his little shop (a minuscule place located in a niche on Larga Street, which stocked suspenders, belts, combs, and ties). Since then, with each step he took, he was little by little disappearing down a road that didn't seem to have an end or a space for him to turn around, and he was farther and farther away from that little piece of clean life that once was his. Everything had happened so quickly: in three years time he had fallen to where he was now. Loss of capital, loss of credit; for a few months he lived off the sale of anything he had that was of some value: furniture, a ring, a clock, two paintings, books, clothes. And then life went rapidly downhill. The monies loaned to him by his friends were gone; then his friends were gone. Evicted from his *pensão,* he had been given shelter in the basement of an acquaintance's house. Then his suit started to wear out, fraying at the elbows and knees, around the collar and in the seat, everywhere his body rubbed most against the fabric; the soles of his shoes developed holes, the toes came unsewn, and the laces broke and were substituted with pieces of twine; at first he had washed his shirt every other day, then every other week, until finally it couldn't be washed any more and it ended up rotting off his back; his little collar had become yellow, turned up at the ends and frayed around his neck; he pulled it off and threw it in the garbage along with his useless, twisted tie; his hair had grown long, his face went unshaven—nowhere on his person was there any sign of neatness or respectability. In the beginning, he had hopes of returning to a situation similar to the one he had lost; as time went by, his expectations lowered. He presented himself for a job at a variety of places: "Do you have a permit? You don't? Impossible." A permit to do the paperwork in a bakery, a permit to measure cloth, a permit to weigh whatever in shops, a permit to wrap up purchases, a permit to push elevator buttons, a permit to deliver packages, a permit to answer the telephone in doctors' offices, a permit to ride a bicycle, a permit to shut a car door. No, he didn't have a permit.

For a time his pride wouldn't allow him to accept manual labor or to lower himself to the status of a servant; he refused to polish the Major's house, to sweep the streets, to wash the cars at the mansion on the corner. Later he wanted to accept anything to earn a few pennies that would ward off hunger; but by then people started to withdraw from him, frightened by his ragged appearance, by his eyes, which were sunk deep in their sockets, lost in the confusion of hair on his face. People's respect disappeared as his wardrobe diminished; his anxiety to please grew as the good will of others decreased. The more he sought to enter into the Order, to return to the social organization that he admired so much, the more they pushed him back, the more they drove him away.

Suddenly, he recalled the episode with Joli, which he hadn't thought about since he was a child. He discovered that his story was exactly like that of the dog, Joli.

Joli had been a small, white mutt with black spots, in whom one could still see, although very tenuously, the marks of the Tenerife breed. Like all the children in his house, he was crazy about Joli; when he was nine years old, he had fought with his own sister, who was ten (today she was a nun, a barefoot Carmelite; it'd been nearly twenty years since he'd seen her), as well as with his brother, who was seven (he died young, the year the influenza struck), just for the privilege of carrying Joli in his arms and sleeping with him at night, hugging him in his bed. But Joli wasn't a faithful dog; he had inherited from his bohemian ancestors a taste for wandering, adventure, and short-lived love affairs with bitches from nearby streets. At times he disappeared, not to be seen for weeks. The children went out in search of him, running through the entire neighborhood: "Joli! Joli! Has anybody seen Joli?" they asked from door to door, and generally they returned triumphantly, pulling Joli behind on a rope. Their parents fussed over Joli and petted him, welcoming him home. Other times, Joli returned on his own, as if nothing had happened, without any remorse, wagging his tail and leaping about; then he'd come back into the domestic fold, grow fatter over a period of time, until he felt the lure of the streets once again. He'd disappear only to reappear, later, oblivious of any wrongdoing and confident of forgiveness. He'd enter the house, barking, with his tongue hanging out like a little piece of red ribbon, jumping and making a great fuss over everyone, who, in turn, reciprocated his affection. On one occasion, he disappeared and stayed away for two months. After long, futile searches, the children lost interest in him, giving him up for lost; then, finally, he returned—filthy, covered with mange, his coat falling off in chunks, open sores on his flesh, and covered with flies that he brushed away with his sad tail and humble ears. The three children now looked at Joli with disgust; their mother came and drove him out of the house and their father proclaimed: "That filthy dog will never come inside again." Although rejected, Joli was persistent. Now that they no longer wanted him, he overflowed with love for everyone, for the house, for the children. He got into the garden, coming in with his coterie of flies, wagging his tail, giving his little barks. The children's father would take off his belt and whip Joli across his back. Then Joli would take off, yelping, only to return as soon as he could. For weeks he circled the house, sleeping at the front gate, following along and jumping after the family, who ignored him as they left the house. When they returned, he'd try to come into the house with them; he stayed beneath the window, crying with the tiniest of whimpers. Then he'd go around to the back, scratch at the kitchen door and stick the tip of his nose through the crack. When the children heard his cries, they felt sad and wanted to take him in. But, as they peeked out between the blinds, the ugly, disgusting, mangy dog they saw no longer resembled their former playmate, who had slept in their beds, wrapped up in their arms.

One day, Joli got the door open and entered the house, but he came in without his old confidence and happy manner and barks and little leaps—he cowered on the floor, dragged his stomach along, and stopped in front of them with meek, beseeching eyes. "Why don't you love me anymore? Aren't I Joli? Your Joli?" That's how the children understood his look, and their hearts grew soft, and the little girl began to cry; but their father came into the room and kicked Joli, who rolled head over tail down the five front steps, then crouched in the gutter, howling. Little by little, his cries became a gentle weeping, and he stayed there, with his eyes on the house, as he chased the flies away with the little flicks of his ears. He remained like that for a week, eating the leftovers the children secretly threw to him, until death finally arrived; his ears grew still, his snout lay between his front paws, his entire body became rigid, with his open eyes fixed on the locked house.

His story was just like Joli's.

He kept walking. His feet hurt him more and more, and his body begged to stretch itself out and rest in any corner. He crossed the street and sat down on the steps of the Municipal Council building. He needed to think about his life, to find a solution for his situation. He had only a few nickels in his pocket, nothing else in the world, and he couldn't figure out where he could get help. He was perplexed: "How could *I* have come to this?" He didn't understand it. He had fallen so slowly, so little by little, that at first he couldn't see how it had happened. His fall hadn't been as violent as Joli's, who had rolled down the steps all at once after a swift kick in the backside. He had fallen one step at a time, in a succession of little noiseless tumbles that didn't bruise him very much. After each tumble, he hoped he would stop, that he wouldn't go down any further, that he might even go up again. But there he was, without clothes, without his friend's basement, without a job, without a permit, and with just a few nickels in his pocket.

He clutched his face in his hands. His head throbbed and there was a foul taste of cigarette butts in his mouth, which surprised him since he hadn't smoked since late yesterday. Still refusing to accept his impoverished condition, he hadn't reached the point of doing what other bums did—picking cigarette butts off the ground that were still damp from other people's saliva. His apprenticeship would be carried out little by little. This was a new situation, to which he would adapt himself. For the time being, he displayed all the hesitations and shyness of the novice. Later, he would learn how to reach out his hand, ask for leftovers, and fall back on charity and social institutions. He still had loathings, scruples, and class prejudices, which would disappear just as the other signs of bourgeois respectability had disappeared: his collar, his tie, and his shaven face. He had failed to exchange in time his tattered coat for a T-shirt, or to swap his shoes, run down at the heels, for a new pair of clogs; he hadn't wanted to do it, preferring to hold on to the last vestiges, the last symbols of his lost position. Just a little while ago, he had been part of a class that judges moral character in terms of apparel; he had clung to his cashmere suit, his shoes, his collar, as if they could save him from becoming déclassé. The moment had arrived when he understood that certain objects, respected when new, produced exactly the opposite effect when they became worn out. Because of them, he had become a bum—a man outside any class; now he wanted the T-shirt and the clogs that would make him look at least like a workman.

Seated there, on the stairs, he began to realize that his integration into the lowest class could bring him some comfort. Because of his love of Order, he liked things that were labeled, that belonged to a specific place—things with a name and a clear function. What left him so utterly distressed was the feeling of being unattached to life, of not being part of any organization, of being outside, of being unable to say "we," of not perceiving any usefulness or rationale for his own existence. He needed to adapt to some humble corner, to stop being a bum, a solitary individual whom rich and poor alike drove away with the same distrust, and in whom no one recognized a kindred spirit.

The more closed the social structure demonstrated itself to be, the more desirable it seemed to him. He wanted to return to it, to fit perfectly within it. By what misfortune had he, the friend of Order and Institutions, come to be here, on these steps, without a home, without a job, without his own place in the world, fleeing from the police and scaring ladies coming out of the theater with his very appearance? In former times, men had tipped their hats to him, women had smiled at him, a few had even loved him. He was the same man, the same as before; it was only his clothes that were torn, only his shoes that were filled with holes, only his beard that was scruffy and long. His moral standards hadn't declined along with his body; he was able to detach himself and contemplate his own spectacle, which he did with a certain constrained fear. He remembered Joli, his beseeching eyes, his tail lightly wagging, his whole frightened being that seemed to say: "I'm the same Joli. . . ." But in the children's eyes, he was no longer Joli; he was a mangy dog surrounded by flies, who was losing his coat in chunks.

And the same question, the same question without an answer, like an obsession, came to him: "What am I going to do tomorrow? What's going to happen to my life?" He didn't see any solution; but there must be some solution. The world seemed too perfect not to have a solution for his situation; it was like a puzzle in which each piece has its place, and fitting together with others, each piece contributes to form the overall design. Why was he alone, unable to adjust, to fit into the well-defined space? He didn't see the defects in the design, he didn't notice the misfit pieces or the gross, weak, provisional whole. Despite what had happened to him, it was still a great world, and things had their proper place; things and people. Even society's defensive stance against him, the bum, the unwholesome element—even that, at bottom, seemed to him a praiseworthy attitude.

He was falling asleep. Not even cigarettes were as desirable to him as a bed with its pillows and covers, where he could stretch out very slowly, first one leg, then the other, belly up, his whole body stretching out long, one arm behind his head, the other extended out on the mattress.

He went up the steps of the building, looking for a place to sleep on the narrow balconies forming a semicircle. On one side he found a black woman huddled over, covered with newspapers, with a little boy in her arms—a three- or four-year-old, a thin little thing with a cloth tied around his head. The woman sat up and looked at him distrustingly. "Excuse me, young lady." He moved away, over to the other side. He found people there as well, a little mulatto boy about twelve years old, still wide awake. He lay down next to the child, forming a pillow with his doubled-over hat, and was so dizzy with sleep that he barely noticed when the child, who was frightened by his presence, picked up his newspapers and went down the stairs in search of a bed somewhere else. He fell quickly into a deep, heavy, dreamless sleep, a dark, silent hole.

The sun was up when he was shaken by brutal hands: "This here isn't a hotel. Go home and sleep." Startled, he opened his eyes and saw a policeman.

He raced down the steps without watching where he was going. He crossed the street.

The collision happened so fast that he barely took in what had occurred. He heard the squeal of brakes and then he rolled over and over in the street, finally coming to rest in the gutter, just like Joli.

He didn't realize that the answer had come, that his situation had found a solution. He remained there, stretched out, his mouth open and drooling blood. He saw the policeman blowing his whistle, the people crowding together and then being driven back and contained by the rope that cordoned him off. He felt them going through his pockets, searching him all over, and heard a voice say: "He doesn't have any documents." He vaguely thought the only ironic thought he ever dared think: "Can it be that I'll need a permit for *this* too?" Then he lost consciousness and was wrapped in silence and solitude.

Later, he heard the ringing of the ambulance. The bell rang far, far away, sounding as if it were wrapped in flannel, as if it were coming from a distance and, in order to reach him, had to cross the gray mist forming in front of his eyes. From behind the mist, which lifted for a few moments only to become thick again and forever close off his vision of things, he had a last look at the perfect world. He saw a rope holding people back, like prisoners of a space the authorities granted them; he saw the policeman blowing his whistle, the traffic lights changing from red to yellow to green, the white ambulance, the two stretcher-bearers with their starched aprons, the nurse with a bag, the doctor with the syringe in his hand, bending over him, the trolley cars moving slowly along the tracks; he saw the hangers-on leaning over to look at him; a garbage collector dressed in blue denim and leaning on a broom; the buses passing along on the other side, filled with people going to work—everything he saw was a testimony to an absolute order, to the exemplary organization of people and things. . . .

Lygia Fagundes Telles

Lygia Fagundes Telles is one of Brazil's best known authors, and in 1985 she became the third woman elected to the Brazilian Academy of Letters. Born in São Paulo in 1923, she has written numerous volumes of fiction. Her most recent work is the novel *As Horas Nuas* (1989) (The Naked Hours), which is narrated by an aging actress and her cat.

Fagundes Telles writes about the lives of the middle and upper classes in urban Brazil, and her most powerful works, such as *Ciranda de Pedra* (1954) *(The Marble Dance),* are concerned with women's sexuality. In more recent years, she has adopted an experimental style—as in *As Meninas* (1973) *(The Girl in the Photograph),* her celebrated novel about three women whose experiences with drugs, sex, and violence are described within the context of a turbulent right-wing dictatorship. Her latest works have a magical, supernatural quality, and she seems increasingly drawn to the animal world. Her volume *Seminário dos Ratos* (1977) *(Tigresa and Other Stories)* contains some of her best stories, whose gothic atmosphere is generated by obsessive, frightening images of insects and animals.

In both her novels and her stories, Fagundes Telles is adept at portraying the subtle tensions and conflicts between family members; for example, in "Antes do Baile Verde" (1965) ("Before the Green Ball"), which was awarded the first-place prize at the Cannes International Women's Fiction Festival in 1965, she describes a self-centered daughter's frustration with her ailing father, whom she ultimately abandons on his deathbed. Several of the stories in her collection *Antes do Baile Verde* (1970) are about incompatibility, distrust, and deception between the sexes. The monologue translated here, "Apenas um Saxofone" (Just a Saxophone), was first published in 1969 and subsequently included in that volume.

Just a Saxophone

(1969)

It's grown dark and cold. *"Merde! voilà l'hiver,"* according to Xenophon, is the sort of thing one ought to say now. She learned from him that a dirty word in a woman's mouth is like a slug in the corolla of a rose. I'm a woman, consequently I can say vulgar words only in a foreign tongue, and if at all possible, I should make them part of a poem. That way, people will see my originality and erudition. An erudite slut, so erudite that if I desired I could utter the worst possible obscenities in ancient Greek. Xenophon knows ancient Greek. And the slug would go unrecognized, as is fitting for a slug in a forty-four-year-old corolla. Forty-four years and five months. Good Lord, it went by fast, didn't it? Fast. Six more years and I'll be a half-century old; I've been thinking a lot about that and I feel a secular chill as it comes up through the floorboards and into the carpet. My carpet is Persian, all my carpets are Persian, but I don't know what those damn things are good for since they don't keep the cold from settling into the room. It was less cold in our bedroom, with the walls covered with oakum, and the little jute carpet on the floor. He had covered the walls himself, where he had tacked up portraits of ancestors and pictures of the Virgin by Fra Angelico, about whom he was passionate.

Where is he now? Where? I could order a fire to be made in the fireplace, but I dismissed the butler, the housemaid, the cook—I dismissed them one by one, flying into a rage and sending the bunch of them packing, get out, get out! I remained alone. There's firewood somewhere around the house, but it's not just a matter of striking a match and touching it to the logs like you see in the movies; the Japanese fellow always spent hours fooling around there, blowing on the wood until it caught fire. And I barely have the strength to light a cigarette. I don't know how long I've been sitting here. I unplugged the telephone, wrapped myself up in a blanket, grabbed a bottle of whiskey, and here I am drinking very, very slowly so as not to get drunk, not today, no, because today I want to be clearheaded, seeing one thing then another. And there are things galore to be seen from inside as well as outside, in fact even more from the outside, like that shitload of things I bought from around the world, things that I didn't even know I had and that I'm only seeing now, just now that it's dark. It's as if we are getting dark together, the room and I. An atrocious, affected, pretentious asininity of a room. And what's more, rich, to the point of transcending mere wealth. I opened a bag of gold for the decorator to go wild with and he really went wild, the fag. His name was René and he'd arrive very early in the morning with his fabrics, velvets, muslins, brocades, "today I brought a fabric from Afghanistan for the sofa, it's absolutely divine! Di-vine!" Not only was the cloth not from Afghanistan, but he wasn't quite the fairy he made himself out to be—everything was mystification, calculation. Once I suprised him alone, smoking near the window, with the tired and sad expression of an actor who had had it with performing. He was taken aback when he saw me, as if I had caught him red-handed stealing the silverware. Then he reassumed his bubbling persona and went out swishing from side to side to show me the oratory, a fake antique oratory, made just three days ago with little holes in the wood, imitating three centuries of dryrot. "This angel can only be one of Aleijadinho's, just look at its cheeks! And the drooping eyes that are just a tiny bit crossed. . . ." I agreed in the same hysterical tone, although I knew perfectly well that Aleijadinho would have needed more than ten arms to make so many angels like that because Mado's shop has thousands of them, every one of them authentic, "just a tiny bit cross-eyed," she says, echoing René's falsetto voice. Deluxe colonial style. Knowing I was being taken, I couldn't have cared less—on the contrary, I felt an acute pleasure in being sold a bill of goods. Yesterday I read they're eating rats in Saigon and that there are no longer any butterflies in the country, never again will there be even the smallest butterfly. . . . Then I broke down crying like a madwoman, I'm not sure whether because of the butterflies or the rats. I don't think I've ever drunk so much as I have lately, and when I drink like that I get sentimental and cry easily. "You need to take care of yourself," René said the night we got drunk, and it's only now that I'm thinking about what he said to me because why should I take care, why? Next I hired him to decorate the country house. "I have the ideal furnishings for this place of yours," he informed me, and I bought the ideal furnishings, I bought everything, I would even have bought Marie Antoinette's wig with all its mazes made by moths and the dust as well, for which I wouldn't be charged anything, a mere contribution made by time, of course. Of course.

Where is he now? At times I'd close my eyes and the sounds were like a human voice calling to me, enveloping me, Luisiana, Luisiana! What sounds were those? How could they seem to be a person's voice and, at the same time, so much more powerful, so much purer. And sincere, unpretentious, like waves renewing themselves in the sea, apparently the same, but only apparently. "This is my instrument," he said sliding his hand over the saxophone. And cupping his other hand, he placed it over my chest: "and this is my music."

Where, where? I look at my portrait over the fireplace. "Your portrait has to hang over the fireplace," René declared with an authoritative air, for at times he was authoritative. He introduced his lover to me, a painter, at least he led me to believe he was his lover because I no longer know anything now. And that ephebe with the curls on his forehead painted me all in white, a Dame aux Camélias returning from the field, with a long dress, a long neck, everything elongated and illuminated, as if I had the angel candlestick on the stairs lit up inside of me. Everything has turned dark in the room except for the dress in the painting—there it is, diaphanous like the shroud of an ectoplasm, hovering delicately in the air. An ectoplasm much younger than I, without a doubt the young bullshitter was clever enough to imagine how I must have looked when I was twenty. "You look a little different in the painting," he conceded, "but the fact is that I'm not just painting your face," he added, subtly. He meant by this that he was painting my soul. I agreed at the time, I was even moved when I saw myself with the electric hairdo and glassy eyes. "My name is Luisiana," the ectoplasm now says to me. "Many years ago, I sent my lover away and since then I died."

Where? . . . I have a yacht, I have a silver mink jacket, I have a diamond tiara, I have a ruby that had once been incrusted in the belly button of a very famous shah; until just a little while ago, I knew the name of this shah. I have an old guy who gives me money, a young fellow who gives me pleasure, and on top of that I have a learned man who gives me philosophy classes, and whose interest is so platonic that he went to bed with me after the second class. He came so humbly, so miserably, with his dusty mourning suit and his widower's boots, that I closed my eyes and lay back, sighing, come Xenophon, come. "I'm not Xenophon, don't call me Xenophon," he begged me, his breath smelling of Valda cough drops, but he was Xenophon, there was never anyone so Xenophon as he. Just as there was never a Luisiana so Luisiana as I. Nobody knows about that name, nobody, not even my pimp of a father, who didn't wait for me to be born to see what I was like, nor my poor soul of a mother, who didn't live long enough to register my birth. I was born one night on the beach, and that night I was given a name that lasted briefly, only as long as our love lasted. In the wee hours of the morning one day, when I got loaded and went to talk to a lawyer to make sure no other name would appear on my tombstone except that one, he gave a detestable little laugh, "Luisiana? But why Luisiana? Where did you get that name?" He controlled his anger at being awakened at that hour, and he got dressed and very politely took me home. "As you wish, my dear, you give the orders!" Then he gave his little laugh, after all, he probably thought, a drunk but rich slut has the right to put whatever name she wants on her stone. But I no longer care what he thinks, him or the other rabble around me; public opinions are this carpet, this lamp, that painting. Public opinion is this house with its saints pierced by a thousand responsibilities.

But I used to care a lot. Because of public opinion, I have a grand piano, I have a Siamese cat with a ring in its ear, I have a house in the country with a swimming pool, and in the bathroom is toilet paper that the old guy brought from the United States, decorated with little gold flowers and encased in a plastic music box that plays "The last rose of summer! . . ." whenever anyone unrolls the paper. In addition to the rolls, he gave me some cans of caviar, "It's necessary to sugarcoat the bitter pill," he said, laughing in his customarily gross way. He's incurably gross; if it weren't for his spitting out dollars, I'd have already told him to go to hell with his golf clubs and his lavender-perfumed underwear. I have shoes with diamond buckles and an aquarium with a coral garden at the bottom, and when the old guy bought me a pearl, he thought it highly original to hide it in the bottom of the aquarium and then send me off to find it: "You're getting warm, warmer, No, now you're cold! . . ." And me, making like a little girl, laughing, when all the while I wanted to tell him to stick the pearl up his ass and leave me in peace, leave me in peace! Him, the ardent youth with all his ardors, Xenophon with his minty breath—I wanted to drive them all out of the house, like I did with the staff, all of them a bunch of bastards, who pee in my milk and laugh hysterically whenever I'm about to fall down dead drunk.

Where, my God? Where is he now? I also have a diamond the size of a pigeon's egg. I'd trade the diamond, the buckle shoes, the yacht—I'd trade everything, rings and fingers, just to be able to hear, regardless how little, the music of the saxophone. I wouldn't even need to see him, I swear I wouldn't ask that much, I'd be happy just knowing he was alive, alive some place, playing his saxophone.

I want to make it perfectly clear that the only thing that exists for me is youth, all the rest is foolishness, sequins, glass beads. I can have two thousand plastic surgeries and it doesn't resolve anything, in the end it's the same shit, only youth exists. He was my youth, but at the time I didn't know it, at the crucial moment people never know nor can they know since everything is natural, like day following night, like the sun, the moon, and I was young and didn't think about it, just like I didn't think about breathing. Does anyone, by chance, pay attention to the act of breathing? Yes, but only when the breathing goes to pot. Then it brings with it that sadness, goodness, I was breathing so well!

He was my youth, him and his saxophone shining like gold. His shoes were dirty, his shirt was falling apart, his hair was like a bird's nest, but his saxophone was always meticulously clean. He also had a thing about his teeth, which were of a whiteness I never saw equaled, and whenever he laughed, I stopped my own laughing just to look at them. He carried his toothbrush in his pocket as well as the diaper he used to clean the saxophone. He had found a box with a dozen Johnson diapers in a cab and from then on he began using them for all sorts of purposes: as handkerchiefs, face towels, napkins, table cloths, and cleaning rags for his saxophone. He also used one as a flag of truce during our most serious fight, when he wanted us to have a child. He was passionate for so many things. . . .

The first time we made love was on the beach. The sky pulsated with stars and the weather was warm. We went rolling and laughing right down to the waves that sizzled on the sand, and there we stayed, naked and embracing one another in the water that was warm like the water in a sink. He got worried when I told him that I'd never been baptized. He cupped his hands, filled them with water, and poured it over my head: "I baptize you, Luisiana, in the name of the Father, the Son and the Holy Spirit. Amen." I thought he was kidding around, but I never saw him so serious. "Now your name is Luisiana," he said kissing me on the face. I asked him if he believed in God. "I have a passion for God," he said softly, as he laid down on his back, with his fingers laced behind his neck and his gaze lost in the sky above: "What perplexes me is a sky just like this one above." When we got up, he ran to the dune where our clothes were, removed the diaper covering the saxophone, and brought it back delicately in his fingertips to dry me off. Then he took hold of the saxophone, sat down all curled up and naked like a baby faun, and began to improvise very softly, forming with the bubbling waves a gentle, warm melody. The sounds grew and trembled, like soap bubbles: Look at that big one! Look at this one that's rounder . . . oh, it burst. . . . If you loved me, I asked, would you stay just as you are, naked, and go to the top of the dune and play, play as loud as you can until the police come? He looked at me and, without batting an eye, he took off in the direction of the dune, and I ran after him, shouting and laughing, laughing because he had already started to belt out the notes.

My girlfriend from dancing class married the drummer from a group that used to play in a night club, and a party was held. It was there that I met him. In the middle of the biggest blowout in the world, the mother of the bride locked herself in the bedroom, crying, "Look at the company my daughter's keeping! Just bums, just scum! . . ." I laid her down on the bed and went to look for a glass of water with sugar, but while I was gone, the guests discovered the bedroom, and when I returned, couples had already poured in and were clinging to one another on pillows on the floor. I jumped over bodies and sat down on the bed. The woman was crying and crying until, little by little, the sobbing became faint and suddenly stopped. Then I stopped talking, and the two of us remained very quiet, listening to the music of a young man whom I still hadn't seen. He was sitting in the shadows, playing the saxophone. The tune was gentle, but so eloquent that I was bewitched, as if under a spell. I'd never heard anything like it, no one had ever played an instrument like that. He was saying with the saxophone everything I had wanted to say to the woman and hadn't been able to: that she shouldn't cry anymore, that everything was all right, everything was fine as long as there was love. God existed, didn't she believe in God?—asked the saxophone. And childhood existed, those sounds now spoke of childhood, look over there, childhood! . . . The woman stopped crying, and now I was the one who was crying. Around us, the couples listened in an impassioned silence, and their caresses became more intense, more real, because the music also spoke about sex, alive and chaste, like a fruit that ripens in the sun and the wind.

Where? Where? . . . He took me to his apartment, he lived in a miniscule apartment on the tenth floor of a very old building, his entire fortune was that bedroom with its tiny bathroom. And the saxophone. He told me that the apartment had been left to him by his fortune-teller aunt. Another day, he said he had won it in a bet, and then still another day, when he began telling a third version, I stopped him and he laughed: "It's necessary to change the stories, Luisiana, improvising is what's fun, that's what we have our imagination for! It's sad when something stays the same its entire life. . . ." He improvised all the time, and his music was always agile, rich, and so full of invention that it began to bother me. "You keep on composing and you'll end up losing everything; you have to take notes, you have to write down what you compose!" He smiled. "I'm self-taught, Luisiana, I don't know how to read or write music, and that's not even necessary to be a tenor sax. Do you know what a tenor sax is? It's what I am." He played in a group that had a contract with a club, and his only ambition was to have his own group some day. Also a high-quality record player to listen to Ravel and Debussy.

Our life was so marvelously free! And so filled with love, how we loved and laughed and cried with love on that tenth floor, surrounded by the Fra Angelico paintings and by the portraits of his ancestors. "They aren't my relatives, I found all this in a trunk in a basement," he confessed to me one time. I pointed to the oldest of the portraits, so old that the only thing left of the woman was her dark hair. And her eyebrows. Did you find this one in the trunk too? I asked. He laughed and even today I don't know whether or not he was telling the truth. If you really love me, I said, get up on that table, now, and yell as loud as you can, "You're all a bunch of cuckolds, you're all a bunch of cuckolds!" and then get down from the table and leave, but don't run. He gave me the saxophone to hold and I fled, laughing, no, no, I was kidding, don't do it! From the street corner, I could hear him shouting in the bar, "Cuckolds, all cuckolds!" He caught up with me in the middle of a group of dumbfounded people, "Luisiana, Luisiana, don't deny me, Luisiana!" Another night—we were coming out of a theater—I couldn't resist, and asked him if he would sing a bit of opera right there in the lobby, come on, if you really love me, sing a few bars from *Rigoletto* right here on the stairs.

If you really love me, you'll take me to a restaurant right now, you'll buy me those earrings right away, you'll buy me a new dress immediately! He was now playing at more places because I was becoming demanding, if you really, really, really love me. . . . He left at seven at night with the saxophone under his arm and only returned in the early morning hours. Then he meticulously cleaned the mouthpiece of the instrument, polished the metal with the diaper, and distractedly fingered the keys, without weariness, without loss of energy, "Luisiana, you're my music and I can't live without music," he said, seizing the mouthpiece in his mouth with the same fervor with which he took my breast in his mouth. I began to get crabby, restless, as if afraid to assume the responsibility for so much love. I wanted him to be more independent, more ambitious. Don't you have any ambition? There's no call for artists without ambition, what future can you have as you are? It was always the saxophone that responded to me, and the argument was so definitive that I felt ashamed, miserable for demanding more. Nevertheless, I kept on demanding. I thought about leaving him, but I didn't have the strength. I didn't. I preferred that our love rot away, that it become so unbearable that, when he went out, he would leave filled with nausea, without looking back.

Where is he now? Where? I have a house in the country, I have a diamond the size of a pigeon's egg. . . . I made up my eyes in front of the mirror, I had a date, my life was filled with dates, I was going to a club with a banker. Curled up on the bed, he played softly. My eyes were brimming with tears. I dried them on the saxophone's diaper and kept looking at my mouth, which I found particularly thin. If you really love me, I said, if you really love me, then go out and kill yourself immediately.

Júlia Lopes de Almeida

Photograph from the collection of Cláudio Lopes de Almeida

Rachel de Queiroz

Clarice Lispector

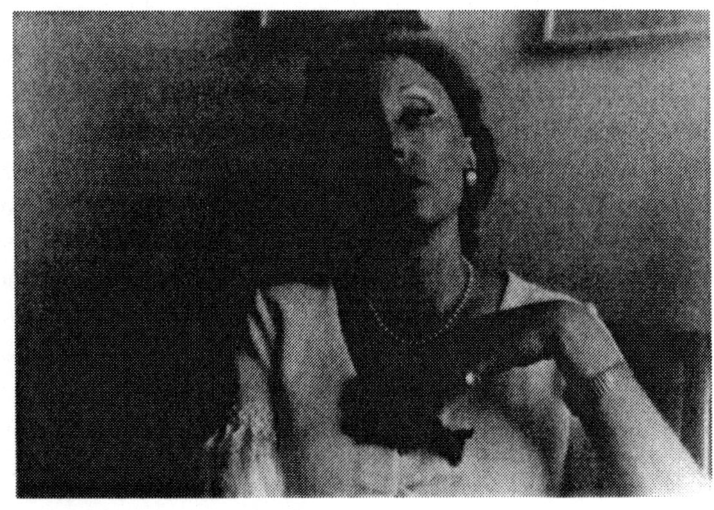

Emi Bulhões Carvalho da Fonseca

Lúcia Benedetti
Photograph by Sascha Harnisch

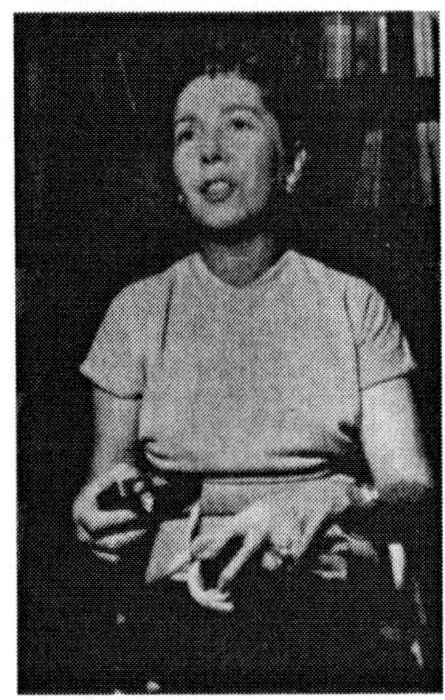

Dinah Silveira de Queiroz

Lygia Fagundes Telles

Adalgisa Nery

Hilda Hilst

Photograph by Gal Oppido

Nélida Piñon

Tania Jamardo Faillace

Photograph by Daniel Faillace Vieira

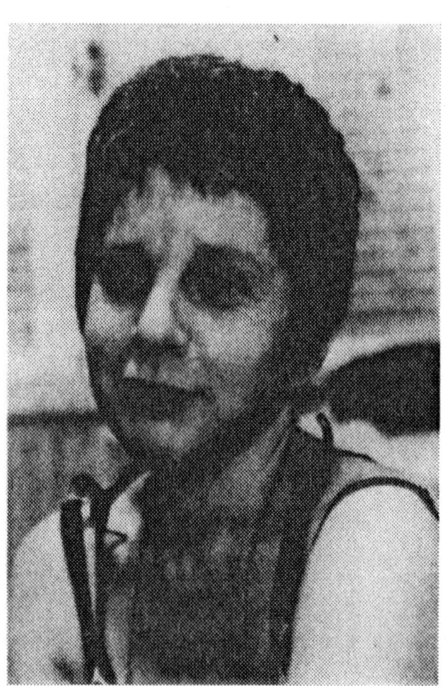

Elisa Lispector

Edla van Steen

Marina Colasanti

Márcia Denser

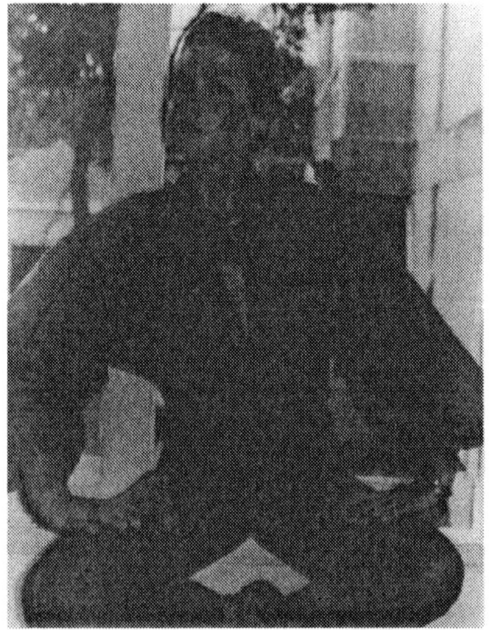

Lya Luft

Sônia Coutinho
Photograph by Marco Rodrigues

Adalgisa Nery

Born in Rio de Janeiro in 1905, Adalgisa Nery married the Brazilian artist Ismael Nery in 1922; and through him, she came into contact with some of the major intellectual figures of the Brazilian modernist period. Following the death of her husband, in 1934, she worked in the Ministry of External Affairs to support herself and her two sons, Ivan and Emmanuel. In 1937, she published her first poem, "Eu Em Ti" (I In You), and, soon afterward, the collection *Poemas.* She also began writing for various newspapers and reviews, where her earliest short stories appeared.

In 1940, Nery married Lourival Fontes, a high official in the Vargas administration. That same year, she published a book of poetry, *A Mulher Ausente* (The Absent Woman), and in 1943 her volume of short fiction, *Og,* appeared. From 1943 to 1945, she lived in Mexico, where her husband was the Brazilian ambassador. In 1953, she began publishing political commentaries in her daily column in the newspaper *Última Hora.* Entitled "Retrato Sem Retoque" (Picture without Retouching), the column was extremely popular, especially between 1960 and 1966 in Rio, where she won repeated elections as the state representative. Before taking political office, she and her husband separated.

In addition to her column and other journalistic writings of this period, Nery published two novels, *A Imaginária* (1959) (The Imaginary One) and *Neblina* (1962) (Mist), the latter a powerful work about a woman who, following an operation, no longer speaks. The novel portrays the effect the woman's silence has on her family, for whom she becomes a troublesome, undesirable object. Also in 1962, Nery published a volume of poetry, *Mundos Oscilantes* (Oscillating Worlds).

Nineteen sixty-six was a difficult year. The military government stripped Nery of her civilian rights because of a column she had written prior to the coup d'etat of 1964, in which she denounced the corrupt business dealings of a certain admiral in the Ministry of the Navy. Nery subsequently withdrew from public life and gave up her long and successful journalistic career. In 1972, she published a volume of short fiction entitled *22 Menos 1* (22 Minus 1), which contains "Premeditated Coincidence," the story translated here. She died in Rio de Janeiro in 1980.

Premeditated Coincidence

(1972)

After dinner, a small group was commenting on the death of an acquaintance who had died under morally questionable circumstances.

A gray-haired man with a calm appearance silently listened to the different opinions expressed about the death. He straightened himself in his easy chair, and with the manipulative demeanor of a person accustomed to solving others' problems, he said, in a leisurely voice:

"This case you gentlemen speak of with such alarm, I, in my position, would categorize as a simple, routine accident. A similar case came to me just last week; the immediate circumstances were different, but it required a solution to a difficult problem, for it involved a well-known figure, who, to complicate matters, belonged to a mandarin social world that believes the error of an individual is damaging to an entire class. Let's just say, in order to simplify my account, that any person's error in his private life can be interpreted by his class as a weakening of the whole community. One needs to exercise great care to avoid controversies in individual cases. As you all know, I am the district chief of police. The strangest and most unexpected events come my way, and they require, in addition to absolute secrecy, much prudence and a measure of diplomacy. I'm not going to cite names or places; besides, none of you gentlemen know the individual and perhaps haven't even read the announcement of his death. For these reasons, I can recount the episode without betraying my sense of ethics. I'm merely doing this to show you how, at times, a police chief comes across a tragedy and feels obliged to transform it into a comedy. I brought about such a transformation in order to save the dead man's reputation and to guarantee the widow her unblemished memory of a dutiful, loyal, and steadfast husband.

"It was four o'clock in the afternoon when I received a telephone call from the son of the deceased, who was in a state of panic as a result of the circumstances and locale in which the death had taken place. I was a childhood friend of the deceased, and I knew he was having an affair with the wife of a humble government employee. This affair had been going for a long time. Every day between two and four in the afternoon, the man, who was a sixty-five-year-old retired officer, religiously visited his lover, a woman without great charms, flacid of body, and with a suburban taste in clothes.

"The dead man's son knew about the ancient affair, and was even friends with his father's mistress. A kind of filial benevolence made the father and son the closest of friends.

"That afternoon, when the overwrought son telephoned me with the news of his father's sudden death in his mistress's house, he asked me to take urgent steps, emphasizing that they should be carried out with the greatest secrecy in order to avoid a scandal. I thought for a few minutes and said:

" 'The first step is to apprehend the husband of your father's mistress.'

" 'But that'll end in a scandal without precedent. Apprehend him? But why? To this day the fellow doesn't know what was going on between my father and his wife.'

" 'I need time to work out my plan. Wait for me in the apartment with the deceased.'

"I immediately ordered a detective, who was in my complete confidence, to go to the office where the humble government employee worked and to bring him to police headquarters, where he'd be detained until I issued a new order. And this was done.

"While the dismayed husband remained in police custody, the dead man's son and I arranged for a hearse to transport the body. We waited until it grew dark, to avoid arousing the neighbors' curiosity; as it was a small street without traffic, the job was made easier. We waited until seven in the evening, when everyone was gathered together for dinner in their homes, with their doors and windows closed. I should mention that the apartment where my childhood friend had died was on the ground floor. Thus, there wasn't the problem of taking the dead man down the elevator. In the darkness and silence of the night, no one from the surrounding area disturbed our macabre task.

"We slid the body into the hearse and proceeded to the morgue.

"At this point, the son got in touch with his mother, giving her the news of his father's unexpected demise in full public view.

"Moments later, the unconsolable widow appeared. Crying hysterically and embracing the cadaver, she praised in a loud voice the unmatched virtues of her exemplary husband, who was incapable of any moral lapses that would damage the family's well-being.

"You gentlemen must have guessed that, during these moments, I didn't look at the dead man's son, and I am certain that he didn't look at me. Our eyes didn't meet for a long time after the widow's lamentations stopped.

"Once the legal steps were taken—a death certificate was furnished by an old family doctor, who had treated the deceased for his various heart attacks—the most difficult part of the problem was resolved.

"They went about making preparations for the dead man's funeral. There was my old childhood friend, dressed up as if for a military parade, lying in a casket covered with flowers and encircled by enormous garlands. Ready for the wake.

"I should mention that all this proceeded in an almost totally normal way. Normal, that is, since I, the district chief of police, used the authority of my office to cover up any detail that could put me in a ticklish situation and even implicate me in a death and burial whose circumstances were unusual. At least, unusual in the eyes of outsiders. Despite the risks, I resolved to carry out my convictions. I would be rendering my old friend a last homage. And there he was in the chapel, surrounded by the tears and grievings of his wife, son, and relatives.

"Suddenly, I remembered the husband of the dead man's mistress, whom I had ordered detained at police headquarters. Now what to do? What to say to the poor fellow? How to get around the facts without injuring the innocent man's dignity? Entering police headquarters, I ordered them to bring the prisoner to me. I came face to face with a thin, middle-aged, gray-haired fellow, with threadbare clothes and the fear of the world stamped on his face.

" 'Mr. Chief of Police, sir. What's going on? I'm a peaceable man with a simple life. I've worked in my government office for twenty-two years without a missing day; I've never received the slightest reprimand from my superiors, and there's not a mark on my work record. I have no enemies. I regularly leave work at five in the afternoon, and before six, I'm in my home. I never stole, slandered, or killed; I didn't do anything to justify being taken prisoner, and to suffer the embarrassment of being apprehended in the office in front of my colleagues and taken directly to police headquarters. I never in my life have entered a police station. What's going on, sir?'

"The man's eyes were watery and he was overwhelmed by a profound shame.

"I thought a few moments, then a brilliant idea came to me.

" 'Sir, before giving you any explanation, I wish to beg your pardon for the lamentable error made by my assistants. In truth, we were looking for a person with your first and last name; he's a government employee in the same ministry where you work, he's married, and has exactly the same physical features as yours. The individual we were looking for was another man, and for the mistake and aggravation caused you, I ask your forgiveness. I hope you understand the coincidence and that you forgive us for the error we committed.'

"The fellow drew in a deep breath and it seemed to me he was going to faint from relief. I ordered coffee brought to him and I kept him company to show my remorse. I talked to him, showing him extreme kindness, and repeatedly begged his pardon. Once he recovered from his tremendous scare, I sent two assistants from headquarters to take him home in an official car.

"But the best part of the story, gentlemen, happened when the ingenuous husband returned home in the company of my employees. The wife, with her eyes swollen and her face crumpled by the panic brought on by the death of her lover in her house, was seated in a rocking chair, awaiting her husband's return and prepared for the terrible consequences of her old love affair. She didn't know anything that had happened after her lover's body had been taken away in the hearse.

"Standing at the side of the policemen who had taken him home, the innocent government employee looked compassionately at his wife and, with a sweet voice, explained to her the delay that, for the first time in his life, had kept him from arriving before eight o'clock at night.

" 'My dear, see how no one is free from the misfortunes of life. See how a coincidence can lead an honest man to prison. The police were looking for a fellow with the same name as mine, the same job as mine, in the same ministry where I work, and with the same physical features as my own. By mistake, a terrible mistake, I was arrested at four in the afternoon in the office, as if I were the person sought by the police. What a coincidence. I always complained to my father for having baptized me with such a common first name, because on top of that, our last name is shared by thousands of people. It seems I was foreseeing today's unpleasantness.'

"Still dressed in her *robe de chambre,* which was the color of egg yolks, and wearing slippers adorned with blue stork feathers, the woman listened to her husband, undaunted. She was now freed of her worst expectations. A wave of relief passed over her face.

"Since then," the police chief said, "I've never heard from or seen those people again. I have an easy conscience for having defended my old friend, for having avoided the just recriminations of his widow, and for having dispelled a scandal that would have troubled his circle of friends."

"But, Chief, sir, I don't understand your reason for ordering the innocent husband to be apprehended as the 'first step' toward the solution of the case," said one of the listeners.

"That's easy. The husband usually arrived home at six in the afternoon. My friend's death occurred at four. While the husband was held prisoner at headquarters, I had time to take measures that would avoid a greater evil. By detaining an innocent person, we sometimes gain an opportunity to forestall a crime or solve a moral dilemma. My actions were humane, for the benefit of the widow herself."

The listeners were left in a great silence, each one possibly wishing in private to be close friends with the chief of police.

Hilda Hilst

Born in 1930 and educated as a lawyer, Hilda Hilst has been writing for forty years. Her career has three distinct phases. Between 1950 and 1967, she published eight collections of poetry; between 1967 and 1969, she wrote eight plays; and since 1970 she has produced five volumes of fiction. She has been Artist in Residence at the university in Campinas (São Paulo), where she currently lives.

Hilst has been influenced by both existentialism and surrealism, and she seems particularly interested in the themes of sexuality and mortality. She experiments with point of view, typography, and syntax, making extensive use of a somewhat Joycean free-associative language. Neologisms, agglutinated words, and exotic names abound in her writings. "Agda," from her 1973 volume *Qadós,* is typical of her unorthodox and passionate fiction.

Agda

(1973)

In memory of Sch. An-Ski

In the direction of many deaths,
many lives, my road now.

Take care of yourself, Agda, it's time you took care, the fruit inside the hand, just give a look, how can you touch with your yellow hand the one who says he loves you, that tenuous one, Agda, begin your routine as always, take care of the pigs, clean the patio, water the cactus, examine the ferns, the anthurium, walk slow slow, you've been looking old for a long time, and especially this morning. Remember your mother almost at the end saying you'll not endure, my daughter, you who take care of yourself so much, orange cream for your face, the other kind for your hands, the light green one for your body, stove cinders to whiten your teeth, daughter, you'll not endure, it's better you die Now Now life around you, clean clean, look at me, and above all else don't love, NEVER AGAIN, you have to be ashamed if someone touches you you already know the sadness of your flesh, everything dull dull, and your hands, look at your hands, they call that keratosis, daughter, it comes with old age, first the spot, then a thin crust, you think it'll go away, the doctor smiles, he says it begins at middle age, madam, it's time, do you understand, madam? You smile. Time? Yes, the time that no one sees, stretched out, mucus-like, more and more becoming transparent. How your Ana smiled when she learned that he loved you, and she smiled even more when you suddenly began to fix yourself up. Can you hem this skirt for me? And if there's time put a gold fringe here, look I already bought it, it'll look nice, won't it? Gold and maroon go very nicely together. Never again, never again they told you. Oh yes, I'm going to clean the patio, I'm going to water the cactus, oh yes, my God, I must forget the touch, the adornment, the golden hoop earrings, I must forget, stab the memory, no you never felt anything and much less now, you feel nothing, no, I don't feel anything, in dreams I saw the new little schoolgirls, they were dressed in green and going to chapel, I was dressed in black, going in the opposite direction, at the end a door-window opening onto the void. Now it will always be the abyss, I look deep down there, what is down there? Dryness, everything consummated. Never again. Never again, pull up the collar of your coat, look at the row of flowerpots on the bench, right, manure wasn't necessary for the cactus, now the coiled white, potbellied one is drooping over, it's necessary to put in tiny stakes, I'll be like that too when I'm satiated, Agda I myself satiated, folded over myself, each time more the abyss, each time more the earth, then after everything the shame, oh yes, shame, he'll tell his friends the old woman howled in my hands, the old yellow woman's breath rattled even at the touch of my fingers, fingers, your hand, my love, your hand isn't necessary over my dull whole, your sun-drenched hand over my shadowy body, I, a root advancing beneath the earth, root-body-flesh, a thing that falls apart, no you musn't touch, don't mistreat the light that leaves your fingers, NEVER AGAIN should I be touched, it's the body itself that can no longer be touched, after all it exists, and could I say I am my body? If I were my body would it hurt me thus? If I were my body would it be old like this? What is the language of my body? What is my language? Language for my body: a funeral of mine, watered, fat, funeral of daisies and lilies, someone repeating a useless cadence: sunflowers for the woman-child. For my body a funeral, and for the BIG LIFE OF THE ONE WITHIN, THAT LIVING WHOLE, what did you say? Agda, it's like this: THAT LIVING WHOLE doesn't go with the body, it's intact, nothing corrupts it, THAT LIVING WHOLE has many hungers, it searches, never tires, never grows old, it penetrates everything that bubbles, even what is still, entering that which seems tacit and adjusted, into the fruit, the pond, the marshy richness that your body doesn't see. THAT LIVING WHOLE is what lives this love, not the body, Agda. Is that true? I examine myself. Small nodule on a vein, knotty vein, varicose nodule, knot, I touch, one thing doctor, that won't burst, will it? It's probable, madam. And another thing, doctor: the flabbiness here, near the armpits, that that there, who knows, perhaps exercises? He smiles: long sleeves. I know, but it's the touch, do you understand, sir? Someone touches you, madam? A thousand pardons, madam, I didn't mean to say, who knows, how about gloves, would they help? A thousand pardons, madam, I didn't mean, that is I mean in order to revitalize that kind of flabbiness, that is, at your age, fifty? fifty-five? To be frank, that kind of flabbiness has no solution, madam, who knows, maybe classical music . . . would be a distraction . . . you don't care for classical music? On the contrary, doctor, I like it a lot, Stockhausen and. Really? Stockhausen's okay, but who knows if Scarlatti wouldn't be better? Fugues, concertos, fifteen cantatas? Someone touches you, madam? he said that. Yes they touched me, my father you touched me, the tip of your fingers over the lines in my hands, your middle finger over my life line, you said, Agda, only three nights of love, you'll give me three nights and then you squeezed my wrist and then you looked toward the wall and at our side the old women were whispering yes his daughter, the head's the same, the little eyes too, pretty daughter so very white. . . . My father, the cement bench, the tiles, the rubber trees, the hospital orderlies in the distance. They smiled. I say: it's me, father, Agda, mother didn't come but she sends you her love, it's me, father, Agda, Agda, she'll come, she didn't come today because she hasn't been well, it's me, your daughter. You will have a long life, Agda, as long as from here to China, everyone will be passing on, you'll say, wait, my friend, it's me Agda, is it true you don't remember? Will they pass on silently? Or like this, looking everywhere, trying to guess where it'll come from, it, THE GREAT DARK THING. He touched your wrist, don't insist on the landscape, the wall, the tiles, the rubber trees, and when he touched you, speak Agda, speak of your desire to lie down right there, yes, but it was pretty, it wasn't simply a matter of lying down, it was a thing spilling out, a passionate thing, he stretched out, tenuous above me. Tenuous like that other one who now says he loves me. Then three nights, Agda, and the discovery of the islands, our dead ones disinterred, you will awaken your very beautiful mother, mothermothermother he's here now, come with us to the beach, the sea urchins beneath the rocks, we three motherfatherdaughter, we three interwoven fiber all twisted, and these flowers here, people put flowers here deep down inside these holes in the ground, there's nothing inside there anymore, all of them resuscitated, the flesh clean, naked, we're all naked and a stupendous happiness, here we go making a house of stone so that time might pass without a trace, we'll say get going time, you don't have any place here, here we are the three, those three, the three as always, not the holy trinity of always, the other three of flesh and astringency, of blood and astringency. Of flesh. I should take care of the pigs, put water on the cactus, examine the ferns . . . if I take you out of this corner, who knows, perhaps you'll come back to life, you wilted so suddenly, could it have been the wind? If I place you there, in the center of the patio, around the well, no, too much sun, these delicate things want shade, shade this instant in the square of the patio, yes he'll come, even though it's the Wednesday of Holy Week, he'll come because I exist, I am my body, Agda's body, body that's going to awaken alongside another tenuous body, the little rosy circles, no, I never had children that's why they're pretty, he's going to touch them, he's going to say they're very pretty, Agda, and when I lie down my face looks smoother, I'll let down my hair, and when I lie down it seems that my mouth is always smiling, I'll keep smiling and I ought to take care at the moment of pleasure, no frowning, no screaming, just a trembling, and for the love of God, Agda, don't let your nostrils flare open, no, I don't look good, my nose is thin, a little like father's, a little like mother's, pretty nose of the two of them, at least this is decent about you, your nose, oh yes, your breasts are decent too, it's necessary to be careful with your mouth, and no watery looks, look into the eye, don't close your eyes, you can show your feet too, they're very nicely shaped, the arch is pronounced and that is also pretty, now your legs, never, remember the little nodules on the veins, small nodule of the vein, knotty vein, varicose nodule, knot. Let Ana clean the patio today, let Ana take care of the pigs today, that's what she exists for, Ana, today you clean the patio, today you take care of the pigs. She smiled, she smiled because she knows that I can't tire myself out today, I ought to put my legs up, put compresses on my eyes, change the bed linen for the white embroidered ones, and put eucalyptus leaves under the pillow case. One thing my daughter: everything's okay, I'm feeling very well, my body, you know, but it's necessary that you tell your mother to tell the doctor that my memory . . . that it's necessary to pull out my memory, understand? The boats are too heavy, they put in a thousand things, I asked them to empty the boats and they placed rocks, ropes, enormous anchors inside, so that I can't, my daughter, I can't reach the island, and another thing, Agda, my dreams, it's necessary to yank the dreams out of me, another life at night, a life of others starts to happen, they call me from many sides in these dreams, your mother always refuses in these dreams, I walk in the darkness, I don't see the rivers and I fall, some keep waving, people I never saw before my daughter, others I know but wouldn't like to see them again, Agda, tell your mother to tell the doctor that the dreams and memory ought to be devoured, I'll stay here on the cement bench and someone will devour the two of them, that way I'll expel the dream memories and someone at my side will eat them. Understand, Agda? Body-limit, outline at rest or tense, how far does the real me go? The inside of my hand, this I know is mine, the inside of your hand, my father, that inside now intimate absorbency of we two, perplexity of sweats, body-limit-poor thing. Suddenly you move, you enter the pig hut, you ask yourself what is this thing, this pig? Suddenly you recall that someone already asked, that many will ask what is this thing, this pig. What is this thing, this I? Young pig, rosy little pig, I pick it up filled with tenderness and I say such a pretty little pig, it would be good to have one like that always in the house, later on, a big stuffed pig, I won't pick it up any more, I say it's good to eat at tomorrow's party, commemorating one hundred years of after tomorrow, the fireworks of the giant bonfire, three days from now the cake together with the large stuffed pig I devour you. Thus this thing this I: rosy baby I give you sweetness, you give me slobber, pee, I love you, later on, little girl delicate pubis, I give you candy, boots, trinkets, I give you smiles, you're smooth all over, hard, buckram, later on, woman I'll give you trinkets again so that you'll give me just that, I give, you give, later on, an old hag, shut up big mouth, you stink yellow one, I won't give you, you won't give me, no one touches you, I ask you: is the pig-body still yours? Agda limit of yourself, your breath rattles; then nothing more from here on? He was your father, the one there on the cement bench, yes yes I already know, walls, tiles, rubber trees, don't pretend, dispense with the landscape, that one was your father, crumbled neuron, prefrontal without antennae, summer summer, useless crossing from the bench to the bed, vice-versa, your father without any thrill, splendid head in an immense disorder, yes thrill yes, he took my hands, he asked me for love, father, how I wanted everything of yours to return to life in me one hundred, a thousand times, that the love OH NEVER NEVER WOULD DIE, now loving this tenuous one is as if I were seeing you grow, it's like seeing you as a seed, everything that is inside you waiting to burst, to burst inside of me, you'll give your all to me, Agda, you're delirious, you once said you weren't, you weren't like that, full of love and disturbed, you said. Or were you? Were you always like that? Like an old woman-thrill? Another thing my daughter, another thing my love: don't sing Slow Boat to China anymore, it's that . . . I don't want to hear Slow Boat to China anymore, we won't go forward, flesh rots, there's not enough time to get there. Another thing: no more repeating this too too solid flesh, nothing about solidity, it's a lie, each day I feel it's getting softer, inside, outside, each day yellower, touch me here and here, you, yes, you're still alive, touch me if it doesn't nauseate you, and my mouth I'm going to open it wide so you can see, here my daughter, nothing more, my teeth crumbled away, the big pleasure-kiss I would give you, that I would no longer give to your mother, Agda-mother-daughter, nothing more is my body, nothing more is me, I was never anything because if I were, I wouldn't be this nothing-body today. It grows late. Even though it's the Wednesday of Holy Week he'll come, green empty ashen shadow over the square patio. Or is it still morning? Yes it's still morning, the sun beating just on this side, Ana, it's necessary to put the birds in the sun, a chicory leaf for each one of them, you always forget, and look how the leaf of the anthurium is turning yellow, Ana, Ana, the anthurium was so pretty. Who's fault, Ana? Your yellow demagnetized hand, your hand is what touches the once gleaming leaf, your hand is what now makes it die, you walked a lot, I walked, yes, but I never saw what they said I'd see, THAT WHITE SERENE FLAME AT THE END. Flame. Desire to see everything again, to see, touch for the very first time. Not the first caresses, nor the second ones, the first. What a great wonder. Later on, my mouth above the shoulder of the tenuous one, that father-lover-son for the first time, that revived sense of myself, that joy stretched out on top of me, that which the BIG DARK THING will not touch because I will be there before it, immense, and I'm going to say and I say: get out of here you filthy thing, death, black broom with wings, that one, never, that one, no, that indelible tenuous one, truly vigilant inside of me, this entire life in my-his-body. It's so, the love of the entire world washing itself in my corner, later on, they'll try to dry up the fountain, they'll say: Agda asks everything that the others asked, she pretends her head is crowned, but she's merely the spectrum she's always been, then let's repeat: who are you, that usurp'st this time of night? When night comes I won't be speaking with the tone of a saxophone, no, body-aroma on the embroidered sheets, lily's mouth, pretty pretty lily's mouth bacchante butterfly and plant, Agda-little-she-horse when night comes, little-she-horse with her little-he-horse—, as if time . . . as if the great body time were merely an immobile whole, irremediably curled up and immobile.

Wait a little, they're already coming to look for me, listen: above all, before they pull out what I just told you, above all, Agda, let your mother give my thanks for the absence of the object. Tell her to tell that to the doctor, take this down, get out a pencil, like this: he thanks you doctor for the absence of the silver and steel-devil-object, that abominable whole, like that, daughter: he thanks you for all of us. And that this-unique-I never again unfolded is happy to exist inside the nothing, that this-unique-I is, use some pretty words, daughter, is . . . stupefied, that's it, now in capital letters: STUPEFIED BY HIS LUCID CRITERION, doctor . . . because that life, Agda, of the abominable-devil-object, that existing multiplied, added weight to this-unique-I, even in your mother's tableware, in the glass of the windows, even in the metal of the trays I always asked her to put on the tablecloth, to wrap up the knives in flannel, everything in that house was a thousand times I-other, at the end of the hallway, in the foyer, even at the side of the bed your mother put the abominable-devil-object, even in the bathroom, daughter, I'd wake up wet because I was coming out of the river, I'd get up and was going to defecate, and there there was the unknown watched other. How many times I spit on that other one, I rubbed shit on that face, or then, listen, I finally said pretty words, I finally said, yes, I'd say: cloud, sail, musk, fugacious, I'd say, dissolve yourself, I'm going to give you a while, hazy I'd say, dilute yourself, I'll give you a while, defiant image I finally said gently, pantomine of nausea I'll break you. I ran my hand through ten fifteen times and he opened his bloody mouth but I didn't stop. Later on I breathed, daughter, my forehead on the tiles, looking slowly, and wouldn't you know the other one was still alive? Crumbled but still alive. Just thinking about him, see my hand, wet, just thinking that he's around there, perhaps just around the wall, trying to cross over the thickness, him and his useless calendar, because that's what it was, daughter, each morning the other one wasn't the same, understand? Yes, because if he didn't change his face he might even have been well received, it's good to have a shadow friend, waving, I'm here, it's good, it's fitting to have one. I don't have a lot of time, recreation hour is already over, they're coming to look for me, now cheese and bread lunch, listen: far from the big house, near the pigs' hut there's a golden earth, at the second post in the fence to the right, dig. I discovered it very late, there wasn't time, your mother called the men, I had to stay here, but you can take advantage of it, swallow the golden earth, swallow it, that was what I heard, swallow it, my daughter, later when you're an old woman take a handful and the abominable-devil-object will show you another face, retrocession, weeded earth. What, father? You go back, daughter, youth again, adolescence, infancy, then the nothing, but it's worth it. Just one time and it's worth it. You'll be a little girl traveling toward the nothing, but the mechanism is easier, little by little you identify with the inanimate, littlegirl-plant, littlegirl-stone, littlegirlearth. Don't forget, take this down: my father told me that many years from now when I'm an old woman I should swallow the golden earth near the pigs' hut, at the second post in the fence to the right. I'll dig. It's still morning. How long should I dig? The earth blacker and blacker, if I had planted rosebushes, imagine, black rosebushes in the center of the clearing, bison, golden bulls, me pretty-Agda daughter-all white under the rosebushes. Agda lavender trudging around the rosebushes. Every morning, every afternoon, high moon, Agda, oldwoman-thrill digs digs under the rosebushes. Of course, gentlemen, I'll show you the place, yes, yes, I worked for her for a long time, yes, my name is Ana, let's get going, you know, the boy didn't want to see her any more, he was right the poor thing, from my room here I heard what was going on there, what he said in Agda's bedroom, he said: I want you just as you are, it has nothing to do with your body, what do I care about your body? It's the lightning in you, the sorcery, the thrill, nothing in you is shadowy, Lively Glow, I exist because you dreamed me inch by inch, I exist because each moment you remake what isn't sad in me. The vertigo of your existing, beloved, I swear gentlemen it was just like that, the boy said it like that. You know, in the beginning people didn't believe it, he was slim, almost a little boy, you'd never guess he was twenty, I laughed because . . . well, he was inadequate, Agda wasn't puny, you gentlemen will see, a lot of woman, the poor thing, I laughed because . . . you gentlemen should know, it's funny an old woman like that and a little lamb, there wasn't any evil here inside of me, no gentlemen, just fun, pure fun, the little fellow was unusual, a pretty mouth, eyes this size, you had to see, big, precious, and his hair, everything sweet, it was sad you know, Agda heavy sluggish, but what fire, gentlemen, before everything happened, before dying in the hole, she shouted: flame at the end, I never saw that serene white flame at the end. Who knows what she was thinking when she shouted that.

I DIG. Constancy. Ten arm lengths deep. How many? Snails. Mud on my face. I have the look of someone half-buried. A gold that doesn't come. Nor the reflex. It'd be good to have a yellow light gilding the snails, the worms, my hand. It'd be good to recompose words, criss-cross them, to say of the light, scintillating faceted filter, to say of the dark, just entrail, to say of the search what it is, the seeker and the sought, revealing the two sides, here you see yourself, here I am looking at you, the joyous orbit shattering fears, here when you were a little girl on top of the wall, hiding your face, the light parching your pupil, violet eyelid folded over, arm, forearm, end of the elbow pointing to the one taking a picture of you. Who was taking a picture of you? Mothermothermother beauty, the beret tilted to one side, curls in your hair covering the rosiness of your ears, mothermothermother beauty, let me touch your tender skin, or . . . fly, fly Medea, get away from me, travel across the spaces, cross all the bridges or go live under the water, let your father's reflex be just for me, *vere dignum et justus est, aequum et salutare,* let it be just for me . . . because . . . because I would keep explaining it to you many nights or just screaming like the other one: woe, woe, Ah me, Ah me! Yes, now I'm knowing myself with this mud on my face, chewing me myself, burning wax consuming my body, consuming me and knowing me without nausea, throat wide-open, livid alchemist, go, Agda, deeper, without your knowing that your body is a sieve, miniscule orifices a thousand and one separating what is of worth, tasting, and letting the other trickle toward the well. Go, Agda, deeper, OH, I'm going, that tenuous body never again over me, oh, never again, life death expelled oh I was lucid, clean, my flesh was smooth, oh the joyous mysteries, the joy of myself, the great joy that is to sink into the old and yellow flesh in this mud and never again will anyone TOUCH ME, NEVER AGAIN NEVER AGAIN

Nélida Piñon

Born in Rio de Janeiro in 1937, Nélida Piñon recently became the fourth woman to be elected to the Brazilian Academy of Letters. She published her first two novels, *Guia-Mapa de Gabriel Arcanjo* (Gabriel Archangel's Guide-Map) and *Madeira Feita Cruz* (Wood Made into a Cross), in the early 1960s; both works exemplify her interest in religious and mystical themes. In 1969, her novel *Fundador* (Founder), about the creation of a new society peopled with fictional and historical figures, was awarded a special literary prize.

Of particular interest are Piñon's *Casa da Paixão* (1972) (House of Passion), about a young woman's first sexual experience, and *Tebas do Meu Coração* (1974) (Thebes of My Heart), which pokes fun at the institution of marriage. Her semi-autobiographical novel *A República dos Sonhos* (1984) *(The Republic of Dreams),* about the migration of a Galician family to Brazil, is widely regarded as her most important work.

Some of Piñon's best writing is her short fiction. Two collections deserve special mention: *Sala de Armas* (1973) (The Fencing Room) and *O Calor das Coisas* (1980) (The Heat of Things). "Near East," from *Sala de Armas,* is a fine example of her mysterious, somewhat oneiric style.

Near East

(1973)

The four little Turks arrived. They didn't care for onions. As if somehow knowing this, I offered them nothing. Perhaps that's why they looked at me thankfully. The little Turks expressed their gratitude by mentioning a piece of plowed land. They always loved the soil. Once they said, and I accepted it:

"Where we come from, besides goats, are large olive trees."

Despite their sunburned skin, I imagined them seeking shade under full-grown trees. I never saw them apart. Though I wasn't able to say what blood or language ties united them. I thought it would be foolish to know, for what good would it do me? Portuguese, they spoke well. French, even better. And certainly not because they'd lived in slavery, more because of an affinity, their look said. They purchased magazines and read. Only then did they speak reverently to me:

"Each day we know the world better."

Not even at the spellbinding sound of these words did I show in my face that my destiny was to love them. I feared they'd consider such a reaction frivolous, and I was careful not to hurt them. My dearest friends. The first little Turks in my life. In the beginning, our friendship was difficult. A friend is never won without a struggle. Especially four little Turks. As others can bear witness, I said:

"A friendship like that I don't need. A friend should spring up like a plant; we know it was difficult to grow, although we didn't see it happen. Just reap and enjoy it, take it home if you want and put it in a vase."

But they persisted. I never asked them: why, my friends? Perhaps they might have answered: since when are we friends? We little Turks band together in a different way, not like you, for what you understand to be friendship is a thorn in our lives.

Their first gesture of esteem came in the form of a basket filled with cheeses and fresh figs. In such abundance that I feared the duty of having to consume so much. Half of it I placed in the refrigerator. Since I lived alone, the solution would be to invite them and some other friends over. To my surprise, they wore ceremonial attire. I feared that I would offend them with my simplicity. After all, I'd invited them for cheeses and fresh figs and the humbleness of my home. I introduced them to the others, who were already eating, and one of the little Turks said, as if speaking for them all:

"Our happiness is like the freshness of these figs and the firmness of this white cheese."

Luckily, I'd informed my friends about the strange behavior the little Turks would adopt without warning. They came from distant lands with special ways that we should respect, never making fun of them. Thus, upon hearing these words, my friends stood up and embraced one another effusively. I never saw them so close to the garden of Gethsemane, and it made me think: I'm a proud woman.

We dedicated ourselves to triumph that night. The men looked at the women as if bestowing love on them because God had made them different. And certainly wouldn't have loved them any the less had they been made totally in the likeness of man. Yes, it was a miracle we owed to the presence of the little Turks.

Months later, they confessed they had a house and I'd soon be invited there. I assessed the situation, taking care not to make a mistake. I owed them discretion. A circumspection that, furthermore, flattered them. Compassionately, I declared, as if in a state of mourning:

"When spring comes, I'll visit you."

That was exactly what they expected of me. All four kissed me, a delicate kiss, and I imagined them as one body with smooth skin, like the surface of a flower. As soon as they would insinuate their rare invitation, I'd be prepared for the visit. I understood their race. I trusted in its difficulties, which were attractive like images that are distorted when seen through a veil. If it weren't that way, what would I have to do with four little, ordinary Turks who smelled of milk without having the vices of the goat, who liked olive oil and cared nothing for the magic spell of the olive.

I met them one day in the public gardens. They were commemorating the anniversary of their village by eating sandwiches as if they were in their own countryside. I stood up to toast the holiday, but the oldest one, with a discreet gesture, said to me with a sadness that made our friendship seem fragile:

"Not yet. Only when we're a free land."

At home, I tried to locate their strange nostalgia on a map. I needed to find the little Turks' land, an indispensable reference point on a never-ending chart. How else could I participate in the sadness they commemorated with sandwiches in the park, the four of them always united, if not by surprising them, saying that one day I'd visit their land and that I, too, would fight for its freedom, or wouldn't my life itself be enough? However, not finding the place, I thought, it isn't important. Their enemies will surely perish.

After that encounter, I didn't see them for a long time. I began to fear I had committed an unintended offense by embracing them forcefully when I should have merely extended my hand in greeting. I sought out the paths they normally walked, without finding anyone to call out to. We never had any mutual friends. As days passed, they shunned those who had attended the banquet of cheeses and figs. But in such a delicate way that I couldn't reprimand them or appreciate them any the less. The youngest one, with my hand in his, had said:

"Blessed is the hand that chooses friends and shares you."

I concluded they wanted me for themselves, as was the custom in their land. Even though I wasn't their woman, I should behave as if I were. And as they hadn't appeared for such a long a time, I imagined them disembarking in their country, fighting the enemy in the mountains, perhaps dying for the freedom they glorified on the day I found them, supposedly impassioned, although I had noted the signs of a prolonged melancholy.

When I began reading newspapers praising the sacrifice of warriors, they appeared at my house in mourning, all four of them. Without saying a word, they sat down in their favorite seats. They never got the wrong chair by mistake, and I watched them, wanting to record some error. At times I changed the chairs around to confuse them. Even so, they were true to themselves. They fulfilled my expectations, because I always wanted them to be consistent, so greatly was I attracted to these little Turks from an enslaved village.

I mourned their prolonged absence, and they knew well my reason for not seeking them out. I waited for them to leave me free to console them by confessing that one day I, too, had followed tearfully the body of a loved one. Nevertheless, we remained silent until they handed me a card and said goodbye. Not a name, not a word, just an address that I supposed was the house where they lived. It wasn't easy reconciling oneself to enigmas or achieving the poise that their race particularly appreciated, always becoming lost in investigations of the firmament. But suddenly I understood that the time had come to visit them.

It was a complex of houses painted diverse colors. Theirs sat at the end of a cul-de-sac. With blue windows. They kissed me on my eyes, blessing the vision that could appraise their abode. With the thin saliva of each of these creatures on my face, I analyzed the house that had opened itself to receive me. I learned the passion of hospitality from those little Turks, as well as a strong feeling which crosses frontiers, in which I came to trust. The inhabitants of enslaved lands gave greater value than we to their possessions, thus their gift and pride.

We ate the repast they selected, and several times I wanted to ask if some of the foods had come from their homeland. I avoided the question so they wouldn't think that the selection of dishes had displeased me, or that I was complaining about the strangeness of the meal, or that perhaps I was demanding more, not satisfied with the abundance they offered me. I learned to go around in labyrinthine circles, as they did and were happy to do. The sole darkness in their life was the memory of their subjugated land. I kept closing my eyes without wanting to, and yet I was unable to tell them I ought to go. My parting would certainly cause them an alternating joy and sadness; how to analyze the feelings of my little Turks in the end?

One of them stood up and said, as if he somehow guessed:

"Certain flowers suffer the night more than others."

They put me to bed in the largest room. Seated round me, the four little Turks watched over my sleep, a fact I discovered only on the following morning, with the coffee on the table. I wasn't able to thank them enough for their zeal. They smiled and I took pleasure in the coffee.

"Do I perchance snore?" was the only question I took the liberty of asking during my entire visit. Embracing me, they said, first one then the others:

"We never know what our friends do."

I longed to understand the ties that bound them together. Or the names with which they had been baptized. Unlike us, they didn't divulge surnames, so I never knew how to introduce them formally or how to correctly address a letter to be sent to them. I simply called them the four little Turks. That's how they were known in our city. They smiled at my pause, when I hoped they'd finally reveal their names.

Later I surprised the oldest in the market. Handling fruits with the intensity of a pagan. Which he wasn't; they all prayed, and I even caught a trace of penitence on their faces. I thought resolutely: today I must know them. But he spoke first:

"I can no longer live without you."

He spoke seriously and his declaration of love honored me. As I watched, he pointed to the fruits: "I take care of them all, each one belongs to a race that has pride in its skin. Sometimes they can rot within hours. Have you ever considered what it's like to be entrusted with such a delicate thing?" He peeled an orange and divided the sections between the two of us:

"Now we are united forever."

It was like an Eastern wedding. Wine was drunk and the goblet was smashed. The others arrived and they imitated him. I felt bound to them all, in a secret matrimony. We walked along the beach, urgent and careless of life, and we loved one another. On that night, I could say without remorse: wasn't it security I was seeking?

For some time I forgot about seeing them. Since the orange united us, we weren't in any hurry to renew our esteem. Weeks later, I began to be afraid. And I didn't dare go to see them at home. Their hospitality couldn't be continuously exploited. The market seemed the best place for our encounter. I put on my *laise* dress, white and impeccable, and it wasn't even summer yet. I trusted in the black hair, the dark eyes of those people. Ready to judge, I needed no one else's judgment. I was surprised by the closed market stall, even though people were milling about. I scoured the market wanting to find out by myself what was going on, not wanting to ask the neighbors. The following morning, I repeated my visit. I could no longer bear the *laise* dress. For days I rendered them the same homage. I felt I was dealing with the dead. And didn't they die whenever they didn't see me?

The visit from the man in black didn't frighten me as I had expected. I said to him: "What do you want?" He responded: "I am of the same race." Among the many races in the world, I tried to imagine which of them he referred to specifically. Not acknowledging my confusion, he went on:

"Now that you know, here's the letter you were waiting for."

Although the drama seemed to be playing itself out, I wanted to rebel, rejecting the message and denying the obvious purpose of the man's visit. I ended up expressing an awkward thanks for his trouble. He, however, showed pity and suggested:

"Perhaps I ought to stay so that we can read it together?"

I don't know now whether I resented his rudeness or appreciated the strange sweetness that had come into his face, the warnings of the world lined on his skin, which was exactly like that of my friends. Following the rituals I had learned, I filled two glasses and we drank cool water in a single gulp. He was ready to leave. Kissing my face, he said and I, too, agreed:

"It's been a long time since I've felt so moved watching a ship leave!"

Pain was etched on my face, I suppose, now that he went away. He still wanted to help me, he, who had plunged the dagger into my chest. I put the letter away in a drawer without reading it. It can still be found there today. I know with certainty its words. One day I will read it without tears.

Tania Jamardo Faillace

Tania Jamardo Faillace was born in 1939 in Rio Grande do Sul, the southernmost state in Brazil. Her novel *Adão e Eva* (1965) (Adam and Eve) retells the biblical tale from the point of view of Eve; and *O 35° Ano de Inês* (1971) (Inês's 35th Year) contains several stories about women driven to madness and suicide. For the last few years, she has been working on a *roman fleuve*, entitled *Beco da Velha* (Old Woman's Alley), about prostitution in Rio Grande do Sul.

Faillace's work as a journalist and political activist in Porto Alegre, the capital city of Rio Grande do Sul, brought her into close contact with the lower classes, whose poverty, frustration, and solitude are common themes in her fiction. She frequently writes about the difficulties children and adolescents encounter growing up in a world of drugs, crime, and sexual violence. Some of her most powerful and disturbing stories appear in *Vinde a Mim os Pequeninos* (1977) (Come unto Me the Little Ones), whose protagonists include abandoned children, teenage mothers, and gang youths. The story "Dorceli," first published in 1975, is included in that collection.

Dorceli

(1975)

A baby with black eyes. Every newborn has gray eyes. Dorceli was born with black eyes. The nurses said:

"What a pretty little thing . . . she looks like an Indian."

The mother wrapped Dorceli in the donated baby shawl and left the charity hospital for good. She continued to walk up one side and down the other in front of the public square. She watched the women go through the large iron gate. Only the women. They had told her. . . . But she, the mother, is too ashamed to go up to the line and ask: "Which of you here wants a baby?" So she says nothing, with Dorceli—who still has no name—rolled in the shawl they gave her, and she dreams someone is questioning her: "Don't you have anywhere to go, my child? So young and with a baby. . . ." Crying, the mother will then say: "They threw me out of the house, I don't know what I'm going to do. . . ." Yes, that's what she should say.

At nightfall, the mother went away. Dalva was her name. She was light-skinned with blue eyes. Dorceli's black eyes made her uncomfortable. Not even as a little girl did she imagine having a child like that. She used to rock her doll and say to herself: "Neusa Cristina." Neusa Cristina, pink and blond with several petticoats under her dress, patent leather shoes, and little dimples in a face with lowered eyes. "Such a well-behaved child!" But the Indian needed a name, of course. An Indian's name, a name with an "I"—Irani, Iraci, Jaci. . . . "Dorceli," suggested the woman who lived in the room next to hers in the *pensão*. Dorceli it was.

Dorceli was howling from hunger. "I don't have any milk," Dalva said, as if to justify herself, and she didn't have any, either. Cow's milk gave Dorceli diarrhea and she almost died. The neighbor woman suggested rice water, and Dorceli was saved. She was wrinkled, with little dry legs, and her rump was full of creases—ugly.

The woman who owned the house appeared: "Look, I don't want to be mean, unfeeling. . . ." The mother picked up Dorceli, the cardboard suitcase, and left again for the front of the hospital. Night fell once again, and she hadn't had the courage to speak to anyone, to offer them the Indian.

When she next looked around, she was on a bus. Her sister's house.

"You're back?"

"Yes."

Her sister took a peek at Dorceli, who was sleeping. Suddenly, Dorceli opened her black eyes.

"Who's the father?"

The mother shrugged her shoulders.

"And now?"

"I have to wait for her to grow a little, don't I? Besides, I'm not feeling so good."

Her sister served supper:

"Clair won't be back 'til later. I'll explain to him then."

Dorceli whimpered.

"She's sick, too, that's why I came back."

Her sister picked up Dorceli and examined her for a long time:

"She doesn't look like anybody."

"So much the better."

"Why didn't you do something about it, before?"

"I was afraid," the mother confessed.

"Nonsense, you just had to look for me. I know good, competent people."

Dorceli squinted her eyes, twisted her whole body, then she let out a prolonged wail.

"I think she's hungry," the mother said. "But she only drinks rice water, otherwise she gets diarrhea."

Dorceli was returned to her mother's neck, her lips drawn back over her gums. The mother gave her a finger to suck on while her sister got to work in the kitchen.

"I can stay here for a while, can't I?"

Dorceli started to bawl again—the mother's fingernail had scratched the roof of her mouth. The mother shook her:

"Be quiet!"—and to her sister: "You think Clair isn't going to like it?"

Her sister used a wooden spoon to stir the uncooked rice in the mug filled with water. A thick veil of starch rose to the surface. The spoon cut through the vapor. Then the sister drained the rice, placed the cloudy water in a cup, added a small spoonful of sugar, and put the cup inside a bowl with cold water. Dorceli was screaming:

"It's coming, it's coming," soothed the aunt.

"Will it be long?" asked the mother. "I can't stand this crying anymore . . . it's been going on for days . . . she didn't let anyone sleep at the *pensão.*"

"It's very hot," clipped the aunt.

Dorceli's head moved back and forth, her feet rubbed against one another angrily, her body arched and became rigid, as if she had meningitis. Dorceli lost her voice, her breath, she was getting purple, as the pain and terror of her stomach exploded through her lungs and out of her throat and against the eardrums of the two women.

"Ready. I don't have a baby bottle, but let's see if we can make do with a spoon."

Dorceli choked, vomited; the rice water came out her nose.

"What a clumsy woman," the aunt said. "Here, give her to me."

Dorceli closed her mouth tight before the spoon, the aunt squeezed her cheeks and slowly sprinkled some drops on her tongue. Then it seemed Dorceli began to understand, but her tongue curled itself up, disoriented as it sucked air, and bumped into the spoon. . . .

"What a hungry little thing!" the aunt commented. "How long has it been since she's eaten?"

"Since noon. Me too." replied the mother. "They threw me out of the *pensão.*"

A little room in the back part of the house. Clair nailed up some boards that were missing, and he assembled a wooden-frame cot; the aunt brought an old quilted bedcover and some sheets.

"Don't mind the smell," said the aunt. "The old lottery-ticket woman used to live here. Later we'll spread a little caustic soda around the floor and the walls and it'll be better."

"What happened to the old woman?"

"She died. It was time. I didn't have the courage to send her away. She'd been here since the days of Clair's mother. But it's over. I'll bring a lamp."

The window didn't have any glass panes, just a crude shutter. The mother kept watching the shadows on the wall. She had lived in an apartment. She used to hear the noise of the elevator at night. Before that, there was the house with the enormous backyard with its unseasonably early guavas. Mother, father, brothers and sisters. A pack of younger brothers, who were insolent and rowdy—and her older sisters, who were overweight, serious, tedious, sewing trousseaux on Sunday afternoons.

"I'm twenty-one years old. Just twenty-one. I need to do something before it's too late, before the blue of my eyes fades and my legs become deformed with varicose veins." Was she feeling the tingling sensation, already? The suspicious tingling that would contract her flesh from within, swell her ankles, and put blue-colored spots on her thighs? To leave now, slowly, circle the house, and head for the street. . . .

Dalva turned in bed. She saw Dorceli sound asleep. And her own flacid stomach, the stomach of a woman who has just given birth. The old woman. The old woman spit on the floor, urinated in the gaps between the floorboards—to kill the rats. "Clair is so good," her sister sighed, awaiting the old woman's death. The old lady had paid five *mil réis* for the room when she was a girl. Dalva had inherited the old woman's room, her offensive body smell.

"I'm going to leave early in the morning, I'm leaving tomorrow, I'm going to go back up to the apartment again, put on some records, I'm going to pretend I don't see the lady manager, there, waiting to ambush me in the hall." Dalva gave a little, low laugh—her stitches still hurt. First, she lay on her back, then on her stomach, then she sprawled herself out on the quilted cover and pushed Dorceli over to the side. Fast asleep, Dorceli rolled over, her nose nearly grazing the head of a nail in the wall. Dalva pulled her toward the center of the bed. Vomit gleamed on the donated shawl. The old woman's smell, the smell of the Indian. Dalva criss-crossed her arms over her face.

"When are you going to go to work, Dalva? You have a daughter now."

Sunday sun. A small mongrel dog nosed the scraps from lunch.

"And you have five," Dalva sneered.

"They're already grown up," her sister shot back.

The children played around the papaya tree. Dorceli was fussing in the room in the back.

"I have to think about my life, I have to resolve that first."

"Okay. But Clair isn't rich, you know. It doesn't have anything to do with you or the child. Why don't you look for her father?"

"No way."

Dorceli always wakes up crying. Once she woke up and saw an eye, a corner of an eye. And a black shadow descending over her face. It was just for an instant. The smooth, broad shadow squeezed her face. Dorceli scratched and tugged at the shadow, kicked her legs, exerting her whole body. The light appeared in a flash and her mother's mouth said: "Now, now, what's all this? Were you frightened?" But the eye was strange, dark, blue and shifting, as if it were watching through the crack in a door. Dorceli quieted down, snoring like a dog with a cold. The eye went away.

Now Dorceli always wakes up crying. To tell the shadow that she's there. The shadow never came back because of that trick, and because of another one that Dorceli invented: she sleeps face down, her rump raised up, and her nose protected in a little airhole.

By day, Dorceli crawls around the backyard. Once the dog bit her cheek hard—Dorceli had been taking her share of his food. The dog was punished and so was Dorceli. Intimidated, they now watch one another from afar. But the dog's coat is warm and everyday Dorceli moves closer. The other children jump over her body. Dorceli laughs, cries, claps her hands, and goes in search of the red slippers. The slippers push Dorceli, who sits down hard on the ground. The feet inside them are very white. Dorceli grabs hold of the legs and tries to put her mouth around them. The legs walk away until Dorceli gives up and cries.

"How this child does cry! Dalva, can't you even do that? Take care of your own child?"

Dorceli ends up underneath an elbow.

"I start working tomorrow, you know."

The light enters between the cracks of the shutter. Dorceli is alert. The mother is going to get up now. Dorceli whimpers to get attention.

"I'm coming, I'm coming."

The red slippers. The mother gets dressed, studying her clothes in the light coming through the cracks in the shutter. She speaks softly, mumbling, her voice makes Dorceli sleepy.

"Shit, it's all ripped under the arms . . . it's time to get up. . . ."

Then the mother lifts the shutter, securing it to a nail in the ceiling. With her back to Dorceli, she looks out at the yard. Dorceli remains very quiet, waiting. Soon she gets tired and cries:

"Mama!"

Dalva shivers. She's looking at the hall carpet, over there, in front of the window. The door with the peephole. The curved sofa, the color of squash.

"Mama!"

Dalva turns around slowly. Dorceli is on all fours on the cot. Her diaper has come loose and leaves a damp trail on the sheet.

Dalva turns in the direction of the bed. Dorceli rocks back and forth, swinging the ballast.

"Be quiet!"

Dorceli bites her hands, kicks her between chuckles. Dalva holds her firmly as she changes the diaper, moving her face away from the thrusts of the Indian, from her slobber, her smell.

Now Dorceli goes under the elbow to the front of the house. They give her a baby bottle and leave her under the kitchen table, while the other children play above her.

Another of Dorceli's habits: sleeping on top of her mother. The mother pushes her off whenever she awakens. Dorceli pretends, rolls, then returns quietly to lie on top of her again. That way, if the mother gets up, Dorceli knows because she never sleeps soundly. Whenever her mother gets up, she hears the noise of the door latch, the dog scratching himself, the springs' dissonant sound. Irritated, her mother sighs:

"Let me breathe."

It happened one night. Dorceli woke up and saw her mother leaving. Then quick steps over the dry leaves in the backyard. Dorceli became rigid, her ears vibrated, her eyes fixed on the darkness of the door. The darkness didn't move around. Dorceli called out. The mother didn't return. Dorceli called again, aware of her own voice and the rustling of the leaves outside. The dog barked outside the door and scratched his nails on the wood. Dorceli continued to cry out. Dorceli couldn't make out anything in that darkness. Dorceli extended her arms and legs, probing black air. Dorceli turned over and slid down the bed, kneading the sheet, throwing the pillow far. The mother wasn't there. Dorceli cried louder and louder. But the darkness was all the same, immobile. The darkness absorbed her cries. Dorceli didn't even hear them any more.

Dorceli is alone. Dorceli knows she's alone in a hollow darkness, without a floor, without a ceiling, without mother. Then, the dog's howls reach Dorceli. But the dog is on the other side, outside the darkness. In the darkness, just Dorceli. Dorceli cries, suffocating herself in order to suffocate the darkness, to lock it up and cover it over with her voice. It's the darkness that rustles over her. Dorceli throws herself at it. Comes the shock, the pain. Dorceli falls out of bed. She doesn't recognize the floor. Only the hardness on her knees and forehead, the pain in her arm, her shoulder, the spongy, moldy darkness, like a shadow already forgotten. The darkness comes over Dorceli's face, squeezing it, as the pain in her shoulder and arm makes Dorceli's whole body ache. Dorceli drags herself toward the dog's howl, her buttocks raised against the darkness, her nose tucked in a little airhole, her mouth crying against her arm, the pain, the mother that went away, the round darkness that blinded Dorceli's black eyes.

The whole family was awakened. The uncle came, then the aunt, then the cousins, and the dog, who now licks Dorceli's tears.

"But where's Dalva?"

Dalva went for a walk. That's what she now says to her sister.

"I have a right, don't I? I spend the whole day working. . . ."

"But you should have said something. . . . Look, Clair had to go out at dawn, get a cab, and take the child to the emergency room. She broke her arm, and she might end up crippled. . . ."

"The problem's mine."

"The problem's yours, but we're the ones paying, we're the ones being put out. We've already got five kids. This isn't right. You're the one who had the child and we're taking care of her, right?"

From that point on, Dorceli began sleeping on top of her mother. At times the mother catches her off guard. And Dorceli wakes up alone, tied to the bed. She cries and cries until someone appears. Later, Dalva discovered something: now she ties up Dorceli and puts the dog in the room. The dog lies down on Dorceli's pillow and she doesn't weep.

"Twenty-four years old," Dalva thinks. "Then twenty-five and twenty-six. . . ." She studies her body in the beams of light that pass through the shutter. The room is the same. The old ticket woman's smell has gone away. The Indian's smell is everywhere. In the chamber pot, in the pillow. The cot is crooked; Clair didn't nail new boards over the termite holes.

"Twenty-four years old," thinks Dalva. One day she went by the apartment. Other people, strangers. She glanced and saw the super's wife. If she had known . . . a child in the charity hospital, a little room in the back. . . . That's just what the woman wished on her, when she looked her over four, five years ago.

The cardboard suitcase is open on the floor. Then it goes back under the bed. "Just rags." Dalva straightens up and looks out the window at Dorceli, who's playing under the papaya tree. She has one arm that's a bit stiff since she was little. Black eyes, very dark, straight hair, she doesn't look like anybody.

Dalva's leaving. She hesitates, then goes into the kitchen at the front of the house.

"I'm going away. I'm going to do something for myself in life. But I can't take the girl. I'll send money, of course."

Dorceli holds a finger still as a little insect walks on top of it. She lowers her head to see the bug's legs up close. They look like broken threads advancing cautiously. Dorceli looks cross-eyed, small-immense in that silent encounter. She sticks out her tongue to see better. A strip of bright light around the threads, a bunch of little pieces of things moving around on the bug's head. It's eating, is it going to eat or scrape Dorceli's finger? It gives a little tickle, total enchantment.

Screams in the kitchen. Dorceli and the dog raise their heads, frightened. The insect is lost in the sand.

"I'm the one who's going to take care of this mess you got yourself into? I'm going to take from my children to resolve your shamelessness? Do you think Clair and I are a couple of idiots? A pair of workhorses? Carrying the family on our backs? Wasn't our crazy old aunt in the back room enough? And you and the little kid for the last three years? Haven't we made cuts here and there to feed you?"

"I was helping, you know that."

"Helping . . . helping . . . you've got your nerve!"

"I'll send you room and board money for the kid. You can be sure of that."

"Oh, I can be sure of that! You're going to send room and board money!" The aunt was shouting louder each time: "But who said this was an orphanage? If I wanted another child, I'd have had one, you hear? For three whole years I took care of the little girl to give you a chance—no one can accuse me of having sent you out into the streets—and I know very well what you've been doing during your free time, you think I don't know? You think the whole neighborhood doesn't know? Do you think Clair hasn't had to take a lot of abuse because of you? And now you're going to leave the little kid here, like someone who's leaving some trash. . . . You're crazy, you don't even see what you're doing! We always gave you the best just for you to show what you are: a whore, a tramp, a slut!"

"You can blow up all you want. I don't care. You'll calm down later, I know. I'll send money. I didn't have to do that. I could've left during the night, if I wanted. But I decided to act right. You already have five kids, one more won't make any difference. And if you really don't want her, you know so many people . . . tell one of your friends that I'll send plenty of money every month. . . ."

"You're not leaving here!"

"Of course I'm going. I have to think about my life."

"Oh yeah? And what about mine, who's thinking about that? You're not leaving."

A chair was pushed against the door. Dorceli heard the clatter of a pan against the ground, the panting of two women amidst the dragging of furniture. Dorceli got up, ran to the kitchen, and began beating on the door with her fists. The door suddenly opened wide and Dorceli fell inside.

"All right. Then go, but take your daughter immediately!"

Dorceli was pushed into her mother's arms. The mother didn't take her. When the mother stepped back, Dorceli threw herself against her: "Momma!"

"See, you heartless woman! So you're bold enough to leave your daughter, huh? Look how the innocent thing is holding out her arms to you, look!"

The mother ran down to the backyard. The aunt took off behind her, dragging Dorceli.

"You're going to take this child! I'm not going to keep her! She's your obligation and that bum of a father of hers, too, whoever he is!"

Neighbors leaned over fences. Dalva ran, her face aflame, the torn sleeve of her shirt exposing a very white shoulder.

"Taxi! Taxi!"

"And she's taking a taxi, like a lady. Here, take her at once, and never let me see you again, you parasite!"

The aunt pushed Dorceli outside the iron gate and locked it.

"No more will enter here!" she bellowed, immune to the neighbors, to the drunks in front of the store, to the dog who barked and yelped at her heels, to the terrified look on Dorceli's face.

"Go with her, go," urged the aunt. "I don't want you here."

Dorceli hesitated, then ran up next to her mother, grabbing onto her legs. The hailed taxi stopped. The mother opened the door quickly, forcing herself not to look at anyone, to pretend no one was hearing her, that no one had heard, that no one knew . . . the charity hospital line, the donated shawl, the black eyes of an Indian, who had come from where, no one knew.

"Mother'll be back right away," Dalva said, skillfully loosening the little fingers that were wrinkling her skirt. "Mother'll be back right away," she repeated. And she slammed the car door shut.

When Dorceli screamed, the world was already empty. And the shadow continued to grow.

Elisa Lispector

Born in the Ukraine in 1911, Elisa Lispector was a young girl when her family emigrated to the Brazilian Northeast. After attending the Conservatório de Música in Recife, she moved to Rio de Janeiro, which was her home until her death in 1989.

In the 1940s and 1950s, Elisa Lispector was perhaps better known than her younger sister, Clarice, who is now considered to be one of Latin America's most distinguished authors. Elisa published her first novel, *Além da Fronteira* (Beyond the Border) in 1945; several others followed, among them *O Muro de Pedras* (Wall of Stones), which in 1963 was selected from more than one hundred entries in the competition for the newly created José Lins do Rego Prize. The following year, the book also won an award from the Brazilian Academy of Letters.

Lispector's fiction is usually concerned with introspective women from the middle class. Her 1975 novel, *A Última Porta* (The Last Door), is a compelling book that explores the difficulty of communication between men and women. In her later years, she abandoned novels for short fiction, publishing three collections: *Sangue no Sol* (1970) (Blood on the Sun), *Inventário* (1977) (Inventory), and *Tigre de Bengala* (1985) (Bengal Tiger). Many of these stories, like "O Frágil Equilíbrio" (The Fragile Balance), focus on the inner turmoil of older, single women.

The Fragile Balance

(1977)

As she sewed, methodically making one stitch then another, she said to herself as if issuing a warning: I must be careful with my thoughts. From random thoughts ideas are born, grow, and take shape. Soon you're right in the middle of a circle, without any possibility of escape.

That's where she found herself as she hemmed her traveling outfit, not knowing for certain how events had linked themselves together up to that point.

She vaguely remembered having said that she intended to take her vacation. To travel. More vaguely still, she recalled picking out one date, then another, and then still another. Always putting it off. One day, without her knowledge, the indefinite project escaped her control and took the form of a sealed agreement that pushed her forward almost against her will. As if she were being exiled. Everybody in the office knew her vacation was set and her trip was planned.

"Now it's packing the bag and getting myself off," she said to herself, wanting to joke about it, but deep down forcing herself to contain an anxiety, an imprecise fear, so subtle that it was almost vertiginous.

Never before had she had a clearer sense that she was in danger, that she might be cut off from the small world in which she had been incrusted for so many years. Even prior to taking the train, she felt as if she were being pushed away. Farther away. Away from what, she didn't know, since there was nothing or no one holding her there.

Then, for the first time, she looked back at that little world, like one who looks over a fence, and was suddenly assailed by an ambivalent reaction, the feeling of an oyster out of its shell, of a decapitated head—and, at the same time, of a wanderer for whom a long indefinite road had been cleared.

She knew she wasn't a mollusk, so she resisted the disturbing sense of becoming a trembling and pulsating bit of gelatin held at the brink of disaster, in order to concentrate on the denser but still risky feeling of human living.

"What I always lacked was cunning," she thought, and her mouth suddenly filled with saliva, as if her passivity made her nauseated.

And because she didn't know how to lie or pretend, she didn't know how to impose herself on people. She was exactly as she presented herself, and everyone made her run in circles. They hoodwinked her, overloading her with work that wasn't hers, giving her advice she didn't ask for. If no one contradicted her on the few times when she dared to offer an opinion, it was simply because she'd never been taken seriously, she knew that now. She was a person of no importance, and who was going to pay attention to her?

The many times she had felt set apart from others, unloved to the point of aversion.

"It didn't even need to be much love," she thought, no longer knowing what she would do with a hypothetical love that went beyond certain proportions. It would be enough if they were to say they liked me, as one likes a potted plant. She had no need to be thought of as the ecstatic, blinding light of a radiantly sunny day. The gentle regard one feels toward a rainy day would do, she thought, sadly.

Her heart pounded away as if she had made the journey to the top of the mountain on foot. All of a sudden, and for the first time, she felt like someone who has drunk more than thirst requires.

After the disconcerting first few days of adapting herself to strangers, in the *pensão* where she occupied a room almost as small and dark as the one where she lived in the city, she went out, wandering aimlessly, not knowing what to do with herself. Frequently, she sat on a bench in the square, which was deserted, it no longer being tourist season, warming her back in the sun, a mixed, childlike expression of abandonment and naive curiosity on her face.

It didn't last long, for beneath her apparent passivity she began to feel the growth of a vague, quiet discontent, a thing hard to identify, distantly resembling the mounting challenge she had faced when, years ago, she had been compelled to leave the farm after the death of her mother and then her father, her brothers left desperately struggling to salvage what little remained from the ruins. With the consecutive weddings of each brother, the arrival of the sisters-in-law, and the birth of nephews and nieces, space became more scarce. Soon, there was no longer any place left for her, the spinster. Then she got up her courage and left.

For those who stayed behind, she became an increasingly distant memory, rescued from oblivion by an occasional card around the holidays.

The past was composed of trembling, panting anguish, arid solitude, and gratuitous renunciation; the present, almost all of it, was woven with daydreams leading nowhere. The future?—she asked herself—from where would a new challenge emerge, and with what strength would she confront it, given her total inability to reinvent existence?

Despite her years, she still hadn't acquired a greed for living like that she had noticed, fascinated, the other day at a refreshment table, where an old lady, with lusterless eyes and disheveled white hair, interspersed her eating with quick and repeated gulps of a cold drink.

At that moment she understood she would never confer upon herself the right to any source of pleasure, to any happiness . . . not even to love, she thought reticently, as if this were a lesser glory; and just by thinking about it, she infringed upon an inviolable rule.

There she was, falling back into the trap of cogitation, she admonished herself one morning. Then she made an effort to hold on to what was going on around her. With a certain sagacity, daring something for the first time, perhaps because she didn't have anyone with whom to quarrel, she went about taking over the square.

Looking at things as if they were hers, not without a certain feeling of displeasure at the abandoned state of the wizened flowerbeds and the greenish bouquets of hortense, and the old trees covered with parasitic vines, she observed the closed summer houses, interrogating the immobile silence of their facades. She studied most carefully a large stone edifice, trying to imagine what was going on in the tormented mind of the engineer who, according to what they told her, had lost it, and who, every morning, went out into the street wearing a dark leather jacket, his hands in his pockets, his head bowed, disappearing with long strides as he made his way to the foot of the mountain.

More frequently, however, her contemplative gaze lingered on the mountain peak, sometimes hooded by dark clouds, sometimes raised up clearly and majestically against the intense blue of the sky. And the neutrality of the distant mountain, lofty and immune to time, imposed itself on her confused well of anxiety, her blind and trembling search for she knew not what, giving her a momentary serenity.

Sometimes it happened that, as she looked intensely at the trees in the golden light of morning, she seemed to make out silver threads, as tenuous and delicate as spider webs, wrapped around the treetops in all directions; then, suddenly, they trembled and were no longer horizontal or undulating, but ascending vertically, detaching themselves from the foliage and shooting off like rays, disappearing into the air while other streaks of light burst from the treetops and glittered like silvery beams. And so absorbed was she in the pulsating life about her that, suddenly, in a language without words, on a journey without traveling, she seemed to be secretly arriving where she had wanted to arrive for such a long time. Something in her grew larger and spread throughout her being, filling her with a sense of the infinite. Any more and the infinite would overflow her borders.

Other times, she was moved by a strange longing, perhaps because she had lost her bearings. "The tree is being," she murmured to herself one morning. "The tree is," she concluded. "The mountain is. And up to what point am I myself?" she asked, intrigued. Would she, by chance, have the courage to reach her limit? she wanted to know. Things are so mysterious and unintelligible, she dared to comment, as she ventured along a road that was so narrow she was barely able to pass by.

At that point in her reflections she perceived a shape standing still at the other side of the deserted square. Tall, thin, a gabardine cape fluttering in the wind, a face half-hidden in the shadow thrown by a hat, also of gabardine. In spite of the distance, she sensed he was looking at her. She knew that he couldn't make out her features from such a distance, and was merely speculating on who she was; neither was she able to get a hint of his face, and could only attribute the persistence with which he stared at her to a probable attraction between opposites. That quiet confrontation could last indefinitely, if it weren't . . .
suddenly, as if set in motion by a secret directive, she began reliving all the miscarried encounters of the past, and became so disoriented that she could no longer say if they happened in reality or in dreams barely dreamt, and, settling over the fear that remained from her sense of isolation and over the bitterness caused by consecutive misencounters,

was a strange and crazy hope of something so vague and at the same time so exciting that she didn't dare think of it

. . . because the man was moving, heading in her direction. Closer with each step. Closer.

With a light step, as precise as that of a trapeze artist or a professional ballet dancer, the man advanced in her direction. Until she could now make out an indefinable half-smile. Her heart beat more strongly each moment, in warning. But she was going to resist, she decided. She was running the risk of she knew not what, at the vague beckoning of something that could happen.

Suddenly, to her own shock and surprise, and before she could gain control, she got up off the bench, as agile as a hunted rabbit, and, hastily fleeing with quick, light steps, she headed for the first boulevard, surely cutting off whatever she might discover or definitively lose, but in any event, avoiding a break of the fragile balance that over the course of so many years she had tried in vain to establish.

Edla van Steen

Edla van Steen was born in 1936, in Florianópolis, the capital of Santa Catarina in southern Brazil. She has resided in São Paulo for nearly thirty years, where she has worked in theater and cinema as an actress and scriptwriter. She has written several volumes of stories and novels, and is the editor of *O Conto da Mulher Brasileira* (1978) (The Brazilian Woman's Short Story), one of the first anthologies dedicated to contemporary women's fiction.

Van Steen writes about heterosexual and homosexual love in contemporary society. Many of her stories have been anthologized, and two have recently appeared in collections devoted to Brazilian erotic literature. She also writes children's books, and has translated into Portuguese works by Katherine Mansfield, Henrik Ibsen, and Robert Louis Stevenson.

One of the most interesting aspects of her fiction is its unusual form. The technique of the story "A Bela Adormecida" (The Sleeping Beauty) is clearly influenced by her extensive work in theater and movies.

The Sleeping Beauty (Script of a Useless Life)

(1978)

For Lenita

1st SEQUENCE

Agile hands gather up small objects on top of the furniture; carpets are hurriedly rolled up and chairs are placed close to the walls. The maid executes this task with the efficiency of someone who has done it before. At times, she uses her sleeve to wipe away the sadness that persists in running down her cheeks. She does it now, when she stops to look at the garden as if she'd just seen me. She's distracted by the harsh sounds of the men taking silver coffin racks, tall candlesticks, and a crucifix out of rough wooden boxes.

The family and the coffin won't be long in arriving—she makes the sign of the cross and returns to the kitchen.

It's three in the afternoon on a cloudy autumn day. Fábio penetrates the devastated atmosphere and sits down in front of the empty racks. He's moved by his own solitude, in a place that now seems strange, as if he were witnessing the scene and not participating in it. Then he sees his figure reflected in the mirror. He gives a sigh and tries to turn his attention to details of the room. Isn't my self-portrait attractive? Perhaps my painting has stirred up hidden memories in him, for he doesn't even notice Mariana, dear childhood friend, who's standing at the wide-opened door, surprised by his presence.

2nd SEQUENCE

Little by little the house and garden fill with people. Does Fábio regret having come? Reencountering so many acquaintances, under these circumstances, is painful. I was astonished by his being the first to arrive. I never imagined so much attentiveness. He must have acted spontaneously, because, had he thought about it, he would have been the last person to show up. I'm moved by his tragic look, so individual, so integral, so self-contained. I kiss his forehead, gratefully. He brushes away the suspicion of a caress, interesting himself in the recent arrivals. In particular, he stares at the governess, who has just appeared at the front door, bringing Luís from school. Poor child, he's going on six years old. He's frightened by Aunt Miloca's crying. Coming up to the boy, she embraces him, tearfully. Luís brutally pushes her away, runs to Matilde and gives her his hand. Hard German woman. She totally disapproves of the behavior of my poor dear aunt, who's from another era and controls her nerves less. I wonder about the child's reaction. Children are unpredictable. Who knows, he may think that all these people are commemorating some event. The governess takes him upstairs. It's his bath time. She did well. A kid shouldn't participate in these things.

3rd SEQUENCE

Mariana and Alice have retreated under the fig tree. They isolated themselves on purpose. Alice talks about the visit I made to her last night, my complaints, my dissatisfaction with my canvases, my invitation to go to the movies. A Bergman film. We argued a lot about the Swedish filmmaker—probably because she didn't want to come to grips with other problems. Fear that I'd question her about her affair with my husband? Goodness, I'd never do that. She never opened herself up about personal matters, carefully maintaining an appearance of harmony, good sense, and happiness with Augusto. I stay with the two women because they don't notice the arrival of the coffin. I detest emotional displays. Moreover, it'd be cruel. No one has the right to enjoy their own death, or to stage it. Not even after having read Machado de Assis. Of course, the idea is seductive despite its lack of originality. I'm not so exceptionally gifted as to refuse to try something just because earlier models exist. I was born, I grew up, and I died romantically. What else could I do? But I was also a human being who obstinately drove herself to the limit in order to overcome her deficiencies. If I wasn't the best, I had patience. The paintings show my effort, my considerable command of the *métier*, my dedication. Dead, I may cause a sudden rise in the value of the canvases, which would no longer have the slightest importance.

I accompany my women friends. Groups speak in low voices, reverently. Strange, I don't know why certain individuals came. How did they find out so soon?

Oh, my God, Marcos is coming in. He looks beat. Naturally he's tired out from disentangling all the legal business of the body. He crosses the veranda, indifferent to the gestures of condolence. He doesn't see anyone but Fábio. He knew about my friendship with Fábio and never accepted him, the egotist. He permitted himself barbarities with Alice, and I. . . . She looked down when he passed by. For a few seconds I see my husband from below: He's crying. Well, I'll be! Don't go overboard, thank you. Fortunately that old warrior, Augusto, is diverting his friend with an emotional embrace!

Mariana withdraws: is she also thinking about our chat last night? She was harsh, said she couldn't stand my constant crises, that I should do something, go to a psychiatrist, get a separation and a job. Mariana's one of those practical, executive types. She works in advertising. She's crazy about books and records, a real expert on music. We tried to introduce her to a conductor, hoping this would inspire some enthusiasm in her. No way! Today I ask myself if, of the three of us, she wasn't always the wisest.

In a little while it'll be dark. I don't know why they don't serve the coffee. Incredible, the maids can't even think on their own to fulfill their obligations! I hope my governess takes the initiative. Ah, didn't I tell you? Good Matilde. I sought her out last night, before. . . . She's grown old before my very eyes. She'd never admit that I was a thirty-year-old woman. For her, I was still the little girl she had raised and to whom she used to read fairy tales.

FLASHBACK I

Heloísa, as a child, is lying down with a book of illustrations of Siegfried on her lap.

The governess has just finished tidying up a drawer:
"Shall we throw out these clothes?"
The little girl jumps off the bed and goes to the mirror. She places a tiara on her head.
"Matilde, do you think I can have a prince?"
"You've gotten into your mother's things again!"
"If you don't say anything, she'll never know. Where can that red cape be?"
Governess gives a chuckle. Cut.
Image showing hats, clothes, fur stoles, etc., strewn about the floor. Governess and Heloísa, both dressed up, are laughing. Matilde says:
"Then she married the enchanted prince and they had a pretty daughter and lived happily together for many years."
Close-up of the little girl, fascinated, at the mirror. Little by little her physiognomy becomes sad. She turns toward the governess and, with a grave air, pronounces:
"It's no good. I'm not going to have any prince. You're dumb."

I was a scoundrel yesterday. I hid my inability to live from her. Sorry, Matilde. I pass my hands over her white hair, but my second mother doesn't perceive the caress, so preoccupied is she with gathering up the dirty coffee cups. Anyway, what's the use of regrets?

4th SEQUENCE

My English teacher arrives. I can't understand it, the news spread so quickly!

I follow Mariana to the dining room with its highback chairs, inherited from my Grandma. The empty fireplace enhances the atmosphere of solitude. She goes over to a glass bookcase, the kind that has doors, and pulls out my old book of stories as the last light of day enters through the stained-glass windows.

"Will you let me see the glass coffin?"

A young Mariana consents. Back then the fire colored the walls with an orange glow. Those two little girls had their whole lives ahead of them. And growing up wasn't easy, was it, Mariana?

I feel someone watching us. I turn toward the door and see Matilde, her face wet with tears. Mariana, was I the one who resaw the scene from long ago, or was it she?

I go into the library: Marcos is smoking. How does he remember me?

FLASHBACK II

I walk across a deserted square. The sun filters through the leaves of the trees and is transformed: I want to pick up the stars on the ground, but they extinguish between my fingers.

A gentleman passes by on horseback and doesn't notice me. An unknown figure of a man walks toward me and embraces me: he has a red beard and moustache.

5th SEQUENCE

I go to the garden. Incomprehensible situations reduce me to a small size. What kind of a damn memory is this that, instead of registering real events, marks down hallucinations?

Fábio is leaning against the post on the veranda. He's fifty years old with the bearing of a priest. He's wearing velvet pants and a leather jacket. He's a photographer, a sorcerer, who almost bewitched me with his magic potions. How is it possible that I've lived an entire lifetime believing that I would find happiness only by being in love?

One shouldn't tell fairy tales to children, I said yesterday somewhat angrily to poor Matilde, who didn't get my accusation.

6th SEQUENCE

Fábio heads toward my studio. A mutual friend intercepts him on his way. They shake hands: the look of collusion, of one who says "I know you two had a thing," is nauseating. Fábio continues to walk, impassively. He enters the studio and turns on the light, which, to a certain extent, annoys me. I'd choose darkness. He sounds out the possibilities and sits on a pillow, in front of the stereo.

FLASHBACK III

Heloísa can be heard as the image shows the studio and the paintings.

(Voice in off) "Do you understand? No one was interested in the other paintings, which were better. The exhibition was a failure. That inferior phase sold out completely."

(Fábio turns to Heloísa, who is working) Heloísa: "I'm trying to get away from this, but I can't. I no longer want to do portraits, women or horses."

Fábio: (Approaching the painting) "But you're doing. . . ."

Heloísa: "Nothing worthwhile, look!" (Pause) "What would give me pleasure would be to paint a landscape. To go to the country and be at peace, like when I was a child."

Fábio: (Turning his back to her) "You don't want to paint the landscape, you want to be in it."

Heloísa: "You're absolutely right." (She throws down the paintbrush) "A question of destiny, horoscope, or who knows what. If I'd met you before Marcos, for example, perhaps. . . ." (The two exchange looks)

Heloísa goes over to him. They remain quiet and constrained. It grows dark. Cut.

That's it, so unnecessarily close . . . "I love how love loves." Darling person, so much poetry. "When I saw you, I had already loved you before. I found you again when I met you." That's the big mistake: believing in fiction.

Fábio goes over to the table and returns a cup of brushes that has fallen over to its proper place. He looks at the unfinished landscape. Ha! What inspiration! That painting was going to be good, wasn't it? Homage to Gauguin. I look for a reaction in him, whatever it might be, but he merely gives me that damned look of boredom. "Love, say something so that I might feel you!"

The dead don't have desires.

7th SEQUENCE

The business card on top of the little desk . . . I totally disconcerted that fortune-teller. No wonder, I was so upset. A stranger gave me her address in the supermarket, and I didn't think twice. When I came to my senses, I was waiting for her wrinkled hands to cut the greasy deck of cards.

"You're very sensitive, but you don't believe in anything that you do. Past, present, future are mixed together, just like reality and fantasy. . . . Life and death travel side by side. . . ."

I almost clapped my hands with glee. The woman was perceptive, a genius.

"Can I see my death?"

"Well. . . ."

"Which card is it?"

"This one."

"A queen."

For a few moments I imagined death embracing me like flesh and bone. Its embrace was tender and comforting. That was the day I felt the first temptation.

"Life is nothing more than a big movie, a lie just like all the other ones. Only some sequences are logical, you know?" The woman heard me and was startled.

What designs might she have foretold!

8th SEQUENCE

I'm going to go back to the wake. If Fábio wants to stay in the studio. . . . Provided that he takes care: some memories can bring back the dead! What am I saying? It's just an expression. They say that in the seconds just before death, human beings experience a general retrogression, a long flashback, in which they recall important facts. Could it be? I'm really angry, my memories are so insignificant.

It's nighttime already. Looking from the studio, I can see the house assuming the attitude I most like, that of mystery. A shape appears, against the light, on the window of my bedroom. I don't need to know who it is, the figure is enough for me.

FLASHBACK IV

Heloísa, a child once again, in the corner of the garden. It's dark. The scenery is bathed by a diffused light from the moon. The little girl plays as she softly hums.

Heloísa's voice in off: "Everybody was afraid of my eccentricities. I grew up so alone. . . . If it weren't for the crazinesses, I don't know."

Zoom, close-up of the stone sculpture in the little girl's hand: an ugly, pornographic dwarf.

Little girl: "Who knows, maybe one of these days you'll change into my enchanted prince, just like that horrible frog that the princess took to her bed?" (She laughs)

The image draws back and shows the little girl and the house, gloomy and covered with ivy.

9th SEQUENCE

I cross the yard with the ease of one who flies. What are these happy groups of people whispering? Banalities. I have the impression they've forgotten about me. Even so, I'm grateful for their company. I look about the room: my mother dries her swollen eyes; my father takes a nap, his bearing dignified despite his eighty years. One day he exclaimed: "I'm worn out from burying friends. If I live much longer, I won't have anyone to carry me to the grave." Two aunts, in black, murmur unimaginable secrets. And Marcos? In the library. The ashtray overflows. From my angle of the room, the smoke rises up under the lighted lampshade and escapes bluish-looking through the top. There's an atmosphere of a horror film.

FLASHBACK V

Gallery. Heloísa finishes hanging the last painting. She comes down off the folding stepladder and examines the exhibited work. Cut to the in-

auguration. The artist receives the customary greetings, without euphoria.

She insistently searches for someone. Alice approaches.

Heloísa: "Have you seen Marcos around? Funny, he didn't come."

Suddenly she leaves in the middle of the exhibition and gets her car. Cut.

The house is dark. As she goes through it, she turns on the lamps. Marcos is in the library, drinking. Leaning against the door jamb, Heloísa waits as he drains the glass.

Marcos: "I didn't go today, nor will I ever go again. Do you want to know why?"

(He gets up) "I know you're dying to ask and don't have the courage, right?"

(Facing her) "Let's. . . . Out with it! Okay, here's the truth: I think your painting is crap. I detest your little intellectual friends and I'm fed up with playing the part of the artist's husband. I hate that aura of superiority you have, that 'good' convent education of yours, that high-class faginess. Besides that, I can't stand your gardens or your infantile stories. Fairy tales! I'll never ever be the enchanted prince you'd love me to be. Never, do you understand? Never."

Close-up of Heloísa crying.

10th SEQUENCE

I enter the kitchen. It's a fascinating place, where one supposes everything can be cleaned, washed, restored. Near the stove I hear the hot water deliciously running in the sink. The maid, her back turned and wearing white knee socks, is ageless.

Oh, if only my soul could dry gleaming bright from the detergent in the dishwasher!

FLASHBACK VI

Bedroom. Marcos and Heloísa are in bed. She sleeps. He caresses his wife's back. He intends to awaken her. Sleepy, she lets him lean over her.

Heloísa: (In a close-up, ecstatic) "If you don't love me, why do you tease me?"

11th SEQUENCE

Midnight. Nothing is happening. The situation is equally horrible for the dead. And if they stuck a needle into my heart? Blood would gush forth. Fábio and Mariana are over there on the veranda.

"Did you still like her?"
"Still."
"Up until when did you think she was going to make up her mind?"
"Until yesterday."

These things depress me. There were so many disagreements. The fragrance from the plants stirs in me an old longing, not localized. I'll wander through the streets moaning and will no one respond to my moans? Where, love, where did you hide yourself? Where?

FLASHBACK VII

A narrow street up which Heloísa and Fábio walk. A row of old houses. From time to time she suspects that a window is half-opened and that someone slyly looks out, then immediately closes the shutters. Suddenly a door is opened wide. Apprehensive, she interrupts their dialogue, but soon thereafter she resumes speaking.

Heloísa: ". . . the difficulty with loving, then, consists of the expectation created around the one being loved, which doesn't always correspond to our fantasies. . . ."

Close-up of Fábio, astonished.

12th SEQUENCE

My son sleeps. He's an enchanting little boy. Just like his father. He doesn't take after me at all. I was a simple incubator. I pray that he discovers reasons to live—I pull up the cover for the last time . . . —and let life be less harsh for him than it was for me.

13th SEQUENCE

Wakes reach their greatest degree of poignancy at dawn. The candles burn without bending, there's a kind of deterioration in the people, the furnishings, the objects. Alice prepares to caress Marcos, but she stops the gesture in midair.

"Don't you have any sense of propriety?"

"Shh, please don't talk that way to me, dear."

"Respect the dead, you. . . ."

She grows pale. She doesn't know the kind of neurasthenic with whom she's been involved.

14th SEQUENCE

"You went too far," Mariana says, offering Alice a cookie.

"I don't know what you mean to insinuate."

"I heard you and Marcos."

"So?" She gives her friend a defiant look.

Mariana returns the look.

"Don't you feel any sense of guilt?"

"Stupid. Everybody knows Heloísa had problems. Our affair never bothered her, on the contrary. . . ."

"You could at least have some scruples today. . . ."

Alice remains indignant.

"Look who's talking! And what about you, did you get over the crush you had on her?"

Mariana frowns, painfully.

Goodness, I never thought about that possibility!

FLASHBACK VIII

Mariana's apartment. Lying on the sofa, Heloísa listens to Bach's 5th for the third time. Mariana looks at her friend with unlimited tenderness:

she's so pretty with her Nordic features, her diaphanous blue eyes; that's what her eyes were, diaphanous, and her hair fine like silk—she touches the strands lightly, fearing, perhaps, that they might dissolve. She feels she can touch the sadness on Heloísa's tortured face, if she so desires.

Moved, she leans over a little more. She stops, in time, the kiss she's ready to give.

15th SEQUENCE

As if wanting to disengage herself from something, Mariana grabs her purse. I feel like stopping her from going, but Fábio will do that for me, I know. Standing there outside, he couldn't wish for another opportunity: someone with whom to entertain himself.

"She went to see you yesterday too?"

Mariana replied yes, explaining further:

"We went for a drive through Morumbi. She was tense, in one of those famous depressions of hers. I advised her to go to a psychiatrist. Know what she said? 'No one has the right to dwell in the secrets of others. No, happiness and suffering are always obscure and unfathomable.' I felt tragedy coming. I tried to make her take a taxi home. Honestly, she drove without the slightest precaution."

FLASHBACK IX

Speeding car. Day is about to begin. Heloísa doesn't obey any of the traffic lights. Suddenly, she hears the sound of the crash.

When she recovers her senses, a man is holding her head in his arms. He has a red beard and moustache. Hadn't she seen him before? Drying the thick, warm liquid running from her chest, the unexpected hobgoblin examines Heloísa, completely seduced, as if he had a perverse witch in his lap. She thinks about saying "It's late," but she has to renounce her body, now sterile.

FINAL SEQUENCE

On this luminous morning, the house is filled once again. The funeral procession is about to depart. I walk among the people, conscious of the futility of everything. I'm going to take a look at me: in the glass coffin, covered with flowers—why do I have my hands bound?—I'm resting, lightly asleep.

There, under the old fig tree, a translucent lady awaits me. In a little while, I'm going to wake up and embrace her with an eternal smile.

Marina Colasanti

Born in Ethiopia in 1937, Marina Colasanti spent her early childhood in Italy, moving to Brazil in 1948. Following her studies at the National School of Fine Arts in Rio de Janeiro, she became a journalist and has written extensively on women's issues for a variety of magazines. In 1975, she began her association with the woman's journal *Nova*.

In the early 1970s, in the *Jornal do Brasil,* Colasanti began publishing *mini-contos* (mini-short stories), a genre which she is credited with having developed. Interesting examples of her work in this area are collected in *Zooilógico* (1975) (Zooillogical) and *Contos de Amor Rasgado* (1986) (Torn-Up Love Stories), which are witty, provocative sketches in the fantastic tradition. She has also written a prize-winning volume of fairy tales, *Uma Idéia Toda Azul* (1979) (An All Blue Idea).

Colasanti was one of several new writers to appear in *Muito Prazer* (1980) (Very Pleased to Meet You), a best-selling anthology of women's erotic fiction. "Menina de Vermelho, A Caminho da Lua" (Little Girl in Red, on Her Way to the Moon), which appeared in that collection, is an unusual and unsettling depiction of preadolescent sexuality.

Little Girl in Red, on Her Way to the Moon

(1980)

This is a story I don't want to tell, a little story without facts, thick like menses, for which I don't intend to claim responsibility. I tried to rid myself of it, to submerge it and the disgust it makes me feel. I didn't succeed. Unnecessary as it is, it nevertheless persists in being. That's why I placed an ad in the newspaper. It said: Narrator wanted. Modesty and a pleasant appearance required. Salary to be negotiated. Inquire . . . address . . . et cetera.

Only one applicant appeared. I would have preferred a woman, but I didn't have a choice, so I took him. Male, and a bit green as he was, I felt obliged to insist on what I wanted: stylistic concision and a docile attitude. I also insisted on dressing him in new clothes. Thus, I present him with a pink skirt and a scarf on his head: a mother of two little girls whose parts will be small, a mother taking her girls to play in a tiny amusement park on a Saturday afternoon—on the very afternoon and at the exact moment when the story wants to happen, and where the narrator becomes, by contract and choice, responsible for it.

The park, I instruct my associate, is small. You couldn't rightly call it an amusement park because it lacks colors and that minimum amount of merriment necessary for entertaining. It has few distractions. A carousel propelled from above by a kind of giant fan installed in a shaky armature. And a large plastic bubble. I don't want you to describe how the light fell, whether full on the face or in profile, and you needn't get lost in romantic considerations about the decadence of parks. I merely want you to get across, by means of the propeller-fan perhaps, the somewhat sordid poverty of the place. And please, don't start off with temporal references.

"A pity having worn high-heeled sandals, I thought, feeling the dust settle between my toes, a viscose sweaty paste forming on the inner sole. I shook my foot in vain. My little girls ran ahead, undecided among the playthings, ready to ask for one then the other, excited by the unexpected possibilities. In truth, there wasn't much. In the space squeezed between two walls—a vacant lot with weeds and the smell of urine in its corners—turned a horseless carousel with packing-crate seats attached to the propeller. Canoes, pendant from chains, cut through the air like scythes. The perforated targets on the shooting stand seemed to have been gnawed by hungry rats. Circling an enclosure, fishing poles with string awaited any fishermen who might want to hook keys and plastic mugs. At the back, however, the large, inflated bubble was an attraction worth the asking price of ten *cruzeiros.*"

Don't give too much value to the bubble. It's old and dirty like everything else around there, purchased from another, larger park, after it was already visibly worn out. And be careful with the clichés: "cut through the air" isn't good, you could have used a more original metaphor. Nor do you need to be so delicate. It's better to say pee than urine, especially in this story. But let's go on. You, the mother, want to pay for your daughters to enter the bubble, where they can jump up and down. That's the purpose of the bubble. You look around, but see no ticket booth, so you call out, then clap your hands. A man comes. I know you'd like to describe him, an old fellow, or a man thus and so, who looks sideways and is very short. But I don't want you to. For the time being, I'll only allow you to say that he wore pants belted at the waist with a rope. That's enough.

"White and yellow with transparent windows. Dirty white, with patches—that's just how the lunar surface would be, an immense, inflated mattress in which a leg could sink, beneath the dome of a bubble. For overhead was written: Walk on the Moon for Cr$ 10,00. And I, wanting to pay for my two astronauts' trip, searched for the ticket booth, a fake kiosk in the midst of that nothing; finding no one there, I returned, trying to attract attention by my simple presence. There were so few people in the park. I thought about calling out, clapping my hands, but inhibited by the thought of my own noisemaking, I stood there beside my girls, looking around with an air that I meant to be authoritative, but which I knew was only forsaken. Could that be the attendant, the man who went by without looking at me, more concerned with hitching up his pants?"

I don't know why you omitted the detail about the rope. It's powerful and says a lot about the character. That "hitching up his pants" of yours says little, it dilutes. And don't be so long-winded. The reader wants climate, pressure. Forget the descriptions. Let's go on, now put your daughters in the bubble.

"He took my money without smiling, his head slanted like an egg in the nest of his shoulders. And pushing a plastic" Stop, stop! I don't want him to be serious. No way. Change that. It's vital. The man smiles, he laughs strangely the whole time, in a mollifying sort of way. And he says things you don't understand. He has a malign air, crafty or perhaps it's servile, you choose the best word, but he's always smiling, with his false bonhomie. "He smiled and reached out his hand for the money, his head slanted like an egg resting in the nest of his shoulders. He raised a loose flap of plastic, a white tongue, and straining his arms, he opened the slit in the bubble.

"A blast of air; sirocco laden with sweat. The breath of the moon. Escaping through the bloodless lips of the slit, its windy howls covered over the words the man spoke as he gesticulated, his mouth opened wide and his nose bristling with hair. Did he want the time? I pointed to my watch. I was shouting, trying to respond in that corridor of wind, when suddenly his dry hand grabbed the arm of my little girl" Very good, I like that hand introducing the sense of desire. Only I don't know what you're going to do with it, what it wants. Make up your mind, but remember that your daughters aren't characters. "My little girl, who was already on her way in. Pulling her about, he slid one hand down her leg and closed it around her knee, the other hand, claw-like, reaching for her ankle.

" 'She has to take off her shoes,' I finally heard, as he unbuckled her sandals; pushing the little one inside, he sealed the slit, stopping the wind. 'You can only go in without shoes on, otherwise the plastic tears.' "

Wonderful, the two are finally playing, isolated in the bubble and safe. You can leave them there for the time being. We aren't going to need them. But look, you hadn't noticed, at your side, another little girl, who's looking through the window at your daughters jumping around. Dressed in red, the shade of carmine, she's wearing a leotard of sorts and is barefoot. Her teeth are decayed. She's ten years old. Watch out for the age, because her eyes have the look of someone older. Small breasts.

She wants to go into the bubble. Passionately. She has no money. But she wants to go in and she's going to have to pay another way. She knows this. You don't.

"They roll around, laughing, the two of them sinking into the floating mattress, their arms open, their steps staggering, their cries held within the curving dome. But I'm not the only one with hands cupped over the window watching the little girls on their journey. At my side, she, too, looks on, greedily.

"She was already in the park when I arrived, a little figure in red, playing with other children in the flying canoes. Ten years old perhaps, older looking from a distance. The carmine-colored lipstick is heavy on her lips, but her breasts are still not breasts, and her hips await filling out. Why does she have a red mask raised up over her forehead if carnival is already past? The waxed cloth, cut in the shape of leaves, crushes the damp strings of her hair, as if a butterfly were perched opposite the slanted eyeholes. She doesn't seem to feel cold, although she's exposed in the brief leotard. She watches on tip-toe, her whole body leaning against the curved surface, her bare thighs glued against the bubble, her mouth open, soft with desire."

She's there at your side, and you two don't have anything to do with one another. But she's a child. Don't forget that, she's a child the whole time, in spite of whatever happens. And like a child, she comes close to your side, mother that you are, seeking support or, who knows, money. "A child, like my own. Who looks at me and smiles, blushing—or is it the makeup?—saying inconsequential things, to which I respond more with attention than words, because we don't have much to say to each other. A little girl who isn't mine, and whom I soon abandon for lack of anything to say. Silent the two of us, prolonging our smiles and turning our heads away little by little, pretending we're no longer looking at one another." You don't look at her directly, to avoid getting involved; to avoid including her, a foreign element, beyond what was expected, in your Saturday. But neither do you let go of her. Looking out of the corner of your eye, sneaky and voracious, you follow her, savoring, little by little, as your understanding slowly unfolds, the smooth metamorphosis in which a new game begins.

Start moving her about. Take her away, bring her back again. Don't let her stand still. Like a child, she roams the whole park as she seeks out the playthings. Like a woman, she approaches that which she desires, forging the key that will make it hers.

"However, I see her when, forgetting the bubble, she darts off. She goes over to the carousel, which is turning, empty of children. Unable to get inside, she watches it from the fence, her hand leaning on the latticework, her face raised in profile. With trotting feet, she slowly circles round to the clamorous beat of the music, a pony far more graceful than the wooden figures, decorated with mirrors, that were part of the carousel in its better days. But she doesn't stay long. Her body has its urgencies, whose tempos are far quicker than the one-two-three of a waltz. She runs, sprints, shakes her wispy mane. Looking at the Moon from afar, she bends down, picks up a forgotten strip of wood, and throws it violently against the wall." That's it, she's champing at the bit. Her body whinnies, raises back, and stretches taut. She gallops about, preparing herself. Then, with lowered head and softened step, she comes in search of the greener grass. "And I sense her return. Brought back slowly by desire, she comes closer, as if by chance, turning round and round. She's put on a more gentle expression, washed clean her gaze, and made her chin look like an infant's.

"First she goes to the window. Just like before, she rises on the arch of her foot, but it's only now that I see that's not necessary. The transparent eye, through which the interior of the bubble can be seen, is close to the ground. Raised up and leaning over, she nevertheless isn't interested in the game played by the two little girls. She looks through sideways, toward the man." It's the moment of her first attempt. She doesn't have much hope in succeeding, but she's going to try. It's a way of testing the old man, of saying I want. Invent a dialogue. Make it short, because it isn't with words that they understand one another. Just enough to make the first contact clear. "Then, slowly, feigning indifference, concealing her advance with a coiling movement of her legs, she approaches the entrance. Her hand sneaks under the plastic tongue." Not sneaks, it inserts, it enters, it penetrates. "Her hand inserts itself under the plastic tongue, and her thigh slowly advances, bringing forth her hips, her entire body subtly forcing open the sides of the slit in an attempt to pierce through.

" 'You can't,' says the man in a low voice, without moving from his place. Startled, she gives him a little laugh.

" 'Only on the next turn,' he says, showing his teeth. 'After the other two who are in there.' "

Everything is still very tenuous, very imprecise. It's hard to see that which, because it is forbidden, is concealed. But little by little, seduced, you see. In the way they have of almost not looking at each other, in her spiraled moves, you see. Be very clear now. This isn't the time to be polishing one's style. The thing is simple: a man and a little girl intertwining their desires. Lift them up, give them line. There's more than enough in which they can tangle themselves. But work the little girl more. I want her to be the primary thing, the strongest, the sweet spider.

"The little girl comes with slow steps, spinning the silk with which she will capture the man's look. She stops, sticks out a leg, arches her bare foot, and with polished toenails, traces spirals in the dusty ground. Staked like the point of a compass, the other leg forms the axis of her soft body. She doesn't look at him. She adjusts the mask with her fingertips and fluffs out nonexistent curls. Then, all of a sudden, she lowers the red visor over her face and through the slits directs the green light of her eyes until it reaches the target—the man's attention, to which she fixes herself. Now, the end of the line firmly secured, she lowers her chin onto her chest, giving a little smile, and slowly begins to turn." No, it wasn't you I needed for telling this story. If I wanted it that delicate, I would have written it myself. I advertised because I needed someone who wanted to ferment manure, to fertilize a vile fact. And here you come with this medieval tapestry, slipping between words, masquerading with images. Are you embarrassed? Incompetent? What's the matter with you? A professional narrator who's afraid of a little girl. But the little girl's seducing an old man because she wants to walk on the Moon. See if you can get that into your head. And get it into the text. "Resolute, designing her own movement in the deep furrow in the ground, she turns round herself and closes the circle. Until she has her back to him.

"It's with her back to him, her hips raised, that she waits for his greed to glue itself above her legs. She's in no hurry. She sucks her finger, pretends to chew a nail, a little racoon with ruined teeth. She lets him closely study her skin, allows his look to sink into the rosy conches behind her knees, to climb high past her thighs and between them for a second. Only then, quick and modest, does she pull down the leotard in defense of her virtues. And raising her head, she smiles at me with her little open face."

Okay, now you can be ashamed. You're a mother, you're watching and you don't do anything. You could have called to the child, talked to her, paid for her ticket. But that would be acknowledging you know what's happening, that while she was playing with fire, you were fascinated with the details, sharpening your pencil to capture the line of her eyes, the position of her foot, more interested in using the scene than in preventing it. Now she smiles at you, just like a child. She doesn't want to please you. She wants your alibi. Smiling back, you sign her certificate of innocence, affirming that, yes, she's a child just like the others, a good little girl, who deserves your affection. And nothing you saw happened. Weakened, you smile. "A little girl like my own, playing in the amusement park on a Saturday afternoon. A child with chubby thighs who asks for your smile. That's what I'm seeing, only that. There's no reason for this dryness in the mouth, this taking note of. . . ." Her mouth isn't dry. She's damp, secretly secreting juices in the sun at the park, imprisoned with the man in the viscose web. She sweats in her axillas. Put that down, the word axillas—no, better put armpits, which you hate even more, because you think it's too obvious. I know you don't want to write as I command, that you already consider yourself the author. But the facts—the one who has the facts is me. And without me you have nothing to tell. Without me you don't exist. ". . . this taking note of masks and feet. Nothing, there is nothing to fantasize over. No concrete gesture. Just a red leotard stretched over her breasts, and two cloth flowers tied to her wrist with a ribbon. A wrist the man now holds, not forcefully, but firmly, bending himself low over her ear, which is covered by strands of hair. A wrist she gives him, momentarily docile, before pulling her arm and body away with a refusing laugh, shaking his words out of her ear, but bringing with that very gesture his dark hand, which quickly embeds itself in the curve of her waist."

Take her away, don't let her stay at his side too long. She insinuates herself in stages, advancing a little more each time, but not yet yielding. Not him. He remains immobile. He's the center, the power. He doesn't move, he doesn't hurry. He knows she'll return until she gets what she wants. And he has his price.

"A moment passes and she's already moving away, dancing, scratching her neck where the golden hair is creased by the elastic haloed round her head. The sole customer at the shooting stand puts down his rifle and concentrates his attention on the brunette target of a young woman in charge of the guns. The little girl makes her way over there. I watch her as she draws near and, crouching like a cat, goes up to the fellow. I don't know what they say. I see the guy put his hands under her arms and slowly raise her up from behind. Until, pressed between him and the counter, she's able to reach the rifle, and, leaning it against her shoulder, she fires it.

"Does the other man notice? It seems not. Without turning his head or seeking her out with his eyes, he moves with flat-footed steps, taking money from parents who, little by little, arrive. He unbuckles sandals with a smile, a benevolent doorman to the Moon that she wants above all the other playthings in the park, and that he knows will bring her back.

"Back she comes, cutting diagonally through the park. She brings running with her another little girl, who follows, holding onto her one moment, then fleeing, pursued and pursuing. They don't go far. In the space next to the bubble, which has become tight with parents and children, they run in circles, seeking one another out, offering themselves, then twisting their bodies out of reach, touching one another between shouts, trying to win the game of hide and seek. Crashing around and tripping, they bring disorder to the small line of people already formed, until the man leaves his post next to the entrance, and, publicly exercising his role as good guardian, puts a halt to their playing.

"The other girl goes away while she, quiet and serene, joins, as if by right, the barefooted children, tickets in hand, waiting well-behaved for their turn to penetrate the cosmos. She doesn't ask nor does she look at him. She lightly bobs her head to the music playing in the park. Then she grows still, the red mask raised like a crown on top of her head. Slowly, she calls to him with a silent whistle, her gleaming, pointed tongue parts her lips, pauses at the corner of her mouth, and caressingly licks off the remains of the lipstick, passing, forcing, urging, sucking the carmine-colored flecks into her own juices.

"The lunar time has run out for my girls, who, emerging like newborns with the winds through the slit, come to me, their cheeks aglow.

The line advances orderly. The man will finally let her enter along with the other children who, facing forward, dive into the warm breath. But she'll be the last one, held back until the end, so he can put his arm into the opening, feigning assistance, and touch her among the pieces of plastic. Then he'll let her jump her twenty minutes in the softness of the bubble, her cries drowned out, without even looking through the window."

Now you leave the park, a mother who has fulfilled her duty, on her way home with her children by the hand. The little girl goes alone. The Saturday is over for her as well. She'll return on Sunday, to reap more where she has sown.

It's over, when I, the narrator, want it to be. I've withstood it silently up to now, swallowing your insults. But the end has come, author. And it's no longer a history, it's a short story. What is it that you had? Facts? But everyone has facts—they happen all the time, right in our face. What you don't have is a voice. I'm the one who has that. These may be your facts, as you saw them or made them up. But now it's my short story, a story made out of my words, that I'll finish anyway I want.

"It's late when I leave, taking my children by the hand. She remains. There in the distance, in the canoe that rises with chains stretched taut, her red figure bloodies the air."

Márcia Denser

Márcia Denser was born in São Paulo in 1949. In the late 1970s she became fiction editor for the woman's journal *Nova.* She has contributed to various newspapers and magazines in São Paulo and has published two collections of her own fiction: *Tango Fantasma* (1976) (Phantom Tango) and *O Animal dos Motéis* (1981) (The Animal of the Motels). She is perhaps best known for having edited two collections of erotic fiction by women: *Muito Prazer* (1980) (Very Pleased to Meet You) and *O Prazer é Todo Meu* (1984) (The Pleasure Is All Mine). With these anthologies, Denser called attention to women's widespread activity in a genre normally associated with men. She also introduced several new authors to the Brazilian reading public.

Although Denser is a writer of erotic literature, she disdains romantic ideas of sexual love and portrays the sex act as a quasi-mechanical function, bordering on the grotesque. There is a hard-boiled quality about her stories, which are typically narrated by women. A good example is the story published here, which originally appeared in *Muito Prazer.*

The Vampire of Whitehouse Lane

(1980)

If the Japanese film hadn't been showing, I wouldn't have had any interest in going out with that guy, a poet, who billed himself as *maudit* just so he could mooch caviar canapes off the upper crust. A sham guru, a cosmic charlatan, follower of an esoteric Oriental sect, a prick like so many others, he used everything to his own advantage. At least he wasn't stupid. He gave transcendental "massages" by appointment, or even without appointment, to ladies who suffered from constipation, lovers' dumpings, and other, more general pyorrheas. He wasn't at all stupid. Somewhat ugly, he must have been starved for real meat, but at least by passing himself off as a spiritual type, he got his crumbs. His conversation was incoherent, full of pedantries, but despite his syntax—a tangle of meanderings that obviously had no goal—one sensed the guy's eternal hunger. He had a kind of vague, pious anxiety, and his talk, which seemed to go round and round, might have found a target, if he hadn't had his sights on something else. While his mouth went on about the evolution of cosmic energy, his eyes (the windows of his soul) were fixed on some point just between my breasts; the talk of cosmic energy came and went, up and down, never getting lost, coiling itself up, then unfolding itself, arriving nowhere, since the true object of his sterile chitchat remained out of his reach. His tedious discourse could be hypnotizing: I felt like a petulant child who doesn't want to go to sleep, or an animal reluctant to fall into the trap.

That Japanese film was really good, a poetic monument, a profound study of human passions, etc. I could have talked about it *ad nauseam*, but the Poet merely exclaimed: "It was awesome! So awesome! How awesome!" He pitched the tone of his voice in such a way that the words exited his trachea and exploded with a dry, hoarse sound, like an oral fart, so that the word "awesome" seemed to contain, if not the meaning of the entire universe, at least of the entire film. This was at the *end* of the movie. *During* the movie he was all the time trying to grab my arm. A real drag. I asked myself: why did I go out with this guy? It was one of those tedious holidays when all my best friends, all the interesting guys, and all my available female acquaintances were traveling, leaving only the neurotics, the bores, and the vampires in the city. It seemed like a good reason. Then, again, I still didn't have a clear image of the Poet in my head, I merely had my *suspicions.* At the zero hour I was overtaken by a fucking panic to please—more concerned with the effect I could create than with him as object, properly speaking. I can end up fascinating Dracula himself, without realizing what I'm doing. Getting rid of the monster is another story altogether.

Like in a classic horror film, an icy wind passed over us as we left the theater. I confess I wasn't surprised when the Poet suggested we pass by his apartment to get his pullover. Poor little thing. I had tried to lure him to a wine and cheese place, but he didn't go for it. I didn't want to seem prudish. Or, who knows? At bottom, at bottom maybe I wanted to see just how much I could fascinate him—and I should know where my desire to fascinate takes me.

At the apartment (if it weren't for all the crappy political posters, the place would have been pretty nice. A bit too "artistico-indifferent," like so many others I've been in that belong to little poets, theater actors, fags. They're all the same. It must be the fairy godmother) I took full advantage of my ability to fascinate. The Poet supplied me with my writings, and I subjected him to an intermittent reading of the best parts of my work for some two hours. My stories are good, but read like that, on the carpet, drinking a good red wine, a fire in the hearth, air conditioning, Peruvian pillows and blankets, soft music, and a guy wanting to fuck me at my side, there's nobody who can resist them. Then *he* submitted me to more than two hours of *his* poems, unpublished no less. If they'd been good, it would have been worth all the effort—the pose of fascination, the feigned attention (I felt like bursting out laughing each time he cleared his throat and put on a circumspect air, as if preparing himself to read a speech, an obituary, a will—in any event, something very, very serious), the excess wine, that apartment, the arty Japanese film, the holidays, those deep craters that pitted his face, the slightly sweet oily smell that came out of them, his habit of speaking about himself in the third person, as if he were a ghost, the fact he was bald on one side and the little remaining hair formed a tuft behind his left ear. But they weren't. They really weren't. Hollow, vague ravings, they were like disconnected concrete poetry full of heavy-handed reticences. In every poem, and given equal emphasis, were entrails and blood, cosmos and eternity, and all the conventional poetic sounds. When anything started getting hot, he'd always throw in words like God, Space, Eternity, Death, forgetting all about prepositions and making everything deliriously obscure, as if he alone possessed the key or code for its deciphering. To novices, young girls and the *nouveau riche*, the stuff seems best when it's least understood. Pretty words are the same as pretty ideas. It's Gongoric, it's elementary. The Poet understood this principle well and applied it to exhaustion. *Mine,* in particular. Actually, some of his poems were pretty good, but it was as if the guy had a padlock on his brain. He was a prisoner. He didn't take himself on. Whenever he started putting his hand into shit, there he was with his antiseptic gods and demons to take away sins. His, at least, that is if he thought he had any. Being ugly was one of them. He kept his sense of perspective by defining himself as "pedantic and sophisticated." That way, he could feel he was inaccessible. Only the suckers were fooled.

During our conversation, the Poet mentioned a party. Intellectual friends, etc. I perked up, let's go, and I started to get up off the pillows, looking for my boots under the sofa, scattering blankets and casting a melancholy glance at the empty bottles, but he held me back. Not yet, he said, staring at me with tigerish, petroleum-colored eyes. He was like an aquarium—his glassy corneas exhibiting what was behind his dead, pimply face: diesel fuel.

The god of cowards, the little Snail god, must dwell in me; it was he who made me cringe, and I pulled back all my nerve endings, all my feelings of pleasure and pain, all my happiness, all my crying; and I transformed myself into an arid cliff on a wasteland taken over by bottleflies, shards of glass, garbage, scrub grass, mongrel dogs, and your kisses, Poet.

A far-off buzzing in my ears, an uncomfortable feeling in my back, and a dry mouth let me know I'd had enough. Little by little, I started to detach myself. A task which, incidentally, was quite embarrassing. I would have said hilarious, if it weren't for my active role. We were like actors in a Harold Lloyd movie. Me pulling this way, him pulling that way. A lucky slip on my part (we were standing up) decided the outcome. We went to the party.

The first thing that got my attention was that the owner of the house—a beautiful fellow, by the way—had two silk ribbons attached to his shirt sleeve, whose colors were those of the Brazilian flag. Just like the boys of the TFP, or the Hitler youth, or the young followers of Mussolini. It was like an unction, the mark of distinction of the high-born, the well-endowed, the very rich, the cream, the perfection. As for the rest of you, begone! Long live Nietzche and the Fourth Reich, General Pinochet, Idi Amin, Pol Pot, Gengis Khan, and the Revolution of '64. I tugged at his sleeve: what's that? He smiled with his freshwater blue eyes. Isn't it a beautiful country? Yes. I looked at the table: French wines, Swiss cheese, Hungarian tableware, Austrian lace trimmings, Cuban cigars, Russian vodka, American cigarettes. An extremely beautiful country. What's beautiful is you, I thought cynically, coveting the fascist youth's good looks and his little playthings, among them a pretty blond psychologist wife, who got her degree at afternoon school, and whose height and weight, according to the magazine *Claudia,* were ideal, and who was extremely worried about her duties as hostess. (All evening she neurotically repeated that her "forecast had failed" with regard to the cheese with nuts that was gone before two in the morning.) And how about the intellectuals? The "party" consisted of exactly ten people. Besides the hosts and me and the Poet/Prophet, there was an enormous, Cro-Magnon type, a general's son with the curious name Ciro, who had a black belt in karate. He was introduced to me as a marvelous but disillusioned painter (these people must be positively blind) and an active cocaine addict. Accompanying him was a girl, half-Dame aux Camélias and half-Stepmother of Snow White. She had deep blue circles under her eyes and coarse black hair, its oiliness accentuating her pale, lunar, almost transparently bony face. She was wearing a transparent white shirt (her breasts weren't at all transparent) without a bra, and she kept calling everyone's attention to her feet, which were injured by ballet slippers. The city is filled with little ballet and embroidery classes frequented by young people who have reached the age of marriage and want to keep in shape. Their highnesses give little parties, fueled by wine, coke, and bad dispositions, with their boyfriends, to whom they are capable of attaching themselves for all eternity in exchange for a last name hitched to their ass and an apartment in the Gardens: the men have their anxieties, the women, their interests, and so it goes. Other guests included Roger, the official intellectual, friend of the test-tube Poet. A skinny little guy, insignificant (that word is enormous!), now erased from my memory, he was with an employee of the American government in Brazil, a girl from California with a Puerto Rican face. She must have hated that tropical face with its dark skin, because her black hair was close-cropped as if she were doing penance. Cowering deep in her physiognomy, her dark eyes made her look like a frightened bat. What could she do? Her mother had wet her back crossing the Rio Grande. Roger, the colonized, gave all his attention to this product of Uncle Sam—but I imagine for him anything would have served, a can of Campbell's soup, for example. Any product of civilization, the superior culture, etc. He would never confess his reasons. He didn't see her as a frightened girl in a strange country—of course not, just like I didn't perceive the repugnant features of my guru-poet. I denied what my nose, my eyes, my mouth told me, and stomached him in the name of some idiotic vanity. Also present was a pair of bucktoothed cousins, who were engaged to one another and left early. I'll bet they went home to watch television and grab one another on the couch.

The early morning slowly filtered into that Neoclassic apartment, which was filled with an energetic movement of wine bottles, rounds of coke, rank camembert, and idiotic conversations. Dawn was breaking, and those who remained included the owners of the place, Ciro, Snow White, the Poet, and me, and I was feeling completely omnipotent. A feeling probably shared by all, since the conversation revolved about extraterrestrial life. In the meantime, our host's blond Plaything was scraping the leftover powder off the behind of a girl on the cover of *Playboy* magazine with a little wooden ice cream spoon. An excellent hostess. Handsome Fascist asked the Poet:

"Klaus, you're a guy interested in these things, you know a fucking lot, you must have had revelations, haven't you?"

"Well," he began, "one could say that we" (he always used the plural form, alluding to an invisible complicity, perhaps with the gods) "have various contacts that are truly inexplicable. For example, I'd say that when Dorinha died. . . ."

"Dorinha didn't die," thundered Ciro, his eyes hypnotized by a slicing knife.

"Maybe yes, maybe no," Klaus mysteriously condescended. "Many of us have already come to. . . ."

"Nonsense, there's nothing," I cut in. "I was up there and saw: they're all dead." And turning to my host: "How about a little passage from your favorite author, handsome. . . ."

"What?" Handsome Fascist opened his blue eyes wide.

"She's rambling," Poet shot me a sidelong glance. "But as I was saying, Dorinha. . . ."

"Now I see," I interrupted again. Suddenly, Ciro and Snow White looked very strange to me: he was enormous, truculent; she, on the other hand, was fragile and a little bit zany. . . .

"You two aren't really together, are you?" I said, smiling at the two of them as if blessing them. Disoriented, Klaus showed his teeth and excused his guest.

"Terrible, terrible," panted Snow White.

"Thinking about it, I believe the girl is right." Ciro never moved his eyes from the knife.

"So how is it that you two manage to fu—." A violent jab under the table from the Guru made me swallow the rest of the sentence.

After that, I plunged deeper and deeper into an acidic, hazy babble. Sentences followed one another from here to there, and I accompanied them; they were like little balls in a ping pong game, like little balls that are nothing but little white balls.

I got up and went to the window: that's it, I thought, stifle the hangover, stuff it in your ashy, bitter morning mouth like in a basket of dirty clothes. This is the price you pay for drugs you consume during the early morning hours, drugs that have a secret way of drowning the nausea, the vomit, the acidity of that dark wine you injected into your veins the night before. Then, when dawn breaks, you flush the toilet, having felt just one jolt; then your stomach applies the breaks and groans at the top of a building in Pacaembu. And that was almost all. Almost because I still hadn't finished. . . . / . . . Because the void, after the flushing, is unbearable. The toilet is empty and you're afraid to use it again and infect the world. The nausea that takes hold banishes all reason, intimidates words, and what remained of that early morning was a wrinkled taste of bromo-seltzer, the pearl gray effervescence of an antacid before my eyes, and a secret, corrupt sadness, knowing I was limp, bendable, and once more returning to do things I didn't want, need, or desire to do, but the alcohol and drugs took me there; it was a kind of death included in the buffet service. And with each episode, I died, and I died and I died again, and I came back to assassinate myself, because telling this story is just like attacking the same woman for years, violently, from behind, as though she were a virgin. The tap on the shoulder, the early morning breath on my back: Klaus. They had darkened the room. Silently, he helped me put on my jacket and, like an older, smaller brother, he took me far away from those dangers. In this case, to his apartment.

I remember breakfast on a table with a plastic tablecloth and an enormous piece of farmer's cheese. I was very fucked up and thought the cheese was extremely funny; there was no way I could show up at home in that state. Klaus looked crushed under the weight of compensation. He had the battered face of a Western villain after the final brawl, something between Jack Palance and John Carradine, only worse. A face pitted by resentment and smallpox, and he gets to sleep with the little girl, just like that. It was too much. He won't get it up, I thought.

It was sunny, but cold and damp; Poet, very solicitous, joined together the two twin beds and covered them with blankets as I got undressed. Having no out, I obediently fulfilled a ritual; like a daughter of Mary, a priestess of Astarte, or a little altar boy fed and secretly fucked by the priest, I merely obeyed. I remained face down, closed my eyes, and thought: pure pleasure, pure pleasure. I couldn't see his face now, it would have been unbearable, inconceivable, and I think he was grateful to me. Even so, he couldn't get it up. He was submerged in drugs and alcohol, an excited living sore that pulsated, groaned, and ground its teeth, a poor somnambulant animal imagining himself a human being of flesh, bones, and feces, vanishing between my buttocks in torturous, inefficient moves. Since he couldn't get it up, the animal deposited himself next to my body like a piece of cold meat. Let's wrap this up, I thought. I felt tired, nauseated, sour. The excitement stretched out like a weak string that wouldn't break. I saw midmorning, the color of magnesia, through the window and said: enough, let's go to sleep. He collapsed like a little campaign tent, as if the whole time he had been waiting for the order to release him from standing at attention. Seconds later he was snoring, eloquently. I fell asleep thinking about what I'd gotten myself into. His bachelor apartment on Whitehouse Lane was like a tomb with people sleeping as the sun came up. The only thing missing was a silver stake, but for some crazy reason I didn't want to go home and I didn't want to stay there. Sleep put me in the right place. I was either dreaming about a Spanish gardener or scissors, I don't know which, when I awoke feeling something warm and alert moving between my thighs. I jumped out of the bed as if jet-propelled: flee, I thought, flee, run, vomit, get dressed. I picked up my clothes that were strewn about the bedroom. As I drew on my stockings, I saw out of the corner of my eye Klaus's astonished, pitted face, which looked like a piece of carbonized tree bark against the white sands of the sheets. With a stupid catfish look, the look of a human fossil, his half-opened mouth didn't dare protest or make a sound. To any word of mine would have come the reply of a hermit crab in the voice of a stifled pharisee, and I didn't want to make anything clear. The whole scene already seemed sufficiently ridiculous, like a sinister porn show: him, with a hard dick under the covers and the face of an idiot, watching a girl dressing in dizzy desperation, as if she were being pursued by Jack the Ripper. Throwing on my jacket, I darted out of the bedroom. A very old maid covered with varicose veins opened the front door for me. I raced down the steps. I didn't even think about being on the 15th floor. Gasping, I finally reached the street. Shit, I was free. I laughed to myself: it had been quite funny. Staggering and happy, I laughed for two blocks. People turned around, startled. The perfume of freshly baked buns drew me to a bakery filled with students and little housemaids. Chewing an enormous ham sandwich, I asked the guy behind the counter for the telephone directory. I covered each page with fresh bread crumbs as I searched for Handsome Fascist's number. I don't know why, but I needed to salvage the night. Hello, a sleepy little voice moaned on the other end. I recognized Little Plaything. Listen, princess, I said, tell your husband that I want to make a switch (it was necessary to go the heart of matters, none of these idiotic formalities used with families and dogs: shock treatment). What? the voice said, suddenly aroused from sleep. Then another voice, a man's, machine-gunned something in a muffled tone. With a dry and urgent voice, he spoke in little blows as if he were hammering out orders. Little Plaything confusedly explained something about Klaus's girlfriend and a switch. She was as objective as a schoolgirl. What's going on? Handsome Fascist had grabbed the receiver. He seemed very irritated. I explained the best I could. Finally, I invited him to have breakfast with me, there, at the Fleur de Lys Bakery, which was on. . . . I asked him to hold the line while I went to see the name of the street. When I picked up the phone again, the dial tone responded melancholically to my hellos. Handsome Fascist didn't even have a sense of humor. Too bad, I murmured, he's so cute. The bread was all gone; as I waited for my change I caught a glimpse of my face reflected in the scales on the counter. Blotched with black mascara, the rouge darker on the left cheek, and bluish circles under my eyes. I looked just like Snow White. A bit of rubbing with my finger accentuated my pallor, but it helped. I wasn't scary enough to frighten children. As I went out, I decided to buy another sandwich to eat on the way. It had gotten warmer, and I tied my jacket—a pretty carmel-colored velvet jacket—around my waist; people continued staring at me. Munching the bread, I walked up the street, which was filled with green trees and laced with sun. I recalled a passage from Faulkner's *The Sound and the Fury.* Sweating and burping salami, I finally reached Avenida Paulista. In front of the Vogue House—which is no longer the Vogue House—I tried to catch a cab. No luck. I decided to keep on walking. It's four kilometers to Paraíso, but it's flat. I thought that was reasonable. I entered the Trianon Garden with its pure air, ecology, ducks, teals, chickens, and idle people. Ecology. I bought a small bag of popcorn. A kid about seventeen years old was throwing crumbs to the turkeys—I detest that ultrastupid air that birds have in general—and I asked him if it was worthwhile to throw popcorn. Of course, he said, and sliding his hand into my little bag, he withdrew some and threw it to the birds. He was a dream of a kid, a wood nymphet, with his hair bleached from the sun and the pool at the club and his smooth, brown chest and a little St. Genaro medal beneath his checked shirt. I asked him if he were Italian. My father is, he answered, smiling. He spoke with simplicity and delicacy. As if coming across a girl with a face blotched with makeup, with a carmel velvet jacket tied around her hips and with a half-eaten piece of bread in one hand and a bag of popcorn in the other at eleven o'clock Sunday morning were the most natural thing in the world. He was morning itself: young, fresh, handsome, pure. I felt awful. I wanted to wash my face, take a bath, invite him to walk around Ibirapuera with me, which is the largest park I know of, but don't have any idea where it is. Better to keep on walking. He watched me as I pleasantly moved away, and he didn't say anything. A haze of exhaustion descended over the garden. I felt far away, my house was farther away, Klaus's apartment farther than that, in another world, another time. I settled down on a slimy stone bench and went to sleep. I woke up a second later: someone was poking my back with a hard, pointed object. Not again, I thought. But it was only a broom, and the man must have been the park custodian. I vaguely noticed that it'd grown dark.

"They took your purse and jacket, lady, better tell the police," he spoke with a voice that was monotone and nasal, and he repeated himself over and over about the robbery and the police.

"Why the broom?" I murmured idiotically, still muddled from sleep. My body hurt. "My jacket and purse?"

"You're not well, huh? If you don't watch out, people'll grab whatever you got. I think it's good you report it to. . . ."

"I'm going, I'm going." How to make him shut up? I stretched my legs. My velvet slacks and silk shirt were still intact. Good, I thought, he's gone away. This is the result of poetic vampirism. Jude the Obscure would be in his little apartment now, listening to Beethoven and eating lamb stew with vegetables prepared by Lady Varicose Veins, his waitress. With his battered, disarranged face munching dessert and his hard, bruising eyes, the animal would fall asleep peacefully, surrounded by his communist pamphlets and smoking mentholated cigarettes. It was too much. I vomited spasmodically in a bed of hydrangea. I decided to go home. They'd pay the cab fare there. Then I remembered: they were all traveling. All my friends, all the guys, my girlfriends, etc. I was without a purse, keys, I was cold, hungry, and needed a bath. In the cab, sighing, I gave Klaus's address.

Lya Luft

I

A major theme in all of Lya Luft's novels is social and sexual identity—a theme derived in part from her own experiences as a child growing up in the large German immigrant community in Rio Grande do Sul, where she was born in 1938. The gothic quality some critics have referred to in describing Luft's novels has to do with the atmosphere of sexual fear and uncertainty surrounding her protagonists, whose dramas unfold in the claustrophobic space of the patriarchal home. One of her most unusual works in this vein is *Exílio* (1987) (Exile), a bizarre tale about a woman who leaves her home and moves into a place known as the "Red House." The occupants of this place include an elderly woman, a lesbian couple, and an imaginary playmate from the protagonist's childhood, who returns as a cantankerous dwarf.

Luft's early works, *As Parceiras* (1980) (The Partners) and *A Asa Esquerda do Anjo* (1981) (The Left Wing of the Angel), are particularly effective in portraying the confusion of women brought up speaking German in the home and obeying the German community's strictly moral, patriarchal codes. Although these women are born in Brazil, they are taught early on to see "Brazilians" as "others"; the confusion that inevitably inflicts them is rooted in a hothouse atmosphere of nationalism and puritanism.

From *The Left Wing of the Angel*

(1981)

(The glass of milk on the bedside table. Immaculate sheets on the brass bed where I've always slept alone.

This is the night. It's been three days since they buried Leo, whom I loved but denied my body. What was the most beautiful tale in my childhood storybook called? The Snow Queen.

My father wasting away in his room at the other end of the hall. Footsteps on the stairs: I pretend not to hear them, we never talk about them during the day. My mother sighs, stopping briefly on the landing where the stairs curve.

Now I need to concentrate on this ritual: I'll be relieved and clean after the horrendous birth. Lying down on this white bed and letting my body expel its violator. For a long time it was forgotten. Was it hibernating? I thought it had died, or that it wasn't anything more than one of those fears that used to torment me—I was the most peculiar child in the Wolf family. A family so important that our dead were placed in the Jazigo, a pink stone mausoleum with purple stained-glass windows.

But my tenant revived. Monstrous phoenix that appears in the night, filling my stomach, crawling up to my throat as if someone outside my lips were calling: come, come, come. That's just how I imagined Mr. Max for many years, behind the crack in that door, calling to something or someone that never came.

No one calls to me. No one desires me any longer, now that Leo is dead. I'm alone, calm and strong. I need that strength.

I can hardly believe that my life depends on that glass of milk. A mere glass of white liquid, so innocent compared to what is about to take place.

Would the Snow Queen expose her private parts to give birth or be violated?

No one will know anything. My father nowadays pays little attention to things; when we talk, he sometimes gets distracted and calls me Maria. But I'm Guísela, and I don't have the sweetness or joy of life of my mother who died, leaving this house so silent.

She fell face down on the paving stones, smeared with the yolks of eggs she was carrying in her apron, which was folded like a nest. Her gray hair stained gold, like the tresses of my cousin Anemarie, whom I loved.

But all that was long ago. I'm sitting on the edge of the bed, and when I lie down the old structure creaks as if indecent movements were being made on top of it. My stomach jerks inward.

I take off my shoes that fall to the floor with a hollow sound. Giant toads on the stones. Stomachs exploding in the cemetery. The bronze Angel that watches over our Jazigo points the difficult way to heaven, and pretends not to hear anything.

I breathe deeply. The creature writhes inside me. I'll wait a little longer—to summon up courage. This time neither flight nor evasions will do any good. Nor dreams.

In the meantime, I remember.)

I'm seven or eight years old. At least three times a week I walk along this street to visit my grandmother and study piano in her music room. A ritual to be observed, like so many in an organized family: everything in the Wolf family is well organized to the beat of the curt voice of its matriarch, my grandmother. It's just that I feel myself off the beat, with my skinny body and my large ears that persist in peeking out from my hair, which they make me wear very short so that "it looks fuller."

I'm also left-handed—something they never got me to correct.

So three times a week, besides the usual Sunday visit, when my grandmother gets the whole family together for lunch and late-afternoon coffee, I walk along this street, in front of this little house with a door and window. At its side is a clothing shop window. Whenever we get close, I ask my mother to stop, shall we look at the clothes? She finds me amusing, so small and already interested in the latest styles!

But what I see, what I feel, in a mixture of fascination and horror, is the opening in the door at the side.

I want and I don't want to see Mr. Max. He's at his post, half-hidden by the door, and behind him, I imagine, more than actually see, a darkened hallway from which rancid and musty odors emerge. It's as if Mr. Max were eternally stationed there, waiting for someone who perhaps will never come.

Seeing that I notice him, he squirms a bit and greets my mother: "Good afternoon, Frau Wolf."

That voice: Mr. Max has a woman's voice even though he's a man. A woman's voice, or a little girl's. I don't know whether it's naughty or vulnerable. Sometimes I get up my courage and stare at him, before my mother pulls me by the hand, we have to get going; your grandmother doesn't like to wait.

But I saw Mr. Max: pointed nose, watery eyes that peer instead of looking straight at people. His skinny body with its protruding stomach gives me the impression of sin and impudence.

It's Mr. Max that I'm afraid of, or of what he waits for there at the door that he never seems to leave, exposed and humiliated, perhaps calling out when no one passes by in the street: come, come, come?

It didn't do much good to ask the grown-ups. Mr. Max was one of a number of things that weren't "for children." The adult world was the birthplace of my fears: the questions that hovered in the air, lowering themselves at night to nestle feverishly in my fantasy.

My mother would pull me by the hand, we were going to be late, and the other Frau Wolf would not tolerate stragglers. She herself supervised my piano lessons, she must be waiting at the top of the stairs, her hand merely resting on the cane she used ever since she fell some years back. A cameo brooch, one day she had said that the brooch would be mine after her death. At times I was ashamed of myself for wanting the old woman to die, so that the coveted object could at last be mine: the woman in profile, flowers braided through her hair, everything tiny and perfect, her nose, eyelashes. A woman without a name, but whom I secretly called Anemarie.

The name of my cousin, of whom I would never be the equal. Anemarie, the family's favorite, with her golden hair cascading to her hips when undone. The beloved granddaughter of Frau Wolf studied far away, at a boarding school, and I rarely saw her. But when she came home, life in our grandmother's house was transfigured, and I believed the world could be beautiful.

I can still see Anemarie today, playing her cello in the music room, head slightly bowed, as if she were thinking intently or as if her hairdo weighed too much.

I was overcome with admiration and love, conscious of how much all that was removed from me.

I would never play the piano like Anemarie played her cello. For me, studies and scales were a torment, accompanied by tiny slaps from Frau Wolf's bony hands if my fingers got twisted up, and the touch of her cane between my shoulder blades when I slouched too much. My grandmother, "the true Frau Wolf" as she liked to say, died at ninety years of age, and until the very end, she sat erect on the edge of her chair.

She didn't permit any weaknesses, and she despised anything strange or foreign. I think that perhaps without knowing it, she also despised me because I was ugly and awkward, and because with me—the child of a mother of non-German descent—the blood of the Wolf Family was no longer "pure."

Something in me was amiss, but I didn't know what. Perhaps there were many things. I felt I was like Mr. Max, wrong voice or wrong hand, begging that they love me, come, come, come—the voice behind the opening.

But the openings between others and myself were always insufficient, and all that came from the other side were demands difficult to satisfy.

Oh, the world of freedom, where grown-ups did what only they understood well, while I remained in my room, in bed, listening from afar to the sound of their festivities.

Oh, the allusions, fragments of phrases, generating ghosts that at night would spy from the folds of the curtains in my room, their pupils fixed upon me, calling with a voice from the abyss—come, come, come!

(This afternoon I passed by the building that they erected where the house of my grandmother once stood. I remembered the basement and the mysterious little door. I was fascinated by the basement, an old place with a dome-shaped ceiling, smelling of mildew. Spider webs, broken furniture, piles of bottles, a rocking chair with a hole in the seat that had belonged to my grandfather, riding boots, tarnished copper pans.

In a corner, the little door: so low that only a child or a dwarf could pass through it. No one seemed to know what its purpose was; no one was interested in it; no one had the key. Whenever I insisted a lot, they said I was nosy, what a habit this child has of imagining mysteries everywhere!

I never discovered what was behind the little door. Perhaps it still exists beneath the building. My childhood fantasy was imagining someone imprisoned there inside, shouting without being heard. Or some monstrous being, twisted up in the dust, something without any features.

The house disappeared; no one knows about the basement, with its dome-shaped ceiling and the tiny secret room made for a child or a dwarf. But Anemarie still hovers around there in the memory of the rooms and corridors. Anemarie, her music, her secret. Today she is watched over for eternity by the peacemaking Angel of indeterminate sex.

I get up from the bed and go to the bathroom. The bodily functions continue. So many people I loved are dead; my father wastes away in his room, Leo has been buried. I didn't even manage to cry when they put him in the ground. It's been a long time since I've been to the cemetery: the strange thing is that there's only one slot left in those walls, as if my family were waiting for my father in order to close the cycle.

I'll remain outside.

I return and lie down once again. The cream in the milk begins to rise to the top of the glass. My tenant has quieted down for the moment, before the great attack.

No sound is heard except the ticking of my little clock and those footsteps lost on the stairs.

My mother, perhaps, pausing briefly to breathe where the staircase makes a turn. But I'm not afraid; all the horror now is concentrated in my own body.)

Long ago I once suffered from this dread: feeling myself invaded by some terrible, disgusting thing that made me wake up screaming, disturbing the entire house. The doctor diagnosed it as merely an oversensitive nature and prescribed rest, vitamins, long walks, and sports. But I hated sports. My cousins played tennis, they swam, their skin red and ugly with blisters and freckles, so different from the beautiful golden tone that my mother acquired when she went outside in the sunshine.

Then, because of my health, my parents took me to the beach in the summertime, and that became a habit for the whole family. They rented two large houses. Since there weren't any children my age and Anemarie was already an adolescent, I entertained myself alone.

One of the pleasures of those summer vacations was playing in the sand. For a few moments they forgot about me, and I didn't need to sit up straight, shut my mouth, suck in my tummy, or use just my right hand—the "pretty hand."

I'm sitting in the sand, piling up a wet castle between my thighs. Aunt Helga (Anemarie's mother) and my mother are talking a little ways away, and my grandmother is taking a walk up ahead with Anemarie, the two of them protected by large straw hats.

I feel a primitive, animal pleasure as I stir around that which is prohibited—they always kept me from picking up dirty things, earth, sand, grass, insects.

Totally absorbed, opening little windows in my castle with the aid of a small stick, I suddenly feel someone come up behind me. A cold shadow covers me, a hand firmly grabs my shoulder, and my grandmother says, in a tone that also reprehends my mother and Aunt Helga:

"But what lack of hygiene! Marie, you know that a child, principally *a girl*, cannot sit like that in the sand. Sand is filled with little worms that can't even be seen! Guísela, go wash yourself off, quickly, quickly! I'll bet you're already filled with nasty little vermin!"

My grandmother speaks in German, as always, her guttural words crashing down upon my joy, toppling my castle, and destroying the brief happy moment.

I get up, trip, fall; I have difficulty freeing myself of the weight of the wet sand clinging to my legs. I begin to scream in horror, I feel I'm being invaded by thousands of filthy worms that wriggle, I'm irremediably unclean.

They carry me inside. My mother washes me carefully, consoles me, but I feel myself violated. At night, my body itches, I feel strange sensations in my privates, in my stomach, I'm contaminated.

For many days I'm nervous, my mother tries to calm me, but the doubt wounds deep and remains: am I really clean?

Perhaps the seed took root on that occasion. Or was it some time after, when I heard a maid in the kitchen telling about her friend who was suffering from a strange malady: she was inhabited by an enormous worm that was devouring her from within, and at night it would crawl up into her throat, wanting to leave in search of more food.

They had taught the poor woman a way of extracting the monster from her body for good.

One night, in utter despair, she followed the instructions. Soon, a white being emerged in her throat, a thing without any features, and her husband couldn't contain himself: he put his hand in his wife's mouth, grabbed the thing firmly and pulled in order to help her with the horrible birth. But he only got the tip of the creature, and the rest disappeared back inside her.

I went running so as not to hear the rest. In the hall, on the stairs, I still heard the cries of compassion in the kitchen. In my room, I threw myself on the bed and covered my head with the pillow. I wanted to forget, but I already knew I never would.

During the days I distract myself; at night, however, that torment grips me with its claws, in comparison with it, my old ghosts are innocent playthings. I have the animal within me. My stomach swells and convulses. The doctor doesn't find anything; my family is already accustomed to my "nervous attacks." I'm ashamed to tell the true story, who knows what kind of tests the doctor would make me take? I've heard stories about horrible examinations.

In the meanwhile, the one that inhabits me is there: at night, when I'm in anguish, it coils itself up in my belly, and climbs up my esophagus, leaving my throat raw from the rubbing of its coarse skin.

I awake the following morning with my jaw so rigid that my face muscles ache the entire day.

With the passing of the years, the suffering eased, and I came to feel I was cured. I came to laugh at those crazy ideas I had had as a child.

Could the creature really have existed then? Or is it only now, after Leo's death—when he smashed his car into the wall in the middle of the night, putting an end to the solitude I left him in—that that thing began to live in me?

I loved Leo: but how could I expose myself? Too much fear. As a child, I liked to imagine the Snow Queen, from my favorite story, in a pure and peaceful world where every kind of noise and worry was stifled by the whiteness.

(It's good to be lying down here, alone. It would be good to sleep, without dreams, if it weren't for that which I still have to do tonight without fail, because my body can no longer contain its inhabitant. That sick, long, hairy thing, which stretches and contracts and then lunges again, making me nauseated, a body where perhaps head and tail are indistinguishable, turning over and over in the shelter of my entrails. Emanations recalling those childhood ones from the hallway behind Mr. Max's door.

I want to be free: to be pure like Anemarie, who died and in my memory lives on immaculate.

I'll never marry. I'll spend the rest of my life taking care of my father, making sure that the house is always clean, a never-ending elaboration of a useless trousseau.

Without noticing, I finally turned into a good woman of the house. Though my needles still rust, my embroideries come out almost perfect; I manage to make a multilayered cake almost as good as Aunt Martha's, and I think that my grandmother would be proud of me today.

I also take pride in my posture, just as she taught me: I don't collapse into chairs anymore; I prefer to sit on the edge of the seat with my back erect.

Our house became much too big, we could have sold it, letting them construct in its place a modern building like the one they raised over the dome-ceiling basement and the tiny secret door of my grandmother's house. Where the voice of the bronze Angel still moans, over the paving stones of the garden and the stone bench where one day I longed to kiss Anemarie.

But my father and I stayed in this house. Perhaps if we were to move to another place, the consoling nocturnal presences wouldn't come with us. And our solitude would be unbearable.

I turn in the bed and it makes that indecent creaking. I draw my knees up, that way I can support better the mass of the thing inside me.

Today you are going to leave, cursed thing. It will be a birth in which I will show neither shame nor humiliation because no one will be here, no one will see me opened wide and panting like the women in the movies who fling their legs apart.

Anemarie is dead: her tresses choke the black coffin where they put her when she died, because she was no longer a virgin. I, yes, could have had a maiden's casket, if it weren't so ridiculous. An old maid in a white box.

The Snow Queen.

In the cemetery—this room?—the gentle sound of stomachs exploding.

And Anemarie?)

What happened with Anemarie proved that "family" was merely a word, a series of postures, perhaps above all an affliction. For this mass with so many heads, eyes, mouths, and names, predestined to be slowly joined together in the Jazigo, shattered into tiny little bits: from that moment on we were shadows set apart, elusive, suspicious of one another: did this one know? did that one guess? had someone else been an accessory to the unimaginable plot, the treason?

For Anemarie had betrayed the Wolf family.

Before, it was as if the idealized, almost unreal cello player were our identity. Once the statue had collapsed, we dispersed. Only the Angel's shadow still preserved us, made it possible for us to pretend, in a convincing way, that we were a stable and clean family.

Anemarie and Uncle Stefan fled one night, leaving my grandmother a letter that she never showed to us.

In the morning, she called a meeting, no one knew what it was about, and we all gathered together quickly. My cousin and Aunt Martha were still not there. Anemarie must have been taking care of her ailing mother upstairs, and Aunt Martha probably spared herself by hanging on to the end of a frying pan. The absence of my Uncle Stefan, Aunt Martha's second and younger husband, was not particularly noted.

Frau Wolf appeared at the top of the stairs: behold, we, your audience, are here, I thought. I automatically straightened my shoulders into the correct position.

Frau Wolf sat down on her chair. On the very edge of the seat. We all looked at her anxiously. With a steady voice, she announced that, to the shame of the entire family, Uncle Stefan and Anemarie had run off together. Without a doubt we would never see them again. We should forget that they had ever existed. And we were never ever to speak of the two in her presence.

She asked that we face with raised heads the gossip that certainly would spread about town. Finally people had a reason to laugh at us. With time, however, that would pass.

Without waiting for our reaction, she got up and climbed the stairs once again. However, she didn't manage to conceal the fact that she was supporting herself with the cane.

The confusion was enormous. We were stunned, incredulous. My cousins, some already married, talked among themselves or with their wives. Uncle Ernst, Anemarie's father, immediately left the room; my mother hugged me and started to cry.

My father ran up the stairs behind the old woman, his mother.

I broke loose from my mother and fled to the garden. I had known, I had guessed everything, it hadn't been an illusion: the bronze Angel protected the animal nature of the bodies. A world of marble and stained glass hiding decomposition.

Now I could never again walk through the house without hearing those two, their brief and ardent encounters in the space on the stairwell, their desperate whisperings: what are we going to do? what are we going to do? Perhaps he always went up to her room, who would have noticed?

It was he Anemarie was embracing, it was he she was making love to when she inserted the cello between her open legs.

(I get up and go see my father once again. He doesn't need anything. He seems ready to fall asleep. I don't notice if there is someone seated at his side in the chair.

I go back to my room; no one needs me. I lock the door with a key. Walking around in my socks, my feet are icy like those of the Snow Queen.

I'm not sure if I can withstand what I have to do, but my inhabitant is turning inside me so violently now that I'm suffering convulsions as if I were about to give birth to a child: a fruit.

I fear I'll vomit. That would ruin everything. And if it decides in its impatience to rush forth and leave? I need to act quickly, to make decisions coldly, as Frau Wolf would do.

But I don't know what position to assume. Hate needs to be greater than disgust, fear greater than the feeling of being ridiculous. The best thing for me is to lie face down. I poured the milk into the ash tray. But it's uncomfortable on the bed. I fear I'll spill the milk and ruin everything; perhaps I'll fall off the bed while in agony. And what if there's blood?

Thus, I, who was always timid and horrified by anything out of the ordinary, stretch out, belly down on the floor, and because I'm so thin, the floorboards dig into my bones.

Uncle Ernst used to tease Aunt Helga, in one of his indecent jokes, asking her to put on some weight "to pad her bones—otherwise, it's like I'm mounting a wooden horse." Aunt Helga denied everything, she disavowed everything with her eternally shaking head.

The milk is on the floor in front of me. I feel I'm going mad; a creature on the ground opening its mouth. My inhabitant makes a forceful movement, it must have smelled the bait, the milk says: come, come, come.

Come, you evil thing, I call out silently. And then I begin to suffer prolonged convulsions as if in childbirth, I saw women twisting and panting just like this in the movies, and it comes. Without eyes. Without a nose. Without an identity, it drags itself along my stomach, it's going to reach my esophagus, I can't stand it. I close my mouth and swallow several times, it wants to climb up against my movements, finally it coils itself in my stomach. How it hurts.

I can't take this horror. I get up with some difficulty, I'm heavy, if I lower my eyes I'll see my stomach swollen, as if I were pregnant. My mouth is filled with saliva, with disgust. My grandmother spat on Anemarie's coffin. How can I keep my mouth open?

With my left hand I grab the toothbrush on the sink in the corner of my room. Too long. Angrily, I break off the bristled top, and lying down once more on the floor, I prop the handle in between my jawbones and I taste blood flowing as it pierces my skin.

I'm opened wide. It's a birth, it's coming again, its rough skin scratching my mucous membranes, it manages the curves, it's coming!

I breathe with difficulty, great jerks, a flood of tears, grotesque and desperate, I'm giving birth. I think about Anemarie, it's good you can't see me like this, Anemarie, my angel.

My memory continues active, with my breath rattling in my throat, I remember Leo is dead and that since his death this thing I'm expelling returned to life inside of me.)

* * *

My mother sighs in the hallway. Anemarie plays, her body one with the cello from which bursts forth the voice of the Angel. From the embraces of Uncle Stefan, death burst forth.

Love is death?

Slowly, my inhabitant turns around, the milk is finished, but it is still famished; it turns toward me, the raised part of its body swaying heavily. It turns even more, I know it's going to confront me. My identity—what is my identity?

It's going to stare at me, without eyes, without a nose, without any features. Without an identity like me—what's my name? Where is my place? How should one love? Better snow or fire?

A sigh, a moan passes through the house. Whispers that merge and groan. My inhabitant and I are the only creature alive in this room.

(In the cemetery, at the entrance to the Jazigo, the crack in the left wing of the Angel splits a little more.)

Sônia Coutinho

Born in Bahia in 1939, Sônia Coutinho lives in Rio de Janeiro, where she works as a journalist and translator. Her first stories appeared in *Reunião* (Reunion) (1961) along with those of three other authors. Since that time, she has published several volumes, including the novel *O Jogo de Ifá* (1980) (The Game of Ifá), which draws from her knowledge of Afro-Brazilian culture.

Most of Coutinho's stories, like those in her collection *O Último Verão de Copacabana* (1985) (The Last Copacabana Summer), focus on middle-class women living in Rio and their unhappy relationships with men. In the story from that volume translated here, Coutinho writes a kind of deconstructive fiction, exploring the subtle, interchangeable relations among an authorial persona, a fictional character, a "real" historical subject, and a consumer image of a Hollywood star.

Every Lana Turner Has Her Johnny Stompanato

(1985)

The material for this story: two women. Capable, nonetheless, of multiplying themselves infinitely. Lana Turner and a second one, presented without a name, without a face, or a biography—except for fragmentary data and vague insinuations. Perhaps not even a woman but a mirror, albeit dingy. Or a ventriloquist, who only speaks through the image of the actress, her doll. But don't be misled: the only true character, the point of reference that enables one to weave the disparate threads of this plot into a tapestry, the white screen that displays the endless unfolding of the dream and, therefore, of the reality, that character is me. In other words, Lana Turner.

(Lana, one of the great stars of the classic Hollywood system; without any precursor, an explosive figure in American society of the period, with the role or power of a man. Lana beyond the actual Lana, the symbol, the myth that was created around her: the goddess or she-devil, the vamp with her "it." What was presented of Lana for the consumption of thousands of eager people—to idolize, destroy, or devour—was inside information about a "glamorous life"; "happiness" and "pain" in a grand style.)

Like Madame Bovary for Flaubert, Lana Turner *c'est moi*. That's what the second woman also thought, the other one, the mirror. (Is her name Melissa? Or is it possibly Teresa? Who knows, Joaquina? Or Dorotéia?) Seated on the tiny patio of her apartment, she was leafing through a magazine when she came across, with a sudden shock of recognition and a strange, complicitous understanding (she, independent, mythified, distorted), in a nostalgic report about the great stars of the past, a not very old picture of Lana.

Yes, there was the deeply tanned skin of the Beverly Hills swimming pools—or the beaches of the Zona Sul—the long, red fingernails, the platinum blond hair, and, on her beautiful face, traces of passing time.

But above all, Lana's smile, her actress's smile, almost a frown. A smile combining irony and pain, defiance, strength, and a pathetic impotence; the heroic smile of a survivor. Of a creature willing, perhaps because there was no other way, to see the performance to the end: the show must go on. (What does human existence consist of, if not small rituals, ceremonies and celebrations?)

On a misty Saturday afternoon, watching fraying clouds empty onto the tree-covered slopes of Corcovado, Melissa sees anew—I see anew—in a dizzying whirl of historic scenes, the similarities and differences between her and Lana Turner, beginning with the Anglo-Saxon Puritans' colonization of America and the arrival of exiled Portuguese with Moorish blood to Brazil.

Like a bridge between two hemispheres, mysteriously linking the California of the old gold rush to the Mineiro gold that the *inconfidentes* claimed, I smiled enigmatically at the magazine (and at life), at the face of Lana Turner (the face of Melissa, my own).

The magazine recalls the glorious and anguished trajectory of the actress, her various husbands, her active career (psychologist? publicity agent? reporter? actress indeed?) and her many trips, including some holidays spent in Hawaii in the company of a woman friend. More precisely, in Honolulu, on the beach at Waikiki, where she discovered she was pregnant by her second husband, the trumpet player Artie Shaw, after their separation. "Which resulted in an abortion and new misfortunes," adds the magazine article, summarizing the autobiography, *Lana: The Lady, the Legend, the Future.*

The reporter explains that in her first marriage to the lawyer Greg Bautzer, she didn't feel any pleasure losing her virginity. He quotes Lana: "I didn't have any idea how I should perform. The act itself hurt like hell and I must confess I didn't feel any kind of pleasure. But I liked having Greg close to me and 'belonging' to him."

It happened at the Toriba Hotel in Campos do Jordão, Melissa recalls. And she corrects the report: she didn't even begin to lose her virginity on that honeymoon, the two of them were so clumsy. She felt pain, she confirms: did she have a vaginal stricture? an overly resistent hymen? But she didn't talk about those things at that time, and then everything began straightening itself out, or destroying itself, in silence.

Lana, states the reporter, attained sexual maturity only when she was around forty years old, following an apprenticeship with about eighteen men—which, he adds, seems a modest number by today's standards. This conclusion, he explains, was drawn from inferences, since Lana never directly addressed the subject.

The article goes on to say that Lana's emotional difficulties probably resulted from a series of childhood traumas. "When she was ten years old, her father was killed in a dark alley." The actress's statement follows: "When I saw him in the coffin, I was horrified." Trauma, coffin, father, Melissa reads, feeling a chill. The words, even more than the chain of events, establish a strange connection between her and Lana Turner, like a code to be deciphered.

The impression grows stronger with the next paragraph—a transcription of Lana Turner's "psychological profile" kept by the studio: "Julia Jean Mildred Frances Turner, born February 8, 1920. Confused, unprotected. Insecure since childhood, when she went through periods of physical, mental, and moral oppression, for which she sought compensation as an adult. Her emotional life, a series of frustrated attempts to stabilize herself. She became an emotional burden to her daughter, Cheryl, who tried to give her support."

Confused. Unprotected. Although the years were different, the birthdays were the same. As if beneath the story of Lana Turner lay another one, which was imbedded and parallel—hers, mine. Could it be that Melissa is/I am going crazy? Can it be that in our paranoia we've chosen Lana Turner as an alter ego instead of the customary Napoleon Bonaparte?

Melissa (Erica?) runs to the bathroom, and with renewed confusion scrutinizes her face in the mirror. She, Lana Turner. Not exactly an actress, more like a trapeze artist or a dancer on a slack rope. I smiled at her in the mirror, a face without innocence, but upon which time had conferred a touch of cynical purity.

Where can I go, where will I go, Melissa asks herself, trembling. The years have passed like a cold wind. And, between husbands, trips, an active career, tragedies—oh, so many things have suddenly become definitive. Lost loves, adventures never experienced and, what's worse, no longer desired.

Returning to her lounge chair on the veranda, and sipping a whiskey, Melissa (Dora?) reads further on in the report a comforting comment by Lana: "I didn't have an easy life, but undoubtedly my life is far from boring. I feel a certain pride at having managed to get this far."

Which, according to the reporter, didn't prevent her from attempting suicide by cutting her wrists (Melissa turns up the palms of her hands and looks at the still rosy-colored scars.) Upon leaving the hospital, totally recuperated, "she looked like a virgin, dressed in white, smiling, the ineffable sunglasses helping to cover her face." The report adds: "One immediately saw she was a star. She had what they call star quality."

Then comes the "true version" of how Lana Turner was discovered. Contrary to what was reported at the time, the magazine says, it didn't happen in Schwab's, the luncheonette on Hollywood Boulevard that was frequented by girls who wanted to get parts in the movies. Lana herself explains: "It was in a place called the Top Hat Café—I think it's a gas station today. And I wasn't having any snack. I had just enough money for a Coca-Cola."

But she confirms that, as in the famous story, the fellow at her side asked the classic question: "Would you like to work in movies?" And she gave the classic response: "I don't know, I have to ask my mother."

Next, a stage name was selected. According to the report, the studio had a catalogue of names already prepared, and someone was reading them off. Suddenly, the actress herself suggested Lana: "I don't know where I got it from. But note that it's Lah-nah, I don't want to hear my name pronounced any other way." In 1937, she made *They Won't Forget* and, the following year, she joined MGM, where she became known as the "Sweater Girl."

Then a whirlwind of successes, roses and champagne. But the centerpiece of the report is the tragic episode with Johnny Stompanato, just as Lana was about to lose her ephemeral freshness, in those days when women were compared to flowers (when she'd win, as a prize, the hard mask of the photograph, the mask of a warrior who has survived, with marks on her face like glorious battle scars). One day, "a fellow calling himself John Steele telephoned the studio, courting Miss Turner."

She found him enchanting, says the reporter, and she ended up getting involved. "When I discovered his true identity," Lana commented, "it was already too late." Johnny Stompanato (or Renato Medeiros) was white as bread, clean as bread, with a purity that only a young Mafioso sought by the police could obtain.

(In bed, looking like a small white horse, the perfect body of a man about twenty-eight or twenty-nine years old, with white teeth, brown eyes tinged with green, but almost always dark, and somewhat taciturn. Deliciously serious, with a permanent sense of fulfilling his duty. He doesn't speak, except for an occasional word—he's indecipherable. But perhaps his enduring mystery is simply that of his own life and its absurdity.)

A complete, beautiful man like a small white horse running on the beach as it grows dark. He, whole and full of purity, as youth is pure; he naked, that whole, strong, large, and pure body; he on top of her, large and whole; he entering her, asking: Melissa, Lana, say something to me, while she just groaned and cried, groaned and cried, saying: love, love, love. Soon she's completely inundated with his liquid, which has the slightly vegetable smell of wet grass or palm.

This will do me forever, I won't need anything else, ever, she thought when he left, slamming the front door, a sound she heard from the bed. It was a misty morning beyond the glass doors of her apartment that opened onto a small veranda, and fraying clouds were emptying onto the densely tree-covered slopes of Corcovado. Later, she'd say when he telephoned: Darling, I went out dancing on air that morning. As if, at last, having reached eternity, she needed to die quickly that very moment.

The magazine claims that Lana began a "terrible psychological drama" as she "tried to free herself of the gangster," while he, "utilizing every artifice," refused to leave the scene.

According to the reporter, when she went to England to film *Another Time, Another Place,* she thought she was free of Johnny, at least for a few months. But he managed to deceive the American authorities, and suddenly he showed up in London. Lana went to Scotland Yard for help and Stompanato was deported.

Once the filming was finished, she decided to take a vacation in Acapulco without telling anyone. "In those days," says Lana, "the most direct route between London and Acapulco was Copenhagen. I arrived in Denmark in the early morning. A few passengers got off the plane, others got on. A young man handed me a yellow rose. I took the flower and suddenly I saw a face at my side: it was Johnny. I never learned how he managed to get on without my seeing him, nor how he got a ticket on the same plane and for the seat next to me. But he was there."

The fights between the two of them were terrible, states the reporter. Melissa tried to keep Patrícia, her fourteen-year-old daughter, from hearing them—but she didn't always succeed. One day, the bedroom door was open and the girl thought he was going to carry out his repeated threat to cut her mother's face with a knife. She ran to the kitchen, grabbed a large knife, and pierced the body of the man. His last words were: "What have you done?" The next stage was the struggle in the courts, when Melissa, desperate, asked: "Can't I take responsibility for this whole tragedy?"

However, the press published other versions of the crime. One of them was that Cheryl was crazy about Johnny and the two had even made love; she killed him when she discovered that he had returned to her mother. But Lana, much later, would render her final homage to Stompanato. "He courted me like no one else," she declared. (A woman will forgive everything for a man who gives her the greatest of pleasures.)

After Cheryl was absolved, Lana counted on the company of her former male friends, each of whom regarded her as a living trophy of his great moments in bed. That was when she began thinking that in some other stage of her life, perhaps not too far in the future, she'd need people's kindness, something she herself had never readily offered.

She began to force herself to be nicer. Now her bad temper was no longer compensated by her brilliant beauty, her passion, her youth. The passage of time was extinguishing her intensity, everything becoming softer in smokey, pastel colors, like the upper part (the clouds) of a Japanese print.

Then, as a disguise, she affected a frivolous theatrical mannerism which, if observed closely, was quite "profound." Perhaps the most profound thing in her life was her smile-frown. The sign, who knows, of an achievement no one looks forward to—the wisdom of middle age, which can become the only thing left to us, keeping us alive.

Nevertheless, she continued to telephone frequently one acquaintance, then another, in the middle of the night—hoping for any crumb of kindness, or simply trying to express something inexplicable that was reduced to a handful of dust, banal phrases notable for their insistence on *me, me, me.*

When she thought it over, she knew her effort to keep pleasing men was unimpressive, an immense and practically useless investment of skill and emotion. At any moment, she concluded, she'd stop altogether, stay indoors alone, watch old films on her videocassette, and cook for herself.

Or she would lose herself in long, nostalgic meditations while seated in her lounge chair on the tiny veranda of her apartment/her mansion. Yes, I know the bittersweetness of Lana Turner's solitude, her soft pain on a Saturday afternoon like this one—when, no longer wanted by the studios, definitively divorced, she'd sip a whiskey as she watched fraying clouds empty onto the densely tree-covered slopes of Beverly Hills.

(More than a history, less than a history. A climate. Like an image glimpsed years later and suddenly remembered. The sudden chiaroscuro that, on a certain afternoon, formed on a woman's face, leaving it—merely for a second, completely burnished by golden dust.)

Lana or Melissa (Silvia? Selma? Ingrid? Laura?), a woman whose story I wanted to tell in many versions, as in the Thousand and One Nights. Innumerable, protean, with something of a hydra about her—when one of her heads is cut off, others appear in its place. And whose reality, clandestine and hidden like an obscure meaning, is permanently subjected to interpretation; an enigma one can only partially decipher, based on crucial symbolic words or on inferences from episodes and situations deliberately highlighted in the text, using the same technique as a newspaper editor, who makes a choice—never innocent—of what goes as the lead or at the bottom of the page.

Lana beyond Lana herself, inexhaustible; Lana, so to speak, *of our time*. Or an atemporal metaphor of love and perdition—Sappho, George Sand, Electra. And, furthermore, Lana like the simple whim of this other woman, whose face is nothing more than a mirror, albeit a dingy one—of mine. All of them, nonetheless, capable of multiplying themselves infinitely.

Before closing forever the magazine with the story about the great stars of the past—allowing Lana (Melissa, me) to continue her (our) painful, smiling, and solitary trajectory (to where? to where?), whose significance, beyond these glamorous images and words with mysterious double meanings, I cease to capture—, I give a last look at the photograph of Lana Turner, bestowing upon it the best shade of my irony, like a delicious and bitter private joke.

A little sad, I now conclude that in reality it wasn't Lana Turner I wanted to write about; rather, it was Rio de Janeiro's Zona Sul. All blue, yellow, and green as fraying clouds empty onto the tree-covered slopes of Corcovado and time passes.

List of Selected Works

Almeida, Júlia Lopes de

Traços e Iluminuras, 1887 (stories)
A Família Medeiros, 1891 (novel)
A Viúva Simões, 1897 (novel)
A Falência, 1901 (novel)
Ânsia Eterna, 1903 (stories)
A Intrusa, 1908 (novel)
Eles e Elas, 1910 (monologues)
Correio da Roça: Romance Epistolar, 1913 (novel)
Era Uma Vez, 1917 (stories)
A Isca, 1922 (stories)
A Casa Verde, 1932 (novel with Filinto de Almeida)

Benedetti, Lúcia

Entrada de Serviço, 1942 (novel)
Noturno sem Leito, 1948 (novel)
Vesperal com Chuva, 1950 (stories)
Chão Estrangeiro, 1956 (novel)
Três Soldados, 1956 (novel)
Maria Isabel, Uma Vida no Rio, 1960 (novel)
Histórias do Rei, 1963 (stories)

Colasanti, Marina

Zooilógico, 1975 (stories)
Uma Idéia Toda Azul, 1979 (stories)
Doze Reis e a Moça no Labirinto do Vento, 1982 (stories)
Contos de Amor Rasgado, 1986 (stories)

Coutinho, Sônia

Reunião, 1961 (stories with three other authors)
Do Herói Inútil, 1966 (stories)
Uma Certa Felicidade, 1976 (stories)
Os Venenos de Lucrécia, 1978 (stories)
O Jogo de Ifá, 1980 (novel)
O Último Verão de Copacabana, 1985 (stories)

Denser, Márcia

Tango Fantasma, 1976 (stories)
Muito Prazer: Contos Eróticos Femininos, 1980 (anthology, editor)

O Animal dos Motéis: Novela em Episódios, 1981 (novella)
Exercícios Para o Pecado, 1984 (novellas)
O Prazer é Todo Meu: Contos Eróticos Femininos, 1984 (anthology, editor)

Dolores, Carmen (Emília Moncorvo Bandeira de Melo)

Gradações, 1897 (stories)
Um Drama na Roça, 1907 (stories) ("Aunt Zézé's Tears" from this collection appeared in Isaac Golberg's *Brazilian Tales*, 1921.)
Lendas Brasileiras, 1908 (stories)
Ao Esvoaçar da Idéia, 1910 *(crônicas)*
A Luta, 1911 (novel)

Dupré, Sra. Leandro (Maria José)

O Romance de Teresa Bernard, 1941 (novel)
Éramos Seis, 1943 (novel)
Luz e Sombra, 1944 (novel)
Gina, 1945 (novel)
Os Rodriguez, 1946 (novel)
Dona Lola, 1949 (novel)
A Casa do Ódio, 1951 (stories)
Vila Soledade, 1953 (novel)
Angélica, 1955 (novel and stories)
Os Caminhos, 1969 (novel)

Dutra, Lia Correia

Luz e Sombra, 1931 (poetry)
História de uma Pracinha, 1941 (fiction)
Navio sem Porto, 1943 (stories)
Memórias de um Saudosista, 1969 (fiction)

Faillace, Tania Jamardo

Fuga, 1964 (novel)
Adão e Eva, 1965 (novel)
O 35° Ano de Inês, 1971 (stories)
Vinde a Mim os Pequeninos, 1977 (stories)
Tradição, Família & Outras Estórias, 1978 (stories)
Mário/Vera—Brasil, 1962–1964, 1983 (novel)

Fonseca, Emi Bulhões Carvalho da

No Silêncio da Casa Grande, 1944 (stories)
Mona Lisa, 1946 (novel)
O Oitavo Pecado, 1947 (novel)
Pedras Altas, 1949 (novel)
Anoiteceu na Charneca, 1951 (novel)
Lua Cinzenta, 1953 (novel)

Bodas da Solidão, 1956 (novel)
Três Candeias, 1959 (novel)
O Julgamento é Amanhã, 1963 (novel)
Desquite Amigável, 1965 (novel)

Hilst, Hilda

Presságio, 1950 (poetry)
Balada do Festival, 1955 (poetry)
Roteiro do Silêncio, 1959 (poetry)
Ode Fragmentária, 1961 (poetry)
Poesia 1959/1967 (poetry)
Fluxofloema, 1970 (stories)
Qadós, 1973 (stories)
Ficções, 1977 (stories)
Amavisse, 1989 (poetry)
O Caderno Rosa de Lori Lamby, 1990 (novella)

Lispector, Clarice

Perto do Coração Selvagem, 1944 (novel) (*Near the Wild Heart*, 1990)
O Lustre, 1946 (novel)
A Cidade Sitiada, 1949 (novel)
Laços de Família, 1960 (stories) (*Family Ties*, 1972)
A Maça no Escuro, 1961 (novel) (*The Apple in the Dark*, 1967)
A Legião Estrangeira, 1964 (stories and *crônicas*) (*The Foreign Legion*, 1986)
A Paixão Segundo G. H., 1964 (novel) (*The Passion According to G. H.*, 1988)
Uma Aprendizagem ou o Livro dos Prazeres, 1969 (novel) (*An Apprenticeship; or, The Book of Delights*, 1986)
Água Viva, 1973 (novella) (*The Stream of Life*, 1989)
Onde Estivestes de Noite, 1974 (stories and short texts); *A Via Crucis do Corpo*, 1974 (stories) (*Soulstorm*, 1989)
A Hora da Estrela, 1977 (novel) (*The Hour of the Star*, 1986)
A Bela e a Fera, 1979 (stories)

Lispector, Elisa

Além da Fronteira, 1945 (novel)
No Exílio, 1948 (novel)
Ronda Solitária, 1954 (novel)
O Muro de Pedras, 1963 (novel)
Sangue no Sol, 1970 (stories)
A Última Porta, 1975 (novel)
Inventário, 1977 (stories)
O Tigre de Bengala, 1985 (stories)

Luft, Lya

As Parceiras, 1980 (novel)
A Asa Esquerda do Anjo, 1981 (novel)

Reunião de Família, 1982 (novel)
O Quarto Fechado, 1984 (novel) (*The Island of the Dead*, 1986)
Exílio, 1987 (novel)

Nery, Adalgisa

Poemas, 1937 (poetry)
A Mulher Ausente, 1940 (poetry)
Og, 1943 (stories)
As Fronteiras da Quarta Dimensão, 1952 (poetry)
A Imaginária, 1959 (novel)
Neblina, 1962 (novel)
Mundos Oscilantes, 1962 (poetry)
22 Menos 1, 1972 (stories)

Piñon, Nélida

Guia-Mapa de Gabriel Arcanjo, 1961 (novel)
Madeira Feita Cruz, 1963 (novel)
Tempo das Frutas, 1966 (stories)
Fundador, 1969 (novel)
A Casa da Paixão, 1972 (novel)
Sala de Armas, 1973 (stories)
Tebas do Meu Coração, 1974 (novel)
O Calor das Coisas, 1980 (stories)
A República dos Sonhos, 1984 (novel) (*The Republic of Dreams*, 1989)

Queiroz, Dinah Silveira de

Floradas na Serra, 1939 (novel)
Margarida La Rocque: A Ilha dos Demônios, 1949 (novel)
A Muralha, 1954 (novel) (*The Women of Brazil*, 1980)
As Noites do Morro do Encanto, 1957 (stories)
Eles Herderão a Terra, 1960 (stories)
Verão dos Infiéis, 1968 (novel)
Comba Malina, 1969 (stories)
Eu Venho: Memorial do Cristo 1, 1974; *Eu, Jesus: Memorial do Cristo 2*, 1977 (prose narratives) (*Christ's Memorial*, 1978)

Queiroz, Rachel de

O Quinze, 1930 (novel)
João Miguel, 1932 (novel)
Caminho de Pedras, 1937 (novel)
As Três Marias, 1939 (novel) (*The Three Marias*, 1985)
Dora, Doralina, 1975 (novel) (*Dora, Doralina*, 1984)

Telles, Lygia Fagundes

Ciranda de Pedra, 1954 (novel) (*The Marble Dance*, 1986)
Verão no Aquário, 1963 (novel)

Antes do Baile Verde, 1970 (stories) ("Before the Green Ball" from this collection appeared in *The Latin American Literary Review,* Fall-Winter 1975.)
As Meninas, 1973 (novel) (*The Girl in the Photograph,* 1982)
Seminário dos Ratos, 1977 (stories) (*Tigresa and Other Stories,* 1986)
Filhos Pródigios, 1978 (stories)
A Disciplina do Amor, 1980 *(crônicas)*
Mistérios, 1981 (stories)
As Horas Nuas, 1989 (novel)

van Steen, Edla

Cio, 1965 (stories)
Memórias do Medo, 1974 (novel)
Antes do Amanhecer, 1977 (stories) ("Mr. and Mrs. Martins" from this collection appeared in *Sudden Fiction International,* 1989.)
O Conto da Mulher Brasileira, 1978 (anthology, editor)
Corações Mordidos, 1983 (novel)
Até Sempre, 1985 (stories)

Darlene J. Sadlier

Professor of Spanish and Portuguese and Adjunct Professor of Women's Studies at Indiana University, is the author of *The Question of How: Women Writers and New Portuguese Literature*.

Printed in the United States
39888LVS00002B/292-309

9 780253 206992